Riley Carson

And The Quest For Justice

MEGAN WARGULA

Riley Carson
And The Quest For Justice

BY
MEGAN WARGULA

To Nanny,
Enjoy life's adventures!
Megan Wargula

Front Cover Design by
Andy Suggs

A portion of this book's profits will be donated to animal welfare organizations.

This book is a work of fiction. Names, locations, characters, and situations are the product of the writer's imagination or are used fictitiously. In some cases, real places, names, and organizations are used and written permission was received. Any resemblance to actual events, locales, or persons, living or dead, is coincidental.

Copyright © 2018 by Hound and Thistle, LLC

All rights reserved. No part of this publication may be reproduced, distributed, or transmitted in any form or by any means, including photocopying, recording, or other electronic or mechanical methods, without the prior written permission of the publisher, except in the case of brief quotations embodied in critical reviews and certain other noncommercial uses permitted by copyright law. For permission requests, write to Hound and Thistle, LLC, addressed "Attention: Permissions Coordinator,"
12195 Highway 92, Ste 114-169, Woodstock, GA 30188
www.HoundAndThistle.com

Ordering Information:
Quantity sales. Special discounts are available on quantity purchases by corporations, associations, and others. For details, contact the publisher at the address above.

Printed in the United States of America

Publisher's Cataloging-in-Publication data
Wargula, Megan.
Riley Carson And The Quest For Justice / Megan Wargula
p. cm.
ISBN 978-0997380736
Library of Congress Control Number: TBD

First Edition

14 13 12 11 10 / 10 9 8 7 6 5 4 3 2 1

To Michael, my best friend of the human variety.
Thank you for loving me, laughing with me, and cooking for me.
For championing my causes with me.
Most of all, for letting me be me.

xoxo

"I look to a day when people will not be judged by the color of their skin, but by the content of their character."

-Martin Luther King, Jr.

CONTENTS

CHAPTER ONE

The Big Day

Sitting at the kitchen table with her family wasn't always the most stress-free part of Riley Carson's day, especially since she and her sister, Hailey, always seemed at odds. But today was different. Today, the Carson family would be adopting a new dog, a dog rescued from the illegal puppy mill that Riley and her best friend Finn had uncovered.

Riley couldn't believe the day had come...and how excited she was. If you had asked her a few months ago about getting another dog, she would have said no. She didn't think she'd ever want another dog after her beloved Sammy died in her arms on the last day of summer break. Riley's feelings had changed after she found dogs in need. Today, she greeted the morning with excitement and enthusiasm, her family was going to get a new dog today!

Everything had changed for Riley when she and Finn found the illegal puppy mill in their hometown of Roswell, Georgia. It was their first semester of middle school and they kept finding dogs that had been mistreated, and only one dog had actually gotten away alive. That dog was key to figuring out the mystery—that and a special "gift" Riley had somehow received, but couldn't totally figure out. Only Finn and Eve, her two closest friends, shared her secret. Riley couldn't explain the gift, but

1

after Sammy died in her arms and she saved a stray cat from the class bully, Corey Thornton, Riley was able to touch a dog or cat and "see" what it had experienced. Luckily this only happened when the animal needed to communicate with her. She couldn't imagine being afraid to touch a dog, fearing what she might see. Riley loved dogs more than anything!

"Morning, Roo!" Riley's dad said as he stacked French toast on a plate, calling her by their nickname for her. Riley was built like her dad, tall and slim.

"Good morning, dear," her mom added. She poured orange juice into glasses and looked as beautiful and well-dressed as always. As she turned to Riley, her shoulders sank. "Honey, are you going to wear *that* today?" Riley's mom was the epitome of perfection when it came to appearances, she looked perfect even if she was just going to the mailbox.

Ugh, Riley thought. The ever familiar disapproval of her attire from her mom. Riley thought she'd be used to it by now, but it always stung. Riley looked at her outfit: jeans, sweatshirt, and sneakers. "Is this not okay to wear to go pick up our new dog? I mean, he won't care what I'm wearing," she cut back. The fact that her mother's insistent push for perfection when it came to appearances drove Riley up the wall was no secret in the Carson household.

"You look great, Roo," her Dad interjected. "No need to dress up to go to the vet's." He glanced at his wife a forgiving, "give her a break," emerging from his eyes.

"Oh, honey, you look fine," Riley's mom said, changing her tune, though it was clear to Riley that her mom thought otherwise.

"I'm glad you're excited about getting a dog, Roo." Riley's dad said as he brought stacks of French toast to the table while in the same breath, hollering up to his oldest daughter. "Hailey! Food's on the table!" He looked at Riley with a grin and said, "Your sister is going to be late to her own funeral."

Riley giggled. "Do you think we made the right decision to get an older dog versus a puppy?" she asked, slicing into her French toast.

"I do," her dad said. "Puppies take a lot of time and attention and the dog we're going to meet is around four years old. While he'll still need lots of training, I think it's a good choice. So many people want puppies, I think it's good we're giving an older dog a home."

"You're right, dad. I'm sure all the puppies have homes by now, it's tougher for older dogs to get adopted."

"And puppies want to chew everything up," Riley's mom said as she elegantly cut a bite-sized portion of French toast. "Of course, this dog will need to be potty trained, but since we're getting him right before Christmas break, I think the timing is perfect."

"Yeah," Riley agreed. "I'll have more time to train him." She thought back to the illegal puppy mill she and Finn had uncovered. The dogs were never let out, so they had to go to the bathroom in their cages...cages stacked on top of other cages, so the stench was overwhelming. Riley shuddered thinking back on that awful place.

"Morning," Hailey said as she sat down, finally deciding to grace her family with her presence. Her hair and make-up were so perfect, Riley thought she could be going on a photo shoot.

Hailey tossed her long blond hair over her shoulder and took a delicate sip of orange juice. "So, I was thinking about names, and I think I've come up with some great ones. Tristan, Percival, or Theodore. What do you think?"

Riley looked at her sister with wide eyes. "Are you serious?" she gaped.

"Yes, I'm serious." Hailey looked mildly offended. "You do realize that Yorkshire terriers come from England, don't you? I think we should give him a very English name."

Riley could feel her blood pressure rise with the condescending comment from her sister. "Of course I know where they come from, but those names aren't dog names," she spat back. "They're pretentious."

"Whatever," Hailey said, dismissing her sister. She turned toward her parents, "What do you think? If we go with Percival, we can call him Percy, or Theodore could be Theo or Teddy."

"Well, those names aren't so bad," their mom said. "What do you think, Jack?"

"I like them. But I'd also like to know what names Riley has come up with. After all, she did save the dogs."

"Well, I like Charlie, Ace, or Buster," Riley said, then noticed Hailey promptly roll her eyes.

"Those are cute names too!" her mom said. "Which do you like best?"

"Buster," Riley said. "Because I busted him out of that awful place."

"I love it!" her dad offered.

"That's so lame," Hailey said before taking a bite of her French toast.

4

"Be nice," their mom scolded.

"Let's do this," their dad offered. "Let's finish this wonderful food and we'll decide on the name after we meet the dog. We can see what he responds to and what seems to fit his personality."

"I think that's a great idea," their mom agreed with a look of relief on her face as she winked at her husband.

Riley liked that idea too, especially when Hailey rolled her eyes again. It only seemed right to meet the dog first and see what he was like; maybe none of those names would fit him. She just couldn't wait to meet the little guy! She sure hoped he didn't have to communicate anything with her. Her stomach turned at the thought. The last thing she wanted was to have to conceal her gift in front of her family on the day she would be bringing her new friend home.

CHAPTER TWO

A New Family Member

Due to the sheer number of dogs that were found at the mill, not all of them could be placed in foster homes so the Carsons set off for the veterinarian's office where most of them were being cared for. It was the same vet's office that Riley went to with Finn and his family when they adopted Molly. Rhonda, Mrs. Murphy's friend, was in the parking lot to greet them. Rhonda worked with Angels Among Us, one of the groups that saved the dogs from the mill.

"Hi Rhonda!" Riley was first out of the car, hardly able to contain her excitement.

"Hey there, Riley," Rhonda said. "Are you guys ready to meet your new dog?"

"We sure are!" Riley's mom said.

Though Riley herself was excited, she was equally irritated by her mother's itch to seemingly replace Sammy—something she had been pushing for since shortly after Sammy's passing.

Riley, along with her family, followed Rhonda into the vet's office. She glanced around at the familiar lobby which was fairly quiet for a weekend. "Is he back in the kennels?" Riley asked.

"Yeah, Kevin's bringing him up," Rhonda said. "The one we thought would be a good fit for your family is a four year old male Yorkie. He's in pretty good shape since he's still young, but you will need to teach him how to potty outside and live like a dog should, out of a cage and as part of your family. It's sad because these dogs don't really know how to act like dogs."

A door opened and the vet tech, Kevin, walked out with a little black and tan Yorkie on a leash. "He may be a little timid," Kevin said as he guided the dog into the room. "So just move slowly around him. He's also a little wary of men."

"Well, that's understandable," Riley said. "That man was a creep." Riley thought back to the dark, filthy place where the dogs were kept. Whenever the man was around, the dogs were terrified, and he made it known how much he couldn't stand them. She squatted down and called to the shy little dog and extended her hand so he could sniff her.

As the dog slowly made his way toward Riley, his little tail wagged tentatively.

"Hey buddy," Riley said in a high voice. The dog moved closer and sniffed the back of Riley's hand. She could feel his little breaths on her skin as he investigated her by smelling her. Riley scratched the dog on his chest and he licked her on the wrist. Riley was relieved that the dog didn't have to communicate anything with her and she hoped that meant he felt safe and secure. She sat down with the Yorkie and continued to gently pet him. "He seems really sweet," she said.

"He is," Kevin agreed. "He has adjusted a bit better than some of the dogs and we think it's because he's younger and wasn't kept in such harsh conditions for so long. He's a good little dog, he just needs to learn how to be a dog."

"Rhonda said the same thing," Riley's mom said.

"Yeah, what do you mean by that?" Hailey inquired as she

came over and knelt behind Riley near the little dog.

"Well," Kevin explained. "These guys have never had toys to play with, a soft bed to lay in; they've spent their lives in cages so they need to learn how to live outside a cage. This little guy is doing well around people, but you'll have to get him used to life in a home, outside in the yard, and just playing and being free."

"That's so sad," Hailey said as she pet the little dog. "He feels skinny."

"Yeah," Kevin said. "Most of the dogs were malnourished, so we're working on getting some weight on them. It won't take long, especially if you use treats when training him."

"I read up on training dogs rescued from puppy mills on National Mill Dog Rescue's website," Riley said, referring to the other group that helped with the rescue. "We'll definitely use treats and slowly introduce him to new things and situations. I guess he has to learn how to trust people."

"Yeah," Kevin said. "Luckily he's been in the kennel with us and is getting lots of good treatment, so hopefully he won't associate being in his crate with bad things, should you decide to use one."

"Honestly, we've never used one before," Riley's mom added. She then crouched near the Yorkie, gently extending her hand.

"Well you might not need to," Kevin said. "But it would be a good idea to have one in case he needs a place to feel safe, kind of like a den."

"It'll be interesting to see what he does, because of his previous association with being caged all the time. He may prefer it at first, just because it's what he's used to," Rhonda said.

The little dog was slowly investigating Riley's mom.

"He's definitely shy," Hailey said. "Did he have a name before?"

"Oh no," Rhonda said with a jaded laugh. "Millers don't name these dogs, they are just commodities to them. Money makers only."

"It's so awful," Riley said, with images of the nasty mill in her mind.

"Have you thought of a name yet?" Rhonda asked.

Riley's parents looked at each other and her dad said, "We had a nice little discussion about that over breakfast. That might be the hardest part."

"A little sibling rivalry?" Rhonda asked.

"Oh, just a tad," Riley's dad said with a wink.

"Why don't you try out the names here?" Kevin suggested to Riley and Hailey. He slipped the leash off of the dog. "Each of you can sit across from each other and call out the names, see what he responds to. I'd kinda like to see this guy when he gets his name. I think it's kind of a big deal. He finally gets his own name, it gives him the dignity he deserves."

"Wow, no pressure," Hailey said with a laugh.

Riley tucked her hair behind her ear. "Let's do it." She and her sister sat on the floor about five feet from each other, with the little Yorkie sniffing around the lobby floor.

Accustomed to always going first, Hailey called out her first choice in names. "Tristan, come here Tristan."

"She wants something British-sounding." Riley heard her father mumble to Rhonda and Kevin, who chuckled.

It was her turn. "Charlie, come here Charlie," Riley said.

She patted her knees and the dog looked at her, but didn't come over.

Hailey raised the pitch of her voice. "Percy, come here Percy!" This name also got a glance from the dog, but nothing else.

Riley tried again. "Ace, come here, Ace!" She tried sounding exciting and frisky, but again, nothing.

Rhonda chuckled. "We might be here all day," she joked.

On her last turn Hailey gave it all she had. "Teddy, come here Teddy!" She clapped her hands which seemed to startle the little fella.

Riley's stomach had butterflies. Competition of any kind did that to her and in this case she felt so silly for it. It didn't matter if her name was picked or not, but she would feel pretty great if the dog did react to the name she chose. She took a deep breath and called out, "Buster, come here boy!" Her voice was relaxed and playful.

The dog looked at Riley and cocked his head to the left and then slowly trotted over to her. "Do you like that name?" Riley asked the dog in a high pitched voice. She petted his chest, "Buster, do you like that name?"

His little tail wagged and he crawled into Riley's lap for more attention. Riley looked up at her parents, smiling from ear to ear. "I think he likes it!"

"It looks like we have a winner!" Kevin said. "I like it."

"She picked it because she busted him out of that mill," Riley's dad said, sounding proud.

"That's so cute!" Rhonda said.

"I think it actually works," Hailey said, much to Riley's

surprise. "He kinda looks like a Buster, a little scrappy," she came over to pet Buster in Riley's lap. "And honestly," she confessed, "he doesn't really look like a Percy or a Teddy." Riley couldn't believe what she was hearing. Hailey wasn't used to losing and when she did lose, she usually wasn't graceful about it. Riley's parents clearly felt the same as she saw them exchange glances of surprise.

Riley's heart felt full at the moment as she gently cuddled her new dog. When she lost Sammy, she didn't think she could love another dog again. But now she was more excited about getting a new dog than she thought she could ever be. She snapped a picture and texted it to Finn, *Meet Buster. We're on our way home. Can't wait for you to meet him!*

CHAPTER THREE

New Home, New Life

Finn was sitting on the front porch as Riley and her family turned into the driveway.

"Hey! He's in a crate in the back," Riley called to her friend as the car came to a stop. "Come see him. But just move slowly around him because he's still getting used to people," she said, climbing from the car. "And definitely men," she added.

Finn joined Riley at the car, though he stood back to give room to the little dog. "I have some treats in my pocket in case I need to bribe him," he joked and a lopsided grin appeared on his face.

"Always prepared!" Riley said. She thought back to how glad she was that Finn was prepared when they nearly got into serious trouble when they found the puppy mill. "Thanks," she said genuinely.

Riley's dad opened the rear lift gate and Riley walked up to the crate. Buster was trembling a little. "Hey buddy," she said. "It's okay, you're home now." Riley felt so sad seeing Buster scared. She opened the crate and let him sniff her hand.

"Here," Finn offered, passing over a treat to Riley. She held it in her hand and as Buster ate the treat, Riley gently clipped his new green leash onto the matching collar. "Good boy," she told him. Then she gently lifted him out of the crate and set

13

him on the driveway. "Let's go into the grass and see if you need to potty," she said. She held a treat in front of Buster's nose, enticing him into the grass. The little dog trotted into the grass and Riley gave him the treat. He sniffed the grass, moving slowly, and picked his paws up as the blades of grass touched the bottoms.

"He's never felt grass before, remember," Riley's dad said.

Riley's heart broke a little. "Yeah, he's just not used to it. He looks uncomfortable here," she said.

"Why don't you take him over to the mailbox and see if he catches another dog's scent," her dad suggested. "That might make him go potty there and the mulch might be easier under his paws."

Finn gave Riley another handful of treats and Riley walked slowly to the mailbox while Buster trailed behind her, treading easier on the driveway. It's great he's not fighting the leash though, she thought.

"Let's go potty," she said as his nose started investigating the black metal mailbox post. After a few moments of intense sniffing, Buster lifted his leg. "Good boy!" Riley said. She immediately gave Buster several treats and petted his little head.

"That's a good boy!" Riley's mom said, coming over to join them. Her voice was high and happy as she gently scratched Buster on the side of his face and Riley was happy to see her mother's affection toward their new dog.

"You try and call him over," Riley suggested to Finn who was now seated in the grass a few feet away.

Finn extended a handful of treats and called out, "Buster, come here! Come on, boy!" He patted his knee with his free hand. Buster sniffed the air before heading toward Finn, still cautious about the sensation underneath his feet, Riley noticed. Buster sniffed around the edges of Finn's extended hand and ever so tentatively, took one of the treats and ate it.

"Good boy!" Riley and Finn said, almost in unison. Riley swore she saw confidence building in the little dog.

Hailey had meandered over to Finn and was kneeling beside him, watching Buster make a new friend. "Let's take him inside and show him his bed and toys," Hailey suggested.

Riley stood and called Buster to follow her. "It's great that he got used to the leash at the vet's office," she said and Finn agreed. When they got to the few steps that led into the house from the garage, Riley felt the leash tighten. She looked at Buster who was behind her and planted his four paws firmly on the cement floor. "It's okay, Buster, come on," Riley said in a sweet voice as she patted her leg. Buster wasn't budging. "Aww, it's okay," she said as she leaned down and petted him, then scooped him up, carrying him inside. When they were all inside and the door was shut, Riley put Buster on the floor, took off his leash, and let him explore. He slowly walked around the kitchen, sniffing the floors, and carefully examined his new surroundings.

"Let's all keep treats handy, in case we need to reward him for doing something positive," Riley said as she headed to the pantry to grab treats for everyone. As she closed the pantry door, Buster jumped at the sound and ran under the kitchen table.

"I'm sorry, Buster," Riley said. "Here you go." She tossed a treat on the floor, in front of the table so Buster would come out.

"He still seems frightened," Hailey said. She took some treats for herself and handed the bag to her mom.

"Let's sit in the family room and let him come to us," Riley's dad suggested. "He might be nervous since we're all just standing here watching him."

The Carsons had already been shopping for their new family member at The Downtown Pooch, a cute pet boutique on Canton Street whose empolyees were equally excited to meet the Carson's new dog. They had placed a stylish and soft dog bed by the fireplace in the family room and it was filled with all kinds of toys. Riley was on the large sofa which faced the front of the house and ran parallel to the kitchen table, she could see Buster to her left and the fireplace to her right. After a few moments, Buster inched out from under the table snagging the treat Riley had left for him.

"Good boy," Riley said in a soft, sweet tone. Buster looked at her, timidly came over, and she handed him another treat. "Good boy, Buster!" Riley had found a nice balance, not too enthusiastic that she would scare him off, but encouraging enough to let him know he was doing great. She wanted to jump for joy at his bravery.

Buster sniffed around the family room and after a few more minutes, found his dog bed and toys. Finn was sitting next to Riley and said, "I tossed some treats onto his bed before I sat down."

Sure enough, Buster found the treats and ate them up. "He's doing great," Riley's mom whispered. Buster headed to the center of the room and laid down on the area rug underneath the coffee table.

"Maybe he feels safe under there," Riley's dad suggested.

"Yeah, and he's used to being in a crate, so soft pillows are kinda new to him," Riley said as she thought back to the filthy cages the dogs were kept in. "At least he was in a clean crate at the vet's office."

"I'm going to put these treats in a jar and leave it out so it's easy to get to," Riley's mom said heading into the kitchen. "We're going to have to reward him when he's a good boy and help him find his confidence."

"I wish he wasn't so scared," Hailey pouted. "I want him to sit with me on the couch."

"Hailey, you have to understand where he comes from. I know you didn't want to see where the dogs were kept, but it was rough. I can't wait for him to want to snuggle with us, but we have to do it on his time," Riley said.

"Well, hopefully it won't take long," Hailey said.

"Patience," their dad said. "He'll get there, and we'll help him."

"Yeah," Finn chimed in, "he just needs time. I'm sure Riley will have him trained and sleeping in her bed in no time!"

Riley's parents smiled at her and she felt happiness. She normally would have argued with Hailey, but this wasn't time for arguing; it was time to help Buster become a happy, healthy dog and that was her mission.

CHAPTER FOUR

The Creepy House

Riley and Finn approached the busy intersection of Atlanta and Sloan streets, on their way to the Public House to meet their friend Eve for lunch. Riley couldn't wait to tell their friend about Buster. As they approached the corner, they spotted Eve across the street. Riley and Finn waved to her as they paused at the crosswalk, waiting for the light to change, but to Riley's surprise, Eve didn't wave back. Instead, she paled, panic stricken, and screamed, "No! Stop!" at no one in particular.

Riley could not figure out what was going on, but she could tell Eve had her eyes on something, or someone. She was staring fearfully into the roadway as if nothing else existed.

"What is she doing?" Finn asked.

"I can't tell," Riley confessed, still worried about their friend's odd behavior.

As cars flew down Atlanta Street, Eve's attention turned to the right and she set off across Sloan Street and dashed down the sidewalk in front of Spiced Right Barbecue Restaurant.

Eve's curious behavior had Riley nervous and her stomach turned. She knew their friend was upset, but she couldn't figure out why.

Finn was watching the crosswalk sign intently and looked at Riley when it finally changed and was safe to cross. "Let's go!"

Once on Sloan Street, they jogged across to catch up with Eve.

"Eve, are you okay?" Riley called out as they caught up with her.

"I saw a girl dart through the traffic!" Eve called behind her, panicked. She was still several paces in front of them.

"I didn't see anything, did you?" Riley asked Finn.

Finn looked concerned, "Nope, just cars flying by." He and Riley jogged past the smoker in front of Spiced Right, the delicious scent of barbecue wafting past as the smoke billowed out.

Eve was still ahead, and moving quickly so they picked up their pace to catch up. When Riley saw Eve cut through the parking lot of the always-for-rent restaurant next to Spiced Right, she stopped and said, "Is Eve taking us to The Creepy House?"

A grin spread across Finn's face and he picked up his pace, "I think so!"

Riley groaned and kept up with her best friend. "You know I hate The Creepy House. There's a nasty ghost haunting it, I just feel it when I'm near it. I really don't want to go."

They rounded the corner where the always-for-rent restaurant stood, rumored to be haunted as well and right next door to The Creepy House. Finally catching up with Eve, Riley and Finn stopped to catch their breath and Eve rushed over, still panicked.

"Eve, what is going on?" Riley asked, she panted, catching her breath, and she could smell something. Eve didn't answer and looked terrified, her brown eyes were huge and filled with fear. Riley put her hands on Eve's shoulders and looked into her eyes. "Eve, are you okay?"

"Fire!" Finn said as Riley noticed black smoke flowing out of the attic of The Creepy House.

Then she noticed something else. "Finn, look!" she cried. Riley let go of Eve and dashed toward the house where a small black and white cat sat, scratching at the door to the crawl space beneath the house. "Call 9-1-1," she hollered back to her friends.

As Finn jogged up behind Riley, he said, "Eve's going to call."

The cat was meowing frantically. Though Riley was more of a dog person and had never had cats, this one sounded downright pained.

The door to the crawl space had a latch, but thankfully no lock. Finn unlatched the door and opened it. A plume of smoke came wafting out and Riley and Finn jumped back and covered their faces as they coughed. Riley just barely saw the cat dart inside.

"No! We need to help it!" She looked through the smoke which had dissipated and saw the cat emerge with a tiny black and white kitten in its mouth. "Oh my goodness, she has kittens in there!"

Finn didn't wait. He got on all fours and crawled inside, emerging a moment later with two kittens in his right hand. "Here!" He handed the kittens to Riley who took them over to some brush along the back edge of the parking lot where they would be safe for the time-being. The mother cat followed Riley over to check on her babies before returning to the crawl space.

Finn had yet to return and Riley called his name nervously. She noticed that the mama cat stood by the door to the crawl space, mewing restlessly but too timid to return inside. Riley squatted next to the cat, "Are there more in there, mama?" Then calling in through the opening, "Finn? Do you need help?" She was beginning to really worry about her friend.

As if she was equally worried, the cat let out a strained "Meoaaaw" just as Finn came back out, another kitten in tow. He handed it to Riley and she took it over to the others. As she carried the small creature, she noticed it was quite still, more so than the others.

Finn came up behind her. "I didn't see any more," he said as he coughed a little and wiped his nose and mouth. The smoke wasn't terrible in the crawl space, but it was getting worse.

Riley watched as the mama cat picked up the kitten she had saved and trotted over to the three Riley had assembled in the brush. Finn followed.

As the mama cat tended to her kittens, Riley had an idea. She gently placed a hand on the cat to see if she needed to communicate with her. Riley felt fear and panic and saw four kittens in the crawl space cuddled up with their mama. Riley removed her hand and looked at Finn who had an expectant look on his face. "I think we got them all. I saw four all together."

Finn let out a sigh of relief.

"I don't think that last one is responding," Riley said as the mama cat started licking and nudging the quiet baby. Unlike the other three kittens, it was not mewing.

"What should we do?" Finn asked as the wail of sirens started in the distance. He looked back at the house which was now burning fast then looked for Eve, spotting her near the other building, reluctant to get close to The Creepy House. "Eve, go get a box from Spiced Right, and see if they can give you some wet towels or something!" He looked at Riley. "We need to wipe them down and get them in a box so we can get them to safety."

Riley said a silent prayer and gently picked up the unresponsive kitten, hoping the mama cat knew she meant no harm. Riley held the tiny kitten in her hands, tipping its head downward and put her mouth over the kitten's tiny nose and mouth. She blew three light puffs of air and felt for a heartbeat, but felt none. She gently but quickly pressed on the kitten's chest, counted to 15 then blew into the kitten's nose again. This time she felt a faint heartbeat and saw the kitten's eyes crack open a tiny bit then close again. She decided to let mama see what she could do and set the kitten down in front of its mother.

Riley and Finn watched as the mama cat nudged and licked her kitten all over and the kitten began to squirm, letting out a faint mew. Riley exhaled deeply as Eve came running down to them with a box and some towels.

"They gave me half wet, half dry," Eve said motioning toward the towels, and still looking uneasy.

The kids arranged the dry towels in the bottom of the box and used the wet towels to rub over the kittens to get any soot off their bodies. They didn't dare try this with the mama cat because even though she was showing trust, she was still a stray and might not tolerate it. Riley and Eve gently placed the kittens into the box one by one when they were through, the mama cat watching them closely.

"Here, they gave me this too." Eve reached into her messenger bag and pulled a small, plastic to-go container that had plain shredded chicken in it. Once they put the chicken in the box with the kittens, the mama cat hopped inside and they were able to carry her and the kittens away from the burning house. Riley was surprised, she figured this cat couldn't be that feral if she was trusting them this much. She hoped the mama cat knew they were trying to help.

Finn called his mom and asked her to bring a small crate so they could safely move the little feline family they had just saved. Before he hung up he said, "Call Rhonda, too. She may be able to take them in for now."

As the firefighters battled the now blazing old house, the kids moved to the parking lot of Spiced Right with the cats in tow. Riley was shocked at how fast the fire moved and was grateful they were able to get the kittens out when they did.

As a firefighter was looking Finn over to be sure he was okay, Riley looked at Eve and said, "What did you see, anyway?"

"I thought it was real!" Eve said. "She looked like a real girl and when she darted through the traffic, I thought I was going to have a heart attack!"

"Do you think she led us to the house?" Finn asked as the fireman was inspecting his eyes and nose, his back to Riley and Eve.

Eve nodded, "I think so." She lowered her voice and said to Riley, "She obviously wasn't real, she was a ghost."

Riley felt a chill run up her spine and was glad the fireman was too preoccupied to hear what Eve said. "I'm so glad she took us there, but I hate that place. I mean, I hate seeing it on fire, but it's called The Creepy House for a reason."

Eve looked uncomfortable. "Yeah, I'm sorry I didn't get closer, that girl wasn't the only ghost who was at that house."

"Did you see something else?" Riley asked. She thought about the stories she had heard about the house, and the nasty male ghost who reportedly haunted it. If she were Eve, she wouldn't want to go near him either. The stories about the ghost were bad enough, she certainly wouldn't want to see him.

Eve fidgeted with the strap on her bag. "When I told you guys that I could see ghosts, you warned me that The Creepy House supposedly had a really nasty ghost haunting it so I've always avoided it." Eve breathed in sharply. "I think the story about him being the hangman for the town is true. When I came around the corner, I just felt so much hatred and evil."

"Did you see him?" Riley asked. "Did he say anything to you?"

Eve took a deep breath and swallowed tightly, nodding her head. "He was horrible. He came right at me and screamed, 'Go!'"

Riley shuddered, then looked around. She always got a weird feeling at The Creepy House, but never saw anything. Eve noticed and said, "He's not up here, thank goodness." She rubbed her hands on her crossed arms and looked around as if she wasn't quite sure.

Finn had finished up with the fireman when Mrs. Murphy arrived. She was frantic, but glad to see everyone was fine. She placed her hands lovingly on Finn's shoulders, looking him right in the eyes, "Are you okay?"

Finn smiled lopsidedly, "Yeah, mom, I'm fine. We had to save those kittens." He paused, noticing his mom wasn't yet convinced. "And the smoke wasn't bad in the crawl space." He added, "I wouldn't have gone in if it was."

Mrs. Murphy gave her only child a big hug and then checked Riley and Eve to make sure they were okay too.

"I've checked them all out," the fireman said. "They're all fine. That's a brave young man you have there." He looked at Riley and Eve. "All of you are brave for saving these kittens, but you need to be really careful with fire. It can spread faster than you'd think. Next time, let us do the dangerous work." He winked at the kids before he set off to join the rest of his crew.

After Mrs. Murphy checked everyone over and heard the story, she seemed to realize that they weren't hurt, but still made them call home. Finn's mom spoke with their parents herself, assuring them they were okay. After convincing their parents to let them have their lunch at the Public House as planned, they helped Mrs. Murphy get the mama and her kittens into the crate in the back of her vehicle.

"Rhonda said she'd take care of the cats for a while and get them checked out, so I'm heading that way," Mrs. Murphy said as she closed up her car which was parked in the Spiced Right lot. The cat and her kittens were snuggled up in the crate in the back of her car, ready for some TLC from the biggest cat lover they knew. Finn's mom gave each of the kids a hug before turning to leave. "You three be careful, now," she instructed. "Lunch only. No more adventures today!"

CHAPTER FIVE

Lunch with Friends

The Public House sat across from Roswell's town square and was formerly the company store for the nearby textile mill. The pretty brick building with large glass windows that looked out to the town square was also reportedly haunted and that was one reason Riley and Finn loved going there. The restaurant was busy today, but not too crowded. "I'm starving," Riley said as she read over the menu.

"Me too," Finn said.

"I wish you could help us when Finn's mom has his party here," Riley said as she looked up at Eve. Finn's mom was an event planner and had a holiday party coming up at the Public House.

Eve's expression turned bashful, "I do too, but I'm going to volunteer at the homeless shelter with my dad and Evan. We always do it around the holidays. Plus, someone else is coming with us."

Riley's blue eyes grew wide and she looked expectantly at Eve, "Who?"

Eve smiled and looked down at the table, then up at Riley, "Tim Harrington."

Finn said, "Is your dad going to be okay with that? I mean Tim's great, but he's a bit of a trouble-maker."

"I'm more worried about Evan to tell you the truth!" Eve said, speaking about her older brother. Even though she and Evan had different parents since Eve was adopted as a baby, he was the typical older brother and very protective of her. "You think my dad is over-protective, you should see Evan."

Riley sat back in her chair as the waitress came to take their order. "That should be interesting! I think it's cool that he's going to feed the hungry with y'all." She looked at Finn, "He may be a troublemaker, but he's a good guy."

Finn agreed, "He is. That's cool that he's going with you. I didn't realize he was into community service."

Eve said, "We were working on a science project in class and got to talking about helping the poor and I told him he could come with us. I was kind of surprised when he accepted."

"That's cool," Finn said.

Eve smiled kindly, then offered a change in subject, "So, how's Buster doing? He's so cute!" Riley was happy to talk about their new dog and her face lit up at the mention of him.

"He's perfect!" Riley added before updating Eve on every detail, including how they picked the name, all of Buster's cute attributes, and even his venture into potty training. She concluded, confessing to her close friends, "After Sammy died, I didn't think I'd be this excited," she said, "but after saving those dogs from the puppy mill, I knew we'd be a great family for one of them. And it looks like we are."

"It's almost unbelievable what you uncovered at that mill," Eve said.

"Sometimes I still can't believe what we found," Riley said. "I do have one nagging thought, though...The entrance to the puppy mill that Mister Clinton was using, why wasn't it secured? Anyone could have found it and gone in."

"Don't you remember seeing that old iron gate against the wall, across from where we were standing when we followed Mister Clinton out?" Finn said.

Riley thought for a moment, "No, I guess I didn't. I was so scared and exhausted. It still feels like the whole thing wasn't real."

"It was also pretty tough to get up there without an ATV," Eve said. "And my dad said the old road was blocked off to discourage people from continuing up that way. Even if they did hike up it, they could have found the entrance. Finn's right, my dad said there's an old iron gate with a padlock, no one could have even gotten in."

"No one except Mister Clinton," Finn said.

"That's the thing," Riley said as she took a sip of water then continued. "Do you really think he was doing all of that himself?"

Finn cocked his head and thought for a moment. "I hadn't really thought about it. I just figured that since he works part time for the National Park service, specifically at that park, it was an easy place for him to hide his operation. I mean, it would be easier to do it there than his own house."

"I think he could pull that off by himself," Eve said as she wiped the corner of her mouth with her napkin. "Like Finn said, he had the opportunity with that really hard to find and out of the way place, and his motive is money. Why else would someone run a puppy mill?"

"It's so gross," Riley said as she tossed her napkin on the

table in disgust. "I just don't understand how people could put money above compassion. I don't care if you gave me a million dollars, I wouldn't do what he did to even one dog."

"I know," Finn said, and Riley could read his eyes all too well, he was thinking of what they had seen, something that was hard for either of them to shake. Those images would stay with them forever. "It's horrible." There was nothing more to say.

"Well, those dogs are so lucky that you guys were so brave," Eve said cheerfully.

"And lucky that your dad is such a great detective!" Riley added, grateful for her friend's positivity. "I don't know what we would have done if he hadn't been there, thanks for letting him know what we were up to."

"Of course!" Eve said. "I was happy to help since I couldn't go with you. And it's so cool that your family adopted one of the mill dogs. Buster is so lucky."

Riley felt so happy—and pretty proud—that she and Finn had exposed an illegal puppy mill and helped save so many lives. She was grateful for Eve's friendship. The three of them, this morning alone, had even rescued a family of kittens. And now Buster was in her life, and Riley couldn't be happier!

CHAPTER SIX

Missing Dog

Several days had passed since Riley, Finn, and Eve had rescued the cats from the fire and Riley was happy to hear from Finn that the mama cat and kittens were doing well at Rhonda's house. Rhonda loved all animals, but was a cat lover who had "foster-failed" and kept several cats she had fostered and fallen in love with before they were adopted. Riley was relieved to hear that the one she had given CPR to was flourishing. She had been working hard with Buster around the house, especially with potty training, and he was getting there, already going outside most of the time.

Riley was dressed and ready to join Finn and his mom to set-up for the party at the Public House. Luckily, Mrs. Murphy wanted the kids in black pants and black shirts for the evening, which meant Riley didn't have to wear a stupid dress or skirt. She had a pair of slim black pants that were really comfortable, and she and Finn bought all black slip-on sneakers that were approved by Mrs. Murphy. She was so much easier to please fashion-wise than her own mom.

Finn had asked his mom if they could help with the event and maybe get some time to ghost hunt. Riley was excited that he thought to ask. They could be in the building before and after the event and might capture evidence of one of the spirits thought to haunt the Civil War-era building.

Riley was in the family room waiting for Finn and his mom to pick her up, scrolling through her phone while Buster snoozed under the coffee table in his safe spot. She smiled affectionately at him and then paused on a story about a missing dog.

"Oh, no!" Riley said.

"What's wrong, honey?" Her mom asked from the kitchen.

"This dog named Baby Girl ran off when two people tried to rob her owner at gun point. She got between her dad and the bad guys and saved his life, but when she heard the gun shot, she ran off and hasn't been seen since."

"Oh, that's horrible!" Riley's mom said. "Where did it happen?"

Riley scrolled through the post. "At a hotel off Holcomb Bridge Road. Her family is staying there while their home is being repaired after a pipe burst."

"How awful!" Riley's mom said as she dried a pot she had just cleaned.

"Baby Girl is still missing and in the post they mentioned that losing her was like losing a family member. They're even getting a tracking team to help track her scent." Riley thought back to when Sammy went missing over summer break and how relieved she was that their neighbor, Hawk, found him in his back yard. "Remember when Sammy went missing, and of all people, it was Hawk who found him? I'm so glad he did."

Hawk was a retired Army Ranger who had moved in across the street and up one house. The first time Riley ever saw him was at the ice cream parlor and then she thought he was following her home. She was so scared, she thought some crazy man was following her and Sammy. As it turned out, however, he was their new neighbor and was suffering with PTSD. He wasn't weird, he was just dealing with stuff and happened to be walking home as well. Riley felt so stupid when she realized he was her neighbor.

Riley's mom smiled, "I feel so bad that we thought he was a strange man. We certainly learned a lesson, didn't we?"

"When Hailey didn't shut the door tight and Sammy got out, I was terrified. We're so lucky that he didn't go far and ended up getting his collar stuck on a branch in Hawk's backyard." Riley thought about Sammy, fighting back tears. At the end of summer he had died in her arms and she still missed him terribly. He was her sidekick. "You know, Sammy loved Hawk and Hawk loved Sammy. I'm glad that Hawk was able to meet Sammy because I think he helped him."

"I do, too," Riley's mom said as she walked into the family room and sat on the love seat adjacent to the sofa Riley was on, peeking under the coffee table to see Buster sleeping comfortably. "Any word on when Hawk's going to get a dog of his own?"

"I know he was waiting until he got back from that job he was on, but Finn hasn't said anything. I'll have to ask." Finn's dad's nephew had an organization that matches veterans with service dogs. "I would think by now Hawk should be close to the top of the waiting list."

"I hope he gets one soon," Riley's mom said. "With no wife or even a girlfriend, he must be lonely."

"How do you know all of that?"

Riley's mom smiled, "You may think I'm a busy-body, but

I keep up with what goes on around here."

Riley laughed. "I don't think you're a busy-body! You just... you just make a point to know everyone's business!"

Riley's mom laughed and she smiled warmly at her younger daughter. "It's good to know what goes on in our neighborhood."

Riley loved moments like this when she and her mom laughed together. Her phone buzzed and she said, "Finn and his mom are here." She gave her mom a quick hug. "Bye, mom!"

***

They were in the car for the short drive to the Public House and Riley told Finn about Baby Girl.

We'll have to keep an eye out for her," Finn suggested. "Since she didn't go missing too far from here, we might spot her." Riley could tell Finn wished there was more they could do to help.

Mrs. Murphy already knew about Baby Girl too. "Angels Among Us knows all about her and has their volunteers on alert. Don't worry, I'm sure she'll turn up soon."

Riley really hoped so, she knew Baby Girl's family must be so scared. "Oh, I almost forgot, have you heard from your nephew if Hawk is going to get a dog soon?"

"Oh yeah, what did he say?" Finn asked his mom who had placed a call to her nephew earlier in the day.

"He called back and said that they have a dog in mind for Hawk and are going to bring him up just before Christmas to see if he will be a good fit. They also like to take a look at the house to see where the dog will be living."

"I bet that's why he had that fence installed when he left town for work," Riley said. "He probably wanted to make sure the house would be perfect for his own dog." She smiled as she thought about Hawk getting his own dog because she knew he really needed one.

As if reading her mind, Finn said, "I hope he gets his dog soon, he really needs one."

Mrs. Murphy agreed, "I know, and it sounds like he will have one really soon." They pulled into the parking lot behind the Public House and saw the manager, Mr. Wood, waiting for them by the back door.

"I wish Eve could have come with us," Riley said as she unfastened her seatbelt.

Finn agreed, "Yeah, but she was so excited that Tim Harrington was going to volunteer at the homeless shelter with her and her family, so that's cool."

Riley smiled. "Yeah, and I'm not sure she'd be too interested in ghost hunting."

"Hey guys!" Mr. Wood called as Riley, Finn, and Mrs. Murphy got out of the car.

"Hi Dave!" Mrs. Murphy said as she rounded the back of her SUV and opened the back. Riley and Finn grabbed containers from Mrs. Murphy as Mr. Wood walked up to help.

"I've got the restaurant all ready to go," he said as he helped Mrs. Murphy unload the hand truck and stack boxes on it.

"Great!" Mrs. Murphy said. "We should have a nice group tonight."

The genial manager had a twinkle in his eyes as he looked at Riley and Finn and said, "I even have a table set for Michael and Catherine." He was referring to two ghosts that are thought to inhabit the restaurant.

"Really?" Finn asked.

"Yep, I always set a table for them, and I think they appreciate it." He winked at Finn.

Riley asked, "If you don't set a table for them, do they do stuff to the restaurant?"

"Well, it seems there's always something going on around here, but, yes, there seems to be less activity when we honor them with a prime table."

"That's so cool!" Finn said.

"Alright, my ghost hunters, we've got work to do, so let's get this stuff upstairs," Mrs. Murphy said as she closed the back of her vehicle and started toward the restaurant.

Riley could feel her excitement rising. She'd heard the stories about the ghosts who haunted the Public House and was excited to have access to the restaurant when it wasn't open for business. Maybe she and Finn would be able to capture evidence of the Civil War-era ghosts?

CHAPTER SEVEN

Party Prep

"After we get the centerpieces on the tables, you two can do a little ghost hunting," Mrs. Murphy said as Riley and Finn trailed behind her up the stairs, each with a box in their arms.

"Won't you need more help than that?" Riley asked.

"We'll see. Mr. Wood has the tables set and ready to go, I may just need you to run supplies up here for me." She smiled at the kids as they reached the second floor and set the boxes down.

Riley scanned the second floor. There were beams across the ceiling and a copper bar at the back. Tables were set with white cloths and black cloth napkins. There was a table for two along the left wall with a sign that said, "Reserved."

Mr. Wood came out from the small hallway next to the bar. He noticed Riley looking at the table. "That's the one for Catherine and Michael," he said with a smile upon noticing Riley's gaze.

"That's so awesome!" Finn said excitedly.

"They seem to like it," Mr. Wood said with pride as he set wine glasses on the tables.

"Okay," Mrs. Murphy said as she looked over the boxes they had just brought up. "Let's start putting the centerpieces in the middle of each table." She lifted a pretty floral centerpiece that had fresh pine and winter flowers along with white roses.

"These are so pretty," Riley said as she picked up a centerpiece and took it over to a table on the far side of the room. "And they smell so good!"

"Thanks, Riley! I also have a box of tea candles that will go in these little glass holders. Finn, can you see if the candles are in that box over there?" Finn's mom pointed to the box closest to the staircase.

Finn was looking through the box, "I see big candles, but I can't find any small ones."

"Okay, maybe they are still in the car. You two keep putting out the centerpieces and I'll run and check."

Finn pulled a small plastic box out of his pocket and set it on the table reserved for Michael and Catherine. "Just in case they're here," he said as he grinned at Riley.

"Is that your EMF detector?" Riley laughed when she said this, she knew her best friend couldn't wait to get here, not to help with the event or for the event itself, but to see if he could find evidence of ghosts.

"Yep, and I've got my mini-recorder too, just in case we have a chance to do an EVP session." Finn had an eager smile on his face as he set his recorder on the table along with his EMF detector, switching them both on. EVP stood for Electronic Voice Phenomena, and basically meant it was something you could hear recorded, but not to the naked ear. They had caught an EVP of a man named Mister Oscar, a slave ghost, who it turned out had been following them to protect them.

Riley and Finn finished dressing the tables, setting out all the centerpieces and little glass candle holders. Mr. Wood had gone back to the office down the hallway past the bar, and they heard Mrs. Murphy walking back up the stairs. She was a little exasperated.

"I have no idea what could have happened to those candles," she said as she brushed a piece of blond hair off of her forehead. I know I packed them." She looked around the upstairs, mentally reviewing her inventory. "I have the smaller centerpieces downstairs for those tables, let's get started on them."

"Looks great!" Mr. Wood said, coming from the office. "Are we all set here? I'm going to go downstairs to review the menu and timing with the kitchen and wait staff."

"Almost," Mrs. Murphy said. "I can't, for the life of me, find my box of tea candles." She dug through the last box adding, "Oh well, if we have time, I can run out and pick some up." She looked at her watch and frowned.

"I should have extras in the cellar," Mr. Wood said. "Kids, do you want to check for me while I meet with the staff?"

"Sure!" Finn said. " I didn't even know there was a basement here!"

"It really is more like a cellar, dirt floor, nothing fancy, but it gives us much-needed storage...and, when the building was remodeled, Confederate money was found down there."

"What? That's so cool!" Finn said.

Riley was excited too, "I love that Roswell has all this cool history!"

Mr. Wood agreed, "I do love this place." Riley could tell he was proud to be the manager of such an historic property and she respected that.

Riley and Finn followed the manager down the stairs to the main level and crossed through the main dining room into an alcove that led to the kitchen. Just to the left of the kitchen was a small hallway with a door at the end. Mr. Wood opened the door and flipped the light switch on.

"At the bottom of the stairs, to your left will be a wall with shelving. Look near the bottom, there should be white boxes labeled 'candles'. Just grab a box and bring it up to your mom." With that, he headed into the kitchen.

Riley and Finn headed down the creaking wooden steps. Finn was leading the way. "These steps are kind of steep."

"Yeah, and you can really feel it get cooler down here." Riley said as she held onto the wooden railing, inhaling the musty, earthy scent of the cellar.

The only light other than the one above the middle of the staircase was almost directly at the bottom of the stairs, and it was kind of dim, Riley noticed.

Once they got to the shelves, Finn squatted down to look at the bottom and found the white boxes Mr. Wood had mentioned. "Here they are," he said as he opened the flaps that had been woven shut. "Yep, these are the ones we need."

As Finn stood, Riley had her phone out and tapped the flashlight app. "It's a good thing they don't keep the candles back there." She shined her light past where they were standing and it didn't offer much light but they could see some tables and chairs and a bunch of boxes stacked up. The walls were stacked stone and the entire floor was dirt. "This is kinda cool."

"Yeah," Finn said as he looked around. "Now this place has got to be haunted!"

Riley laughed at Finn. "I haven't heard any stories about a haunted cellar. I think they've got enough ghosts upstairs! Besides, if you were haunting this place, wouldn't you much rather stay upstairs where it's warm and bright?"

"Good point," Finn said as they turned to head up the stairs.

Riley's phone chimed. "I have notifications set to keep me posted on Baby Girl, I really want to help find her. I feel so bad for her family, especially since they are staying at a hotel while their house is being repaired. I'm sure they can use all the help they can get."

Finn thought for a moment as they headed up the stairs. "Yeah, me too. Other than working with Buster and figuring out our reports for school, we've got all break to do what we want."

Riley smiled and loved that her best friend had the same interests as her. While they did have to work on reports for history class, including an oral presentation, they could actually enjoy some free time over their holiday break. Like Riley, Finn loved helping others and knew they would both feel so proud if they could find Baby Girl themselves. "We won't interfere with any of their trackers or anything, but maybe just do our own investigation," Finn added.

"That's a good idea, I would love to help her family...they sound like they really treat Baby Girl like a member of their family."

Finn agreed, "Yeah, all dogs should be so lucky."

They climbed up the rest of the stairs and Riley was the last one up so she turned off the light before closing the door. She shivered and rubbed her hands along her arms, "I got a chill."

"Yeah, it's much nicer up here," Finn said. "Warm and

toasty!"

While they were in the cellar, Mrs. Murphy had moved down to the main level and started decorating there. Riley and Finn joined her in the middle of the dining room.

"It looks so pretty, Mrs. Murphy!" Riley said as she admired the festive centerpieces now dressing up the tables. It had gotten darker outside and Riley noticed the floral centerpieces glowed with tiny light bulbs.

"Thanks!" Finn's mom said with a bright smile. "These are called fairy lights, and while I love them, I want more ambiance. Please tell me you found some candles, they'll create such a nice glow and I really don't have time to run out."

"Yep, got 'em right here." Finn handed the box to his mom.

She looked inside, relief washing over her face. "Great, can you two start down here and put them in the holders, then go upstairs and do the same? I'm almost done with everything down here."

"Consider it done!" Finn said as he and Riley got to work setting out the little candles.

They worked quickly and were finishing up the last two tables downstairs when Riley looked to her left, across the large room and toward the back corner where the entrance to the kitchen and cellar hallway were.

"What's up?" Finn asked as he noticed Riley's sudden glance.

"Oh, nothing. I just thought I saw something, like a shadow," Riley said as she tucked her brown hair behind her ear and set her last candle in its holder.

"It's getting dark," Finn said motioning to the large front windows that looked out onto Atlanta Street. "It was probably just car lights from outside, shining into the room."

Riley turned and looked out the windows, "Yeah, probably. Besides, Michael and Catherine are upstairs, right?" She gave Finn a wry smile.

CHAPTER EIGHT

A Shadowy Surprise

Upstairs, Riley and Finn set out all the candles and Finn grabbed his digital recorder he left on Catherine and Michael's table. "Shoot, I left it on when we went to look for the candles."

"Are the batteries dead?" Riley asked.

"No, I put fresh ones in both of these before we left, they should be okay. Let's do a quick EVP session." Finn checked the EMF detector which was also left on then set it back on the table. Riley joined him, standing in front of the table reserved for the two spirits thought to haunt the restaurant.

Finn held the mini-recorder and started the session. "Is anyone here with us right now?"

As was their normal routine, Riley and Finn remained quiet to leave time for a response before Riley asked the next question. "If you're here with us, can you give us a sign?"

"Look!" Finn pointed to the EMF detector which had gone from steady green lights to red, then back to green. "Can you tell us your name?"

Riley waited and was about to ask another question when she heard a scraping sound by the bar. "Did you hear that?"

"It sounded like it came from over there," Finn said, nodding to the bar. "Like a glass moved or something."

They heard more movement from near the bar and saw

Mr. Wood coming from the office. "Hey guys, I see you found the candles."

"Yes, sir, thanks." Finn said. He turned off his recorder and grabbed his EMF detector. "We were just finishing up, about to head downstairs to see if my mom needed anything else."

"Did you capture anything?" Mr. Wood asked and nodded at Finn's devices.

"We might have. We'll know for sure when we listen to the EVP session." Finn sounded uncertain. "I hope it's okay that we did a little investigating."

"Sure, no problem! I know you two aren't going to do anything to provoke them. Maybe you'll have more time later, when all the guests are mingling."

"Yeah, we're really careful," Riley said. "The last thing I want to do is upset a ghost and have it follow me home!" While she was joking, Riley did truly wonder what would happen if she upset a ghost, or worse, if they came across an evil spirit. For this reason, she always made sure to be respectful. She thought of The Creepy House and the stories of the evil spirit who haunted it. She understood why Eve was so scared the day they came across the burning house - that ghost wasn't one Riley would ever want to experience.

***

Riley couldn't believe how tired she was from helping with the event and it was only half-way over! She and Finn had been up and down the stairs all night, and despite Mrs. Murphy's original assessment that they would probably have most of the night free, they hadn't had a chance to think of doing any more ghost investigating. Riley and Finn were at the coffee bar in the main dining room taking a few moments to sit and rest their feet, drinking some much needed water.

"I hope we will be able to do more investigating," Finn said as he took a long sip of water through a straw. "But I doubt it."

Riley sat to his right on the high bar stools, her chin resting in her hand. "I know, I'm so tired, though. When this is over, I'm just going to want to go home." Riley got a chill and saw a dark shadow flash by her side.

Finn was about to say something when he turned to the left and looked back toward the kitchen.

"Did you see that too?" Riley asked. She sat bolt upright, her blue eyes wide like saucers. "I saw that shadow again!"

"I saw it," Finn said. "It looked like it went back toward the kitchen, but there was no one there." He hopped off his stool. "Let's go back and look around." Riley could sense the anticipation in Finn's voice.

Riley followed Finn to the opening of the kitchen, where they could see the wait staff and cooks, but everything looked normal.

"Did you hear that?" Riley whispered.

"What?" Finn whispered back.

Riley pointed down the short hallway that led to the door to the cellar. "I heard something down there. But the hallway's empty," Riley said. Finn was already moving down the narrow hallway, so Riley followed behind him.

"Look," Finn said. "The door is cracked. Should we check it out?"

"Sure," Riley said as she tucked her hair behind her ear.

Finn turned the light switch on and the dim cellar bulbs

lit up. He pulled his EMF detector out and handed it to Riley, hanging on to the recorder himself and turning it on. "Just in case," he said with a smile.

Riley and Finn slowly made their way downstairs and when they got to the bottom, everything looked as they had left it earlier.

"I swear I saw something," Riley said. She had the image of a small, shadowy figure in her mind.

"I know, me too." Finn pulled out his phone and turned on its flashlight. "Do you think it was just another trick of the lights?"

As he said this, Riley held up the EMF detector which was steady red. "Look!"

"Wow." Finn looked around. "I don't really see anything that could be messing with the magnetic field down here, but who knows."

"Shine your light toward the back wall like before," Riley suggested. She was squinting to see past the pile of old tables and chairs.

"Did you see something?"

Riley looked at the EMF detector which had now gone back to green. "I don't know," she confessed. "I just wanted to check." She craned her neck to see past everything, ignoring the EMF detector.

"Look!" Finn said, pointing to the device. "It lit up again! Let's go back there and take a look."

"Okay," Riley said, "but keep that flashlight on. It's dark back there, and I have a funny feeling."

By the time Riley and Finn reached the pile of old furniture, the detector was steady red. Riley got excited. "Finn, is that a door?" She pointed behind the stacks of chairs and tables to what looked like an old wooden door.

Finn held his phone so it would illuminate the area Riley was indicating. "It looks like it might be!" he said. "Here, let's just move these few chairs, and then I think we can slide the tables out of the way."

There were two rows of chairs stacked in front of two tables, one upside down, on top of the other. They each slid a stack of chairs out of the way and then each of them grabbed a corner of the tables and slowly slid them out so they could get behind. Sure enough, when they got behind the tables, there was an old wooden door.

"Oh my gosh! What do you think is behind it?" Riley felt her stomach flip.

"It probably just leads to another room, let's check," Finn said, always eager to explore.

"Should we really be doing this?" Riley looked at the EMF detector which was still lit up red, though some of the lights were blinking. She took a deep breath, "Okay, but if there are bats, I'm outta here...and back up the stairs!"

Finn laughed. "I promise, if there are bats, we're going back the way we came." The two were referring to the encounter in the caves when bats sent them running right into the boo-by-traps that almost stranded them deep in the cave system. "Who knows, the door might even be locked." Finn grabbed the old iron door knob and turned it...it wasn't locked.

CHAPTER NINE

The Key

The door opened out, away from them and Finn grinned at Riley. "You know we at least have to take a look."

Riley took another deep breath, calming her nerves. "Okay, but let's be quick, I'm getting the heebie-geebies." She felt cold and figured it was the earthen cellar, though there was an odd feeling she just couldn't shake. She rubbed her hands along her crossed arms to warm them.

Finn pushed the door all the way open to pitch darkness. "Get your phone out," he said. "We're gonna need more than just my light."

Riley put the EMF detector in her back pocket and pulled her phone from the other one. She turned on her flashlight app and joined Finn in the doorway.

While their lights weren't the brightest, they shined them into the opening which appeared to be a long tunnel. "Oh my gosh!" Riley whispered in wonder.

Finn stepped through the doorway and into the tunnel, shining his light along the walls and ceiling. "I wonder where this goes."

"This is crazy," Riley said. She shined her light along the wall and ceiling. "These look like the same stones as in the cellar." She slid her hands across the rough stone walls and followed

Finn down the tunnel, the darkness creeping in behind them as soon as their weak lights passed by.

Finn was moving forward steadily, but Riley felt unsettled and she had a weird sensation of dread. Slight dizziness settled over her and she found her voice again. "Finn, I think we need to go. We don't know what's down here. I've got a weird feeling." Finn glanced back at Riley and she could sense he wanted to keep going. "I'm sorry," she said, "I just don't feel good."

"Okay, let's go back upstairs. We can find out more about this later."

Riley turned and figured they were only about ten feet into the tunnel. The dim cellar light gave her a sense of relief momentarily...and then it disappeared. "Oh no, is someone in the basement? The lights just went out!"

Finn jogged up behind her. "Come on, let's go."

"Hurry," Riley called back to her friend. She was moving at a frantic pace now, tripping over her own feet as her light bobbed erratically in front of her.

"Almost there," Finn encouraged, coming up beside her.

They were about two feet from the tunnel door when it slammed shut. Riley and Finn lunged toward the door. Finn grabbed the iron knob. "Thank God it's unlocked." He opened the door and let Riley through. She shined her light around the cellar.

"Hello?" she called. "Is someone here?" No one responded and she saw no one. "Did that just happen?" Riley asked in amazement.

Finn's eyes were wide and he looked around, "Yep, sure did. Either that door slammed on its own...or someone is or was down here." Finn shined his light around the cellar, seeing no one lurking around. "It might even have been someone we can't see."

Riley got a chill. "I'll go turn the lights back on and we need to put this stuff back." She motioned to all the furniture they moved. "Maybe it was here for a reason," she suggested as she headed up the stairs two at a time, her heart pounding.

By the time Riley had come back down stairs, Finn had already pushed the stacked tables against the door. He smiled at her. "Well, that was weird."

"Weird?" Riley stammered. "That was terrifying!" Her stomach was in knots, her nerves shot, but she felt better than she had in the tunnel. She grabbed a stack of chairs and slid it back in front of the tables and Finn did the same with the other stack. "There's no way that door slammed on its own. We're underground and there's no air circulating down here."

"Could there have been air from the tunnel?" Finn wondered.

"I think we would have felt it." Riley was nervous in an unexplainable way. She was sure someone or something had slammed that door shut, but there wasn't a soul around.

"At least there were no bats!" Finn laughed.

Riley jokingly punched Finn in the arm. "You're lucky there weren't." She grabbed the EMF detector out of her back pocket. "Here, I'm done for the night."

As she handed Finn the device, the lights went from steady green to red and flashing. "You might be done, but someone else isn't," Finn said, still grinning.

"Doesn't anything scare you?" Riley asked. She turned toward the stairs as something clanged on the wooden steps.

She froze. "What was that?" She and Finn walked over to the stairs and on the bottom step, there laid a key. An old-fashioned key, right in the middle of the step.

"I know that wasn't there when we came down. We would have stepped right on it, it's right in the middle of the step where we walked." She was flabbergasted.

Finn agreed. "We were looking down too, 'cause the steps are so steep. And look how it's laying. It's perfectly centered on the step, almost as if it's pointing to the tunnel."

Riley picked up the key and examined it with the light from her phone. "It looks old. Should we see if it works the lock to the tunnel?"

"We may as well since we're down here. I'll try it really quickly." Finn grabbed the key and headed toward the door. He moved one stack of chairs this time, and laid across the stacked tables, just reaching the key hole. The key fit right into the keyhole. "It fits," he called back to Riley. "But it won't turn. It must not be for this door."

"Maybe it's the key for the cellar door." Riley suggested as they headed up the stairs back to the restaurant. "Then again, this door has a simple push-button lock," she said as they passed through. "Something you could pop open with a bobby pin versus a real key."

"Strange," Finn said. "Let's hang onto it, just in case."

"Let's ask Mr. Wood to be sure it isn't one of his keys," Riley said as she pushed the cellar door behind her after switching off the lights.

"Okay, but I bet he says it's not. That key wasn't there when we came down. I think it was left for us to find."

Riley felt her stomach flutter. Why would someone, or something, leave us a key?

CHAPTER TEN

Preparing For A New Neighbor

The next morning, Finn was at Riley's house early because they found out last night that Hawk was getting his dog today! Normally they would be very eager to go through their ghost hunting recordings as soon as possible, but this was more important, Riley and Finn wanted to paint a "Welcome Home" sign for Hawk's new dog.

The two friends were in Riley's basement with Buster snoozing under the coffee table where he could watch from a distance. "I'm so excited about meeting Hawk's dog!" Riley said as she dipped her paint brush into some red paint.

"I know, I wonder what kind he's getting." Finn said as he painted the 'W' in welcome. "Can you imagine him with a little fluffy dog?"

Riley giggled as she pictured the muscular retired Army Ranger with a delicate toy breed, then thought about how Sammy had seemed to calm Hawk down. "Well, as long as the dog helps him, it really doesn't matter what kind it is." She looked across the room to see what Buster was up to. "Look," she said to Finn and nodded in the direction of the sitting area across the room.

"He really likes it under coffee tables, huh?" Finn asked as he smiled at the little dog.

"I guess it's where he feels safest. I'm glad he wanted to come down here with us, and I don't mind carrying him down the stairs, he'll figure them out eventually." Buster still hadn't figured out stairs and was wary of going up and down them, which Riley had come to expect. Each time they approached stairs, she tried to get him to go up or down them, enticing him with a treat, but so far Buster wasn't ready.

"I'm not surprised that he's down here with us versus upstairs with Hailey," Finn said as he continued to paint.

"Yeah," Riley agreed. "She's always talking on her phone and I think he likes the quiet." Riley said as she worked from the other end of the sign and was painting the 'e' in home. "I guess with us he can hear the back and forth of our voices, not just the constant chatter of Hailey's one-sided conversations."

"And she talks so loud when she's on the phone," Finn added and they both laughed.

"I was trying to be diplomatic," Riley said as she smiled at Finn, then turned to look at Buster. "I'm just glad Buster's settling in and knows he can go wherever he feels safe. It'll be cool when he's finally able to relax. He hasn't been able to do that yet."

"That's so sad." Finn said as he added more paint to his brush. "But he'll adjust, and I'm glad he has a home. Speaking of that," he added, "any news on Baby Girl?"

"No." Riley's tone was grim. "I checked last night when we got home and again right when I woke up. There have been some sightings in this one neighborhood, but it's amazing how many dogs look like her until you really examine her picture. I feel so bad for her family."

"You never know, someone could have picked her up and decided to make her their pet." Finn's tone grew sad as he added, "Think about it, if someone was passing through, she could even be in another state by now."

Riley knew that was a possibility, especially since the hotel where she fled from was right near a major highway. Sometimes people picked up strays and kept them as their own instead of trying to find the owners. She felt sad just thinking about it. "I know, and the only way anyone will know is if they take her to a vet and scan her for a microchip. But if someone's keeping her..."

"It's like a needle in a haystack," Finn said, completing Riley's thought.

"Totally," Riley said and they both continued to paint. "So, I was thinking about that tunnel last night," she said, offering a change in subject. She was curious to see what Finn thought of the whole escapade after a night's rest. "We were so freaked out about that key...but there's a tunnel under those buildings!"

Finn glanced up at Riley, his eyes bright and she knew she had struck a chord. "I know," he said enthusiastically, "And it's so cool! I fell asleep last night wondering where it goes. It's gonna drive me crazy now."

Riley looked at her friend with raised eyebrows, "Well," she said, "we could always investigate them."

Finn's eyes were wide with anticipation. "Really?" he asked. "Even after finding the caves? And the weird vibes you got last night? Are you sure you're up for more adventure?"

Riley laughed. "I just want to research them to see what we can find out. I mean, tunnels under Roswell would be pretty cool, though I definitely haven't heard any rumors or legends about them. Besides, it's not like we can just walk into the Public House and tell Mr. Wood we want to hang out in the cellar. Let's start researching them and see what we can find."

Finn smiled. "Yeah, somehow I don't think that asking Mr. Wood for access would work." He went back to painting. "I agree. Let's do some research and see what we can find out. That building pre-dates the Civil War, so you never know! Maybe Mrs. Willnow knows something or can get us some good history books?" Riley thought Finn had a great idea. Mrs. Willnow was their school librarian who helped the kids with their research on the Cherokee Caves, and she just might be able to help them with information on the tunnels too.

"Yeah, we'll have to ask her. I can email her since we won't see her at school until after break." Riley loved Mrs. Willnow and the two had grown close over their love of dogs. She started to work on the 'm' in home. "What do you think about the key? Mr. Wood had no idea where it came from, but it was cool that he let us keep it."

"Yeah," Finn agreed. "That was nice of him. It's weird that he didn't recognize it," Finn confessed. "We know it wasn't there before we went into the tunnel. And the door slamming like it did, that was strange."

Riley agreed, and she concentrated harder on outlining the letter on the sign while she thought through the situation. "It's almost like someone was pranking us," she suggested. "Have you heard anything about the ghosts of Catherine and Michael pulling pranks?"

Finn stood to look at the progress on the sign. "No, but

I did hear that there was a spirit on the first floor that used to mess with people in the bathroom, something like the bathroom stall would lock or unlock by itself. From what I remember, I don't think that's attributed to Michael or Catherine."

"Maybe when we listen to the recordings we'll hear something. I can't wait to see what we captured!"

"I know. I'm so excited about Hawk's dog, but I can't wait to see what we got...if anything. After we meet Hawk's dog, let's listen to the recordings and see if we captured anything." Finn looked at his watch. "Right now I want to get this sign done so it can dry before we have to go over there."

"Yeah, let's paint faster," Riley said. "Does Hawk know we're coming over?"

"Yeah, my dad asked if it was okay. He said Hawk thought it was cool that we were going to have a welcoming party."

"I can't believe I was ever so scared of Hawk," Riley said, thinking back to when she thought he was following her home.

"Well, he's quiet and a pretty big dude," Finn said. "And he was following you home...just to his house!"

Riley and Finn laughed. "I'm so glad we got to know him, and I can't wait to meet his dog!" Riley thought again about meeting a new dog and her breath caught in her throat. She stopped painting abruptly and Finn noticed.

"Everything okay?" He looked at her with concern in his eyes.

Riley drew in a deep breath, thinking about her gift to "see" what experiences an animal wanted to share with her. "I hope Hawk's new dog doesn't have anything to communicate with me."

CHAPTER ELEVEN

Welcoming Lennox

Riley and Finn took the "Welcome Home" sign over to Hawk's house as soon as it dried, making it there by 11:30. Riley rang the door bell as she and Finn held the long banner, facing the front door, only somewhat awkwardly.

Hawk opened the door and a soft smile spread across his bearded face. "Hi, guys," he said. "Wow, that's a really nice sign."

"We can't wait to meet your new dog!" Riley said, grinning from ear to ear.

"Yeah," Finn added. "Where would you like us to put this?" He held up a roll of masking tape in his other hand.

"Let's hang it here on the porch so he can see it when he gets here," Hawk said.

"Cool! So, you're getting a boy!" Riley said. "Does he have a name already?" She thought she might be more excited than Hawk.

"Yeah, they're calling him Lennox. If it sticks, I'll leave it. No sense confusing him if he already understands."

Riley beamed at Hawk; he was so respectful of the dog already.

"Here," Hawk said to Finn, "I'll put the tape on while you two hold it." Minutes later, the kids and Hawk had the sign proudly displayed and Finn's parents walked up the driveway to join them.

"That looks great!" Mr. Murphy said as he shook Hawk's hand.

"You two did a great job," Mrs. Murphy said. "Here, we brought you something." She handed Hawk a toy basket with some durable dog toys and treats.

"Those toys aren't for a small dog," Finn observed, glancing over the basket.

"Nope," Hawk said. "Lennox is a pit bull mix, he's gonna need tough toys."

As they were talking, a black SUV pulled up and the Murphy's nephew, David, got out of the car. "Looks like we've got a good welcoming committee," he said heading to the porch. He hugged Finn's mom and dad and shook Hawk's hand.

"David, do you remember Finn's friend Riley? She lives across the street." Mrs. Murphy said.

"Hey, yeah, nice to see you again." David said to Riley with a wry grin, "I heard about your adventure uncovering the puppy mill. Glad you got out safely and that you rescued those dogs. Good job!" He shook Riley's hand and she felt proud. David then looked at Finn, held his hand up and Finn slapped it, giving him "five."

"Are you ready to meet Lennox?" David said, turning to Hawk.

"Absolutely, man. Can't wait." The two men walked to the back of the vehicle while Riley, Finn, and the Murphys stood on the porch to give Hawk room as he met his new companion. They watched in anticipation as David opened the lift gate and then the crate in the back of the vehicle. He attached a leash to the dog's collar and all Riley could see was a giant smile on Hawk's normally subdued face.

A shiny, black dog with a broad forehead and patch of white on his chest jumped out of the vehicle and immediately walked over to greet Hawk. The beautiful dog wagged his tail so fast, his bottom shook from side to side. Hawk was smiling bigger than Riley thought possible as he squatted to pet his new dog. As he got close, the dog licked his face, his tail still going a mile-a-minute.

Riley had tears in her eyes. Not only was Hawk happier than she had ever seen him, but this dog was in love. Riley thought if this were a cartoon, she'd see pink hearts floating above Hawk and Lennox. Hawk took the leash from David and let Lennox smell around the yard. After a few sniffs, he found a spot to relieve himself and continued sniffing along the yard as they walked to the porch.

Finn was first to pet Lennox who gave him kisses and tail wags; then he was on to Mr. and Mrs. Murphy who were so gleeful as they petted the happy dog.

Riley stood back and watched and David seemed to notice. He looked at her and said, "It's okay, he's really sweet. These guys get a bad rap."

"Oh, uh, yeah...I know," Riley said. She realized that David thought she was scared because of Lennox's breed, David had no idea that she was sacred she might "see" something when she touched Lennox. "It's not that," she said, trying to think of something to say. "I'm just enjoying watching him meet everyone." Riley didn't want them to think she was scared of Lennox, so she squatted down and held out her hand, exhaling a deep breath.

Lennox came bounding over and immediately gave Riley kisses. She couldn't resist his love and reached out to touch his back to pet him. As she did, she saw a newborn puppy struggling to get out of a thicket, then someone throw a rock at the poor pup. Next, she saw the puppy in a shelter with four other puppies and their mom, all of them a mix of black and white, Lennox the only mostly black dog. Finally, she saw the puppy a bit older, frolicking around a huge yard with a man. She watched the vision, captivated as she stroked Lennox's back. In the yard, the puppy ran from one side to the next, a man's feet in the frame of vision, and then, the puppy looked up to reveal the man's face...it was David.

"Are you okay, Riley?"

Hawk's voice sounded muffled and Riley snapped out of it and pulled her hand away from Lennox. "Yeah, sorry, I...I," she stuttered. "I spaced out." She looked down to see Lennox's beautiful amber eyes looking right up at her. "You are just the sweetest, luckiest dog!" she said as she scratched him behind his ears. This time, she felt nothing but happiness exuding from the lovely creature before her.

Finn reached a hand over to pet Lennox as well and he and Riley exchanged knowing glances.

"He certainly fits right in, doesn't he?" David said, grinning. Lennox trotted over to Hawk's side where he stood tall, his tail making a thump, thump, thump sound each time it hit Hawk's leg.

"What's his story?" Mrs. Murphy asked.

Riley kept her mouth shut, though now she knew. She had

slipped before when they first met Molly, the dog the Murphys ended up adopting, and she wasn't going to do that again.

"His mom was a stray and had given birth to a litter of five pups," David said. "They were living on the streets for about a month before they were found and given shelter. There are so many pits in shelters, but the puppies got adopted fairly quickly, except for Lennox."

Mrs. Murphy interjected, "Black dog syndrome?"

"Yep," David said noticing Hawk's questioning glance, so he explained. "For whatever reason, black dogs have a tough time getting adopted. The rest of the pups were black and white, like their mom, but Lennox is almost all black and never found a home."

"That's crazy, I've never heard of that," Hawk said.

"I hadn't either until I started working with dogs," David said. "A lot of people gravitate to dogs with more color, patterns, prettier coats, and black dogs get stuck trying hard to find homes."

"It's so stupid when you think of it," Riley said. "I mean, if the dog has a good personality, who cares what color it is."

"Kinda like people, too," Finn added.

"Exactly," Riley agreed, smiling at her best friend.

"Then you have the fact that he's a pit mix," David said, "and he was going to have a really tough time getting out of there. The shelter saw how good he was with people and how he seemed so sensitive and intuitive, so they called me to see what I thought. We did temperament testing and agreed to work with him. He's turned out to be one of our best dogs." David reached down to scratch Lennox on the top of his head, and the dog looked up at him and grinned.

"Did his mom get adopted?" Riley asked, though she was fearful of the answer.

"Yeah," David said. "There are some great pit bull rescues around Atlanta and one of those took her in. I think she's living in the mountains now."

"That's awesome!" Riley said, grateful for the happy ending.

"Kids, let's let David and Hawk get Lennox settled in, we can come back and visit another time," Finn's dad suggested.

Hawk was smiling. "You guys can stop over any time to see Lennox, and I'm sure we'll see you out for walks." He looked at Riley. "I almost forgot, how's your new dog settling in?"

Riley smiled. "He's good, it's only been a week, but he's getting used to things. I'm careful about taking him out for walks because he's still skittish about a lot of things. I mostly take him in the back yard, because he's still getting used to everyday life. He doesn't like men very much, but is good with other dogs."

"Well, if you need help bringing him around strange men, I can certainly help you with that," Hawk said, making everyone laugh.

Riley blushed and wondered if Hawk realized she had been scared of him when they first met. "I might take you up on that," she said. "You can sit with a handful of treats and I'm sure Buster will warm up to you quickly!"

After saying goodbye, Riley and Finn headed across the street and Finn's parents went up the street toward their house. Riley couldn't wait to listen to their EVPs from last night, but she was preoccupied with what Lennox showed her. She thought about Lennox and why she had seen him as a puppy.

Why hadn't that happened with Buster? Maybe because she had already seen what he had suffered? As they walked up her driveway, she asked Finn, "Did it look obvious that I saw something when I petted Lennox?"

Finn looked unsure of what to say, "I mean, I could tell something was up, and it seemed like Hawk did, too, but it wasn't strange, you just looked like you zoned out."

"I've got to figure out if I can control this at all." Riley's thought was interrupted by a chime from her phone. "A new Baby Girl sighting! Let's go!"

CHAPTER TWELVE

A New Spirit

Riley and Finn pedaled as fast as they could up the hill to Founder's Cemetery. "I texted Eve to meet us," Riley said in between breaths. The cemetery was located just outside of Eve's neighborhood and located on a high piece of land not far from Vickery Creek and the old mill workers' homes. It's a small cemetery with lots of houses around it, some dating back to the mill, others more modern.

As the kids made their way up the gradual hill, Finn said, "You know, they say that the cemetery was actually larger and that they unknowingly built some of these homes on top of graves."

"Oh my gosh!" Riley said as a cool breeze stirred up some dead leaves along the road. "That's awful!"

"I know. I guess the graves must have been unmarked or something." Finn said as they made it up the hill and to the entrance of the cemetery, spotting Eve who was waiting on them. "Hey, Eve!"

Eve was standing at the bottom of the steps, looking nervous. "Hey guys."

"Are you okay?" Riley asked as she rolled to a stop on her bike next to Finn.

Eve smiled, "Yeah, you know me and ghosts...plus, you

know my dad. He was overprotective before we got into trouble down at Vickery Creek. Now it's worse." Eve was referring to the evening that she, Riley, Finn, and Molly went to Old Mill Park to see if she could see the spirit of the dog that her friends had found in the creek. When they heard a gunshot, they had called Eve's dad who was not happy. After that, Eve had been given less freedom than ever.

"Does he know you're here?" Riley asked.

"Yeah, I told him there was a Baby Girl sighting and that I wanted to join you guys. I guess he figures I can't get into too much trouble up here." Eve rubbed her hands along her arms as she looked at the cemetery.

"I'm glad he let you join us. We won't do anything crazy... today anyway!" Riley said with a grin, making her friends laugh.

Finn stood astride his bike and looked at Riley. "Where did the notification say that Baby Girl was spotted?"

Riley put the kickstand down on her bike and swung her right leg over the bike, standing next to it. "Someone on the page said a tan dog that looked like Baby Girl was seen in the cemetery."

Finn got off his bike and joined Riley and Eve at the steps that led up to the cemetery. As they got to the top of the steps, he admired the iron arch over the cemetery. "This is cool."

Riley looked up at the black metal sign that read, "Founders Cemetery" and said, "Yeah, it's nice." She looked around the cemetery, more concerned with finding Baby Girl. "Well, we can see all of the cemetery just by standing here." There was a large tree to their left and foliage around the perimeter of the cemetery, but it was a fairly open space without many places to hide. "If she was here, she's not now."

Finn noticed Eve gazing at the large tree, "You know, people have seen ghosts around that tree."

Eve looked away from the tree and headed in the opposite direction. "Well, we're here to find Baby Girl, so let's take a look around."

"Yeah, let's go," Riley said, not concerned about ghosts right now. She scanned the cemetery for any signs of the missing dog.

Finn was still thinking of ghosts as they scanned the area. "Remember that picture someone took on the Roswell Ghost Tour? It totally looks like a man from a different period and it was taken over there," Finn said, pointing to the tree.

"It did," Riley agreed, recalling the unsettling photo. "But we're not here to ghost hunt, okay?" she reminded Finn with a sincere smile.

"I know, sorry," Finn said. "We still have to listen to the EVPs from last night."

Riley nodded, peering left then right, and back again for any signs of Baby Girl. She, Finn, and Eve passed by the tomb of Roswell King, one of the city's founders, and it loomed over them, casting shadows as they passed.

"I would think the only place she could be would be around here," Finn said. He walked around the end of the cemetery and came back through while Riley paused to peer around the tombs, Eve close by her side. "There's a house back there," he motioned with his thumb behind himself before adding, "but you're right, if she was here, she's gone now."

"Let's check along the bushes," Riley suggested, although she was pretty sure they had missed her. They looked around the brush along the perimeter, but saw no signs of the missing dog and as they headed toward the steps, they saw an older couple walking along the street.

"Excuse me?" Riley said from the top step as the couple stopped on the street below them. "Have you seen a large, tan dog around here?"

"No," the woman said, "but we did see an animal control truck drive through about fifteen minutes ago."

Riley smiled politely as the couple continued on. "Okay, thank you."

"Well, that would be good if animal control found her," Eve said as she skipped down the steps, seemingly eager to get further from the cemetery. "They would check her for a microchip and get her home."

Riley shivered as a coolness passed her by. She rubbed her hands along her arms, agreeing with Eve. "Yeah, that would be great." She looked around her, back toward the tree. "Well, she's definitely not here and I'm getting a little creeped out. Let's head back home and keep an eye out for her along the way."

"Sounds good," Finn said. "We can go through some of the side streets, just to see if we can spot her. I am pretty excited to listen to the recordings from last night too!"

"Me too," Riley said. She had an odd feeling sweep over her and she glanced around once more.

"You alright?" Finn asked, noticing her skittish behavior.

Riley looked at Finn, "Yeah, I just got a weird sensation, almost like we're being watched."

Finn looked around, but saw nothing and looked down the steps at Eve. "Eve, do you see anything?"

"Thankfully, no." Eve said, already on her bike, ready to go.

Finn looked around the area again and said, "Alright then, let's go."

Riley and Finn trotted down the steps to their bikes to head back home. As they joined Eve, she said, "I wish I could come with you, but my dad said I could come here, then had to come straight back."

"I feel bad," Riley said.

Eve smiled, "It's okay. I was the one who wanted to go to Old Mill Park that evening...and after you guys found the puppy mill and nearly got hurt..." Her voice trailed off.

"Yeah, we were pretty stupid," Riley said, trying to lighten the mood.

"Well, I'm sure your dad will loosen up after a while," Finn said. "After all, he's a cop and sees all the bad things that can happen."

As the kids rode past the cemetery, Riley noticed the old house that sat next to the cemetery on their right. She swore she saw an old lady on the porch, but looked again and no one was there, although it was tough to see through the overgrown yard. She noticed little glass bottles that hung from the trees then out of nowhere, a dog charged the fence, barking loudly at them and jumping on its side of the chain link fence.

"That almost gave me a heart attack!" Riley said to Finn and Eve as she looked at the pretty steel-gray dog. "Hey buddy, sorry to bother you!" Riley said in a sweet voice. But the dog was not to be calmed and clearly was a good guard dog. Riley glanced at the porch again and this time did see an old woman with a stern look on her face, peering from behind one of the craftsman-style columns. Riley smiled but her smiled was not returned.

***

Back at her house, Riley and Finn were greeted by Buster who came dashing out from under the coffee table to greet Riley. "Are you sure you didn't see that old lady on the porch?" Riley asked one last time as she knelt down to return Buster's greeting.

"I'm sure," Finn said. "I saw the dog barking at us from behind the fence, but I didn't see anyone on the porch."

"That's so weird. She looked mean, and when I smiled at her, she just stared back at me, like she was staring through me." Riley shuddered.

Finn chuckled. "Are you sure it wasn't a ghost?"

Riley smiled, "Positive!" She gave Buster a treat from the jar on the counter and praised him for being so brave. Then she scooped him up and snuggled him. She asked Finn, "Hey, have you thought about what you're going to write about for your report?" Buster licked the tip of her nose and she kissed him and set him down.

"You, of all people, thinking about school when holiday break is just starting?" Finn smiled at Riley.

"I know, I guess it's because I'm nervous about it. I don't want to have to get up in front of everyone to present it. I think my topic will be about the mill workers who were sent away after Sherman came through. It will be easy since I know a lot about it and maybe that will help me be less nervous."

"I'm not sure yet," Finn said. "I want my topic to be something cool that no one else will think of!"

Riley smiled. She loved how exuberant her best friend was. "Do you want to go ahead and listen to the EVPs all the way through, then I'll come down?"

"You don't mind?" Finn asked.

"Not at all," Riley said sincerely. She knew how patient Finn had been and wanted him to get started. "I want a few more minutes with Buster and I need to take him out," Riley said. "And I'll make us some hot chocolate."

Finn smiled. "Cool, I'll go ahead and get started," he said and headed to the basement.

Riley took Buster out to the backyard to potty then tried to entice him to play. He still didn't quite understand how to play and was content to be near her in the sunshine. Riley loved watching his little nose twitch as he gathered all the scents of being outside. He squinted at the sunlight and she thought about that nasty place where had spent the first four years of his life with a shudder. Buster put his tiny paws on her legs and scratched her. She picked him up and cuddled him. "I'm so glad we got you out of there," she said to him. Buster responded by licking her face and Riley figured it was his way of agreeing with her and her heart swelled.

Riley made hot chocolate for herself and Finn before joining him in the basement. She had to make two trips because she wanted Buster to join them and he still wouldn't try the steps. Riley sat on the sofa next to Finn and Buster took his spot under the coffee table upon which Finn had all his ghost hunting stuff laid out. Finn's headphones were plugged into his digital recorder, and he had two notepads and pens laid out.

"Well, did we capture anything?" Riley asked expectantly.

Finn smiled and nodded. "We sure did!" He handed Riley the headphones. "Remember when we were upstairs finishing putting those candles out?"

Riley nodded.

"We did an EVP session. I cued it up where I asked if there was anyone here with us."

"Okay, cool," Riley said and she slipped the headphones over her ears while Finn pushed the play button. Riley heard Finn's voice say, 'Is anyone here with us right now?' then her own voice say, 'If you're here with us, can you give us a sign?'. She then heard Finn say, 'Look!' then ask, 'Can you tell us your name?'. Riley closed her eyes so she could concentrate better. After a pause she heard something, her eyes popped open and her head cocked to the side. "Rewind it a little."

Finn pressed a button on his recorder, then hit play again. Riley heard 'Can you tell us your name?' again and then she heard a voice, but it was faint and it wasn't hers or Finn's. "Oh my gosh!" She took off the headphones and turned to Finn.

"Don't say anything! Here write it down." Riley and Finn had a system where they would write down at the same time what they heard so neither of them would influence the other.

Riley scribbled on her pad and waited for Finn. "Okay, ready?"

They turned their pads at the same time and found that they had both written the same name: "Arnie."

"Who is that?" Riley asked.

"I have no idea, I was expecting Michael or Catherine, if anyone," Finn said. "But Arnie? I don't know, we'll have to ask Mr. Wood. And that's not all."

"There's more?" Riley asked, her eyes wide with anticipation.

"Yep, when we went back to the cellar and found the tunnel."

Riley shivered. "When the door slammed and we found the key?"

"Yeah," Finn said, though he hesitated. "But...I'm not going to say anything, I just want you to hear it." Finn looked at his notepad and cued up the tape to the time frame he wanted and let Riley listen.

She heard Finn's voice say, 'Come on, let's go.' Then she heard another voice, clear enough that she didn't need him to replay it, her eyes popped open and she looked at Finn. He nodded for her to keep listening. Riley heard their footsteps and then the sound of the door slamming and this startled her in the present. She continued to listen and heard something after the door slammed. She had Finn rewind it and play it again. After hearing it the second time, she nodded for him to let it continue to play. She heard Finn's voice say, 'Thank God it's unlocked' then heard them open the door and walk back into the cellar. She kept listening and then froze in shock.

"I know!" Finn exclaimed, reading her expression as she removed the headphones.

Riley had her pad and pen in her lap and quickly made her notes as Finn did the same. When they showed each other their pages, they had written the same thing: 'No. Stay. Girl. Danger.'

Riley shuddered visibly this time. "What in the world?" She was dumbfounded.

"I have no idea," Finn confessed. "I can listen to these over again, but it's pretty clear. When we said we wanted to go, the voice said, 'No.' When the door slammed it said, 'Stay,' and when we got back into the cellar, it said, 'Girl, danger.'

"Do you think *I'm* in danger?" Riley asked.

"I don't know, I mean, it didn't seem like anything bad was happening."

"But I got a really weird feeling in that tunnel, like I just needed to get out of there. It wasn't just because it was dark and dank, it was just really unsettling."

"If you were in danger down there, I don't think it would have wanted you to stay." Finn offered.

"Yeah, but nothing dangerous happened upstairs."

"We found the key..." Finn suggested.

"Yeah, but nothing has put me in danger," Riley said, searching for answers.

"I know, I can't figure it out. I don't know why it would want us to stay down there."

Riley looked at Finn, "The voice, though...do you recognize it?"

Finn nodded and in unison they said, "Arnie."

CHAPTER THIRTEEN

Christmas Eve

Riley thought about that EVP all night and couldn't make sense of it, but it was Christmas Eve so it wasn't long before she put the EVP aside and was thinking of all the fun they would have tonight! This year, Christmas Eve would be different for the Carsons. Instead of a party at her family's house, after church Riley's family headed to Mrs. Powell's house where they would spend Christmas Eve with her and Finn's family. Mrs. Powell greeted the Carsons with a cherubic smile and Riley was so happy to be spending Christmas Eve with her.

"I'm so happy to see you, dear," Mrs. Powell said to Riley, ushering her in the door. "Merry Christmas!"

When Riley's mom told her that Mrs. Powell had lived a pretty solitary life in the years after her husband's passing, it made her really sad. She hated to think that anyone had to spend so much time alone. After Mrs. Powell rescued Lily, a dog that had mercifully escaped the puppy mill before it was uncovered, she started going out again. Riley and her mom met Mrs. Powell when they were dining at Table & Main and Riley saw Mrs. Powell with Lily. Riley and Finn had found Lily as a stray on the first day of middle school, and Lily turned out to be very important in helping the kids find the illegal puppy mill. Lily and Mrs. Powell were very special indeed!

The Murphys had already arrived and were enjoying appetizers and drinks in the formal sitting room and greetings went around the room as the Carsons joined the party. When she came into the room, Riley saw a face that she wasn't expecting... Hawk was on the settee with Lily in his lap.

"Hi, Hawk," Riley said smiling. She walked over and held her hand out to let Lily sniff. "Hey, Lily!" she said.

Lily stood up and wagged her white tail, her black eyes shining like onyx. Lily licked Riley's hand and Riley petted her on top of her delicate little head. She exhaled with relief as she realized that Lily didn't have anything to show her tonight.

Hawk smiled softly and said, "Merry Christmas. Lily seemed desperate to get into my lap, so we've just been hanging out here on the sofa."

"So, I guess Lennox is at home?" Riley didn't want to pry and wasn't sure if Hawk needed to bring Lennox everywhere with him.

"Yeah, I figured I'd let him have the night off." Hawk said, smiling. "He's so good everywhere we go, it's me who needs to get used to bringing him everywhere. We've been out and about a lot, so I figured he could use some down time."

Riley was happy to hear how well Lennox was doing. "I'm sure you'll get used to it in no time. And it looks like you have a good surrogate tonight," she said smiling at Lily who was now curled up in Hawk's lap.

"I sure do," Hawk replied.

Mrs. Powell's house smelled wonderful! From the aromas wafting out of the kitchen to the live pine garlands and fresh Christmas tree, Mrs. Powell's house smelled like the holidays.

Fires were lit in the fireplaces in the sitting room and across the foyer in the library. Riley felt warm and cozy and was so happy that they were all together and she was tickled by Mrs. Powell's sweet affection for Hawk. She had insisted that he sit next to her at the dining table and be her date for the evening.

As they were enjoying their meal, Hailey said, "So Hawk, what did you do in the military?"

Riley noticed Hawk's jaw flex as he glanced at his plate. "A little bit of everything," he replied, looking back up at Hailey.

"Like what?" Hailey pried, then took a bit of mashed potatoes.

Mrs. Powell seemed to notice Hawk's discomfort. "Hailey," she said, "often times, our soldiers see so much that they prefer not to discuss it. My husband was a veteran as well, and I learned that if he wanted to talk about it, he would. Otherwise, it wasn't something that he wanted to rehash."

Riley noticed that Hailey looked embarrassed, looking at Hawk sheepishly, she said, "Sorry, I didn't mean to pry."

Hawk smiled slightly. "It's okay, but Mrs. Powell is right, it's not something I really enjoy talking about."

Riley's mom chimed in to change the subject. "So, how's your new dog?" she asked. "I see you two out running every morning."

Hawk's face brightened. "He's great," he said. "It's nice having someone else around the house, especially since I work from home. He's a big ol' goofball. We have fun together."

"I feel the same about Lily," Mrs. Powell said. "She brings so much life to the house." She looked at Riley, Finn, and Mrs. Murphy and said, "I'm so grateful you found her and got her to safety. She's such a blessing."

This made Riley's heart swell. She loved that not only did Lily and Lennox have wonderful homes, she loved that they were so appreciated by their new guardians. She wished everyone revered dogs this way.

After they filled their bellies with turkey and all the fixings, plus homemade pies from Mrs. Powell's grandmother's recipes, Riley, Finn, and Hawk cleaned up all the dishes as everyone else enjoyed coffee. When they were finished, they settled into the library where the Christmas tree was lit up and enjoyed the fire burning in the fireplace. Hawk sat in an arm chair near the fireplace and no sooner had he sat down, then Lily came trotting out from under the tree and hopped in his lap.

Riley smiled. "That dog really likes you!"

Hawk was petting Lily's fine white fur and agreed, "I think so."

Finn was perusing the books on the shelves and turned to Hawk, "Both of the Powell ladies seem to love you!"

They all laughed at this and Riley was happy to see Hawk relaxed and enjoying himself. "I'm so glad you came here tonight," she told him.

"Me too, beats sitting at home alone."

"Well, at least you would have had Lennox," Riley said as she joined Finn to peruse the books.

"Yeah, he's a good dude. Mrs. Powell said I could bring him over any time, so next time, he'll join us."

"Hey, look," Finn said as he pulled a worn black leather book off the shelf. "This looks like those journals that Mrs. Willnow had at the school library. The drawings in here look similar to the ones in that journal that had the map of where we found the caves."

Riley inspected the book as Finn flipped the pages. "Yeah, it sure does. I remember the pretty drawings of the birds and they look like the same artist." She looked over at Hawk to explain. "We found a journal at our school library that helped us find The Cherokee Caves. This journal looks really similar."

Hawk's eyes grew wide. "Wow, that's pretty cool."

Finn looked at Riley and said, "You don't think that journal was Mr. Powell's, do you?"

Riley thought about it as she continued to scan the pages of the journal. "I don't know, but this looks like the same handwriting and artist."

Finn sat down in the other arm chair flanking the fireplace. "If so, I wonder if Mrs. Powell knows those journals got donated?"

"Let's see if Mrs. Willnow still has them, and then we'll ask. I'd hate to bring it up if we can't get them back to her."

"Good point," Finn said. He stopped at a page. "Riley, look! I think there's some information about some tunnels in here!"

Riley crouched next to the arm chair and read aloud, "The old Civil War tunnels would have been the perfect way to move troops and supplies under the Union's noses." She put her hand over her mouth. "Oh my gosh! Do you think the tunnel we found could be connected?"

"That would be so cool!" Finn flipped a page, then another. "Look, here's a crude drawing. The writer wrote, 'I've mapped out where I think these tunnels could be located based on my research.'"

Riley pulled her phone out of her back pocket and snapped a picture. "I'll send this to you, maybe this can be your topic for your report?"

"That would be cool...if we can find enough information. You'd think if there were extensive tunnels under Roswell, we'd already know about them. It would be a cool topic though!"

Hawk piped up. "What report do you have coming up?"

"We have to write reports on the Civil War...and then give an oral presentation," Riley explained.

Hawk cocked his head. "You don't sound excited about that."

Riley inhaled sharply then exhaled. "I'm not. I hate getting in front of people and speaking. I get so nervous."

"I know what you mean," Hawk said as he softly petted Lily, now curled tightly in his lap asleep. "What are you going to write about?"

"I'm going to write about the mill workers who were sent away by Sherman. Women and children worked for the mill while their husbands and fathers were fighting, and after General Sherman found they were still working for the mill, he shipped them off to other states, mostly Ohio and northern Kentucky. The mill was providing fabric for the Confederate uniforms, so you can imagine that Sherman wasn't too happy about that."

Hawk seemed to stiffen and Lily rubbed her head against his abdomen and he petted her to settle her...and himself it seemed. "He sent the women and children away?"

Riley could tell it upset him as it did her, but it probably had way more impact on a veteran like him. "Yeah, they were sent off and many couldn't return. Think about how far that was back then. They didn't know if their husbands had survived the war and in those days it would have taken a long time to get back, if they even had the means. Sherman basically exiled them. It's horrible to think about."

"It is, and you're right that it wouldn't have been easy for them to return home." Hawk paused. "It's good you're going to write about it."

Finn had been scanning the pages of the book while he listened. "I really think these tunnels might have existed! Hawk, what do you think?"

"It makes sense," Hawk said. "In war you've always got to figure out ways to move troops and supplies surreptitiously."

Finn looked confused. "What does that mean?"

"Secretly, right?" Riley said.

"Yep, without notice. You know your vocabulary pretty well."

Riley felt herself blush, she wasn't used to being praised for her intellect. "I read a lot, and English is my favorite subject."

"Yeah, she helps me proof my papers!" Finn added.

Hawk got up and set Lily on the floor and watched her stretch her little white body. He looked at Riley and said, "We all have our strengths. Remember, not everyone knows everything."

Riley smiled. "Thanks."

Hawk stretched his long arms and yawned. "I'm gonna head on out. Y'all have a Merry Christmas."

"Wait, do you have plans for tomorrow?" Riley asked.

Hawk smiled sweetly. "In fact, I do. Mrs. Powell mentioned that she wanted to see her great niece in Dahlonega, so I offered to take her. She even invited Lennox to come."

Riley's face broke into a huge smile. "Aww! That's great!" Riley was so happy that Hawk and Mrs. Powell were becoming friends.

After they said their goodbyes to Hawk and he left the room, Riley took his seat next to the fire. Finn had the journal on his lap, the fire was dancing in his wide eyes. "I think these tunnels might really exist! When you and Hawk were talking, I read some of the research in here, and I think it's legit," he said. "The only problem is that the part about tunnels is at the end of this journal." Finn flipped the pages to show Riley. "When we go back to school, we need to ask Mrs. Willnow about the journals she has; if they are Mr. Powell's, they might fill in the blanks."

CHAPTER FOURTEEN

Christmas Day

Riley's favorite thing about Christmas day was the scavenger hunt that her dad created for her and her sister. She and Hailey always got one big gift and their dad would set clues out around the house that would lead them to their gifts. After tearing around the house in their pajamas, upstairs and downstairs, then back upstairs, and again back down, they ended up in the basement. Underneath the ping-pong table was a large box for each of them, Riley's box was so heavy, she had trouble sliding it out from under the table.

Hailey slid her box out first, unwrapped it, and after opening it, pulled out tons of tissue paper. Finally, she pulled out an expensive handbag she had been wanting. "Thanks, mom and dad."

Their mom was beaming, excited to give her older daughter this gift. "Do you like it honey? It's the one you wanted."

Hailey's face didn't show any appreciation for the gift. "It's nice, but it's the wrong color. I wanted berry and this is burgundy."

Riley looked from Hailey to her mom and was surprised at how rude Hailey had just been. "I think it's pretty." She was trying to make her mom, whose face was crestfallen, feel better.

Their dad had shed his smile as well. "Hailey, your mom

looked all over for the bag you wanted and this was the closest one she could find. You should be grateful for all you have and all we do for you."

Riley inhaled then exhaled. This seemed to happen every Christmas. She just didn't understand why her sister couldn't just be happy. Their dad was right. Most girls her age would be so thankful for that one gift, not to mention all the other stuff she had already unwrapped upstairs. How could Hailey not see how lucky they were?

Hailey smiled weakly, "It's fine, thanks mom."

"No, if it's not the one you want and you can't be grateful, we'll take it back," their dad said. "There's no sense wasting money on something you don't want."

Riley's mom tried to lighten the mood. After all, it was Christmas. "Oh honey, it's okay, let's let Riley open her gift. I think we got the right one." Riley's mom winked at her when she said this.

Riley's interest was piqued. Surely they didn't get her a handbag, she didn't even carry one. She opened the large box and there wasn't any tissue paper, but a large stack of white t-shirts and Riley got excited; she recognized the design immediately. "It's my design!" Her face lit up as she pulled out a shirt and held it up. In black ink was the "Mill Cotton Not Puppies" design she created after uncovering the illegal puppy mill. "Thanks mom and dad!" She jumped up to hug them both.

Riley's parents were smiling again. "It was your mom's idea," her dad said. "We thought you could sell them and raise awareness."

"I love your stickers, but thought you could make an even

bigger impact with the shirts," Riley's mom said as she smiled brightly, the disappointment with Hailey had seemed to vanish.

"I love them! This is the best gift ever!" Riley was happy about the gift, even happier that her mom had thought of it. The fact that her mom celebrated her artistic ability and her passion for making a difference meant the world to her. They may not always see eye-to-eye, but she knew her mom loved her deeply.

***

Mr. Murphy, Finn, and their dog, Molly, greeted the Carsons and from the minute they walked in the door, Riley could smell a combination of meat roasting and an apple pie baking. Mrs. Murphy had made pretty floral arrangements and placed them around the house. There was a beautifully decorated live Christmas tree in the corner of the family room that smelled like fresh pine, its white lights making the colored glass ornaments sparkle. A fire was roaring in the fireplace and Molly had laid down in front of it after greeting them. The scavenger hunt might have been fun, but as Riley looked around, she took in this moment—this was the best part of Christmas.

Riley had a gift bag for Finn and one for Mr. and Mrs. Murphy. "Okay, so you have to open these together," she said as she gathered her best friend and his parents together.

Finn was faster at opening and his face lit up when he pulled out the shirt. "This is awesome! Where did you get these?" By the time he had pulled his shirt out, his parents had opened theirs too.

Riley smiled wide, her parents by her side. "My parents got me these for Christmas. It was my big gift. I have fifty of them that I can sell!"

"Well, forty-seven now," Riley's dad said.

"We have to pay you for them," Mrs. Murphy said.

"Nope, you can wear them and help me advertise. I'm going to donate a portion to rescue groups."

"I love it, thanks!" Finn said. He looked at his parents. "Can Riley and I go downstairs for a minute? I want to play her another EVP that we captured at the Public House."

"Sure," Mr. Murphy said. "You two and those ghosts."

Riley didn't want to leave Hailey out and said, "Do you want to come too?"

Hailey flipped her hair behind her left shoulder, "No, I'll stay up here with the adults. I don't believe in that stuff."

Riley didn't have hurt feelings, she was only asking Hailey to be nice since there weren't any other kids there. She knew if Hailey had joined them, she'd just make fun of them anyway and discount what they were doing.

When Riley and Finn headed down the stairs to the basement, Molly hopped up and followed them down. Riley heard Finn's mom say, "She follows him everywhere," and Riley smiled knowing Molly now had a loving family.

"Did you find some more?" Riley asked once they got downstairs. "Can you make sense of what we captured?"

"Yeah, I listened to it over and over and I still keep coming up with the same stuff. I thought I heard something really faint right before the door slammed, so I put the file on my computer and enhanced it. Here, have a listen."

Riley followed Finn over to the sofa where he had his laptop on the coffee table. Molly was on the floor right next to Finn, resting her chin on his right foot.

"She is so cute," Riley said to her friend and Finn grinned at her before turning back to his laptop.

"What can I say? She loves me!" he joked.

Riley giggled. "I'm so glad y'all adopted her. You're the perfect family for her and it's a bonus that I get to see her all the time too!"

Finn pressed a few keys on his laptop, then handed Riley the headphones. "Okay, listen closely."

Riley put the headphones on and held them against her ears, her head down and her eyes closed so she could concentrate. She listened all the way through and said, "Play it again." Riley closed her eyes again and concentrated. After hearing it again she slid the headphones off and looked at Finn, her eyes narrow. "I can't tell what it is, but there's something there. It's faint and it almost sounds like a moan."

"That's exactly what I hear. I tried to figure out if it could be some type of machinery from the kitchen, but it's too hard to tell."

"You don't think it's a person, do you?" Riley was spooked just thinking about that.

"No, it didn't sound like a person, but I can't quite figure out what it is."

Riley shuddered. "Well, I definitely got a weird vibe down there, remember? I felt sick. Maybe it has to do with the Civil War?"

"Could be," Finn said. "I'm trying to figure it out in the context of what Arnie said."

"We need to find out more about Arnie," Riley said. "We

don't know if he's good or bad. At least with Mister Oscar, we know he's really looking out for us. Who knows why this Arnie wants us down there?"

Finn agreed. "Yeah, we need to find out more about him. We don't want to get involved with something that we shouldn't."

***

After a nice meal with the Murphys, Riley and her family snuggled up at home in their family room to watch *It's a Wonderful Life*. Riley loved Christmas and was taking in their tree with lots of sentimental ornaments as a fire glowed in the fireplace. Buster was in his spot underneath the coffee table.

"Dad?" Riley asked. "What was Christmas like when you were growing up?"

Riley's dad had his arm around her mom who was tucked under a pretty throw blanket. "It was very similar to how we celebrate, Roo," her dad said. "We went to church on Christmas Eve, then celebrated with family and friends over a nice meal. On Christmas morning, we would open our gifts, then play with them all day and had a family feast that night. We didn't get nearly as many gifts as you two, though," he said with a wink.

Riley smiled at the thought of her dad as a boy, unwrapping his presents. "What about you, mom?"

Riley's mom turned to her. "Well, it was pretty similar to how your dad celebrated, but we had even fewer gifts." Riley could see her mom smiling at the memories. "We didn't even put up our own tree, Santa did."

"What?" Hailey asked.

"That's right, when Santa came with our gifts, he also put up and decorated a tree for us." Riley's mom was smiling at her daughters' wonder at this. "We usually got one gift and a new pair of pajamas. There were candy canes on the tree and that was a big treat for us!"

"Wow, that's so different." Riley said in amazement.

"Were you sad that you didn't get more presents?" Hailey asked.

"Of course not, we were so grateful for our presents," Riley's mom said. "I have the fondest memories of Christmas as a child."

Riley could see the wistfulness in her mom's eyes as her dad gave her mom a squeeze then a kiss on top of her head.

"Mom?" Hailey said. "Thank you for my handbag. I'm sorry I wasn't appreciative of it. It was really nice of you and dad to get that for me."

Riley smiled at her sister. She was glad that Hailey realized how lucky they were to have such generous parents who gave them more than they needed. This was a merry Christmas, indeed.

CHAPTER FIFTEEN

Verdict Reached

A couple days after Christmas, Riley was setting the table for dinner while her mom was cooking, and the television in the adjacent family room was on the local news. After a story about a bad traffic jam in Atlanta, came news about the "Roswell Puppy Mill Case." The case had gotten a lot of press which Riley was happy about. As the headline banner switched to read "Verdict Reached," Riley stopped what she was doing to turn up the volume.

"Mom!" Riley called back over her shoulder as she made her way into the family room, her eyes fixed on the TV above the fireplace. "They've reached a verdict in the puppy mill case!"

Riley's mom was wiping her hands on a towel as she entered the family room. "Let's see what they have to say."

The reporter was talking, "Jedidiah Clinton was found guilty of thirty counts of animal cruelty today at the Fulton County courthouse. Sentencing has already been reached and we are waiting for details."

Riley turned to her mom. "I'm so glad! I hope they throw the book at him!" Her pulse quickened as she waited to hear what the man's sentence would be. Riley thought back to that dark, damp, smelly place and even now it made her stomach turn.

Riley felt her mom's hand on her back, rubbing up and down to try to help calm her nerves. "Honey, just don't be disappointed if it's not as strong as you want...or as it should be. You know these laws aren't that tough."

"I know, Mom, besides, he's friends with Mr. Thornton who also helped represent him." Riley felt discouraged already. Mr. Thornton worked at her dad's law firm and was a very successful attorney who rarely lost—and he was Corey's dad. She sat on the sofa and Buster came crawling out from under the coffee table. He put his little tan paws on her legs and scratched.

Her mom looked down at him. "It looks like he knows you're anxious." She smiled at the little dog.

Riley picked Buster up and he sat facing her, then licked her on the tip of her nose. "Sorry Buster, I just want this man to be put away for ever." Buster licked her again and she softly massaged his shoulders. It really did help calm her down.

The reporter at the courthouse held her finger to her ear, trying to hear through her ear piece. "Okay, we've got the sentencing report. Mr. Clinton will be sentenced to 6 months in jail and one year of community service."

"What?" Riley burst out. "How could they let him off so easy?" Tears pricked her eyes and she tried to calm herself so as not to freak Buster out. The little dog was relaxed in her arms and strained his head to lick Riley's face. He could only reach as far as the bottom of her chin.

Riley's mom gave her a hug. "Listen, I know it doesn't seem fair, especially after all you witnessed in there." She held Riley at arms-length. "The judge gave him what he thought he deserved and you know Mrs. Murphy was talking about how the laws just aren't strong enough. At least he got punished, but most importantly, the dogs are safe."

Riley appreciated her mom's words but she felt furious. "Not all of them made it out of there. Who knows how many died in that place! I wish that judge had seen what it was like in there, Mom." Riley thought she might lose it. "Nothing on video could ever compare to being in that place and seeing those dogs like they were."

"I know, honey." Riley's mom tucked a piece of Riley's hair behind her ear. "The only thing we can do is try to lobby for stronger laws, and keep educating people."

Riley straightened her posture and set her jaw. "That's what we'll do then. We have to. People can't keep getting away with stuff like this." Riley snuggled Buster between her neck and shoulder and scratched his neck. "Thanks for understanding, Mom."

Riley's mom gave her a kiss on her forehead. "Of course, Roo. Sometimes we don't get the result we want, but that serves as fuel to make an even bigger impact."

Riley cocked her head and smiled at her mom. She was glad her mom knew how important this was to her. "Thanks, Mom. You're right." Though Riley felt better at her resolve to do more, she also knew she needed to talk to her best friend about this. "Can I go call Finn real quick?"

"Sure, honey. Be back down in ten minutes, though, dinner's almost ready."

Riley carried Buster upstairs to her room and set him on the bed as she sat next to him and dialed Finn. They had to do something about these weak laws. Even though they were a couple of kids, Riley just couldn't let this go, not after all she had seen. After she hung up with Finn, Riley received a text message that didn't make any sense. The number was blocked and the message read, *We won. Haha!*

CHAPTER SIXTEEN

A Meeting With Eve's Dad

The next day, Riley and Finn rode their bikes down Mimosa to Roswell Square where they crossed Atlanta Street and headed down Sloan Street to Eve's neighborhood. The weather had sharpened and when they got to her house, they were pretty cold and thankful to walk into a toasty home that smelled of chocolate.

"Hey guys, so good to see you!" Eve welcomed her friends with a bright smile, her dark eyes sparkling. Riley and Finn followed her to the kitchen where she handed them each a mug of steaming hot cocoa. "How was your Christmas?"

Finn sipped the frothy, warm drink before answering. "We had a good Christmas, how about you?"

"It was good, Savannah was nice..." Eve's voice trailed off and got quiet.

Riley looked at her, "Too many ghosts?"

Eve looked in the direction of her dad's office which they had passed off the foyer. "Yeah, that place can be intense for me," she said quietly.

"Well, guess what?" Riley asked.

"What?" Eve asked. Her eyes brightened as she motioned for everyone to sit around the kitchen table while she grabbed a mug of hot chocolate for herself and joined them.

Riley pulled out her phone and tapped it a few times. "Hawk got his service dog, Lennox." She held her phone out so Eve could see.

"Oh my gosh, he looks so happy!"

Riley smiled. "He is...and so is Hawk. I don't think I've ever seen him smile so big!"

"That's awesome, I hope he helps him." Eve took a sip of her hot chocolate. "And how's Buster doing?" she asked Riley.

Riley tapped her phone and put it back in her pocket. "He's making great progress. We still have a lot of work to do, but yesterday he let me hold him and sat on the bed with me for a while. That's a big step since he usually stays under the coffee table in the family room."

Eve's face grew sad. "Aww, poor guy."

"Yeah," Riley said with an edge to her voice. "Actually, we are hoping to talk to your dad about Jedidiah Clinton. I can't believe he got such a lenient sentence."

"We know the laws aren't that strong, but boy did he really get off easy," Finn said. He set his mug down with conviction.

"Hang on," Eve said. "I'll go get my dad." She left the room returning moments later with her dad.

"Hey kids," Detective Rycroft said. "How was your Christmas?"

"Good, thanks," Riley said. "Yours?" She was being polite but wanted to get to the matter at hand.

"Really nice, but it's always good to get back home. Eve tells me you want to talk about our laws," he said pulling out a chair at the table and having a seat.

"You start," Eve suggested to Riley as she went to the stove to fetch her dad some hot chocolate.

Riley turned to detective Rycroft. "So, obviously we've heard about Mr. Clinton getting off easy and it's so frustrating."

Mr. Rycroft leaned back in his chair and crossed his arms across his chest. "I know, it's frustrating to me too, but like I told you after we found the dogs, our animal welfare laws aren't that strict to begin with."

"You did," Finn said. "And my mom warned us of the same thing, but he got off *so* easy."

"Yeah," Mr. Rycroft said, "and part of that is because he had a good lawyer who also happens to have standing in this town. I know it's hard to understand because right is right, and wrong is wrong, but sometimes power and influence have a real impact. In fact, more often than we'd like."

Eve brought a mug of hot chocolate over for her dad.

Riley looked at Eve's dad and said, "If the laws were stronger, would that have forced the judge to impose a stronger sentence? Like is there a minimum?"

Mr. Rycroft uncrossed his arms and wrapped his hands around his mug. He looked at Riley, "There are minimums and quite frankly, a judge wouldn't want to give such a light sentence that it could look like favoritism, so they do have to work within a certain framework."

"What can we do to make the laws stronger?" Finn asked.

"You'll want to start by contacting your city council members. There are city, county, and state laws and they need to be addressed. Email your council members and be brief but tell them what you want to achieve and why. Hopefully there will be one or two who care about the issue and will speak with you about it." He took a sip of his cocoa. "Then you'll want to reach out to your county commissioners and do the same thing."

"You said, 'hopefully one or two will care about the issue,'" Riley said. "Why do you think so few of them would care?"

Mr. Rycroft exhaled deeply, "Well, it's just that a lot of times, issues that help make money or bring in business can be more important to politicians than issues like this, animal welfare. This isn't an issue that will help bring in income or business, so..."

Riley noticed the tension in Mr. Rycroft's face as he tried to explain local politics to them. "But don't they know what was going on in their town?" she asked, her voice growing louder.

"My partner, Glen, and I took video of the scene," Mr. Rycroft said. "The city council members and mayor know what went on, and hopefully it made an impact on them. Because this issue is so fresh, it would be a good idea to tackle this now."

Riley put her chin in her palms and thought about all that Mr. Rycroft had said. "Well, we can't just sit back and not do anything. We have to at least try."

Mr. Rycroft smiled at her. "I like your attitude." He held up his mug and Riley clinked hers against his.

"To at least trying," she said.

Finn and Eve brought their mugs up and said in unison, "To trying!"

Riley heard footsteps, looked up, and her stomach filled with butterflies.

"Did I miss something?" Eve's brother, Evan was standing in the kitchen doorway with a grin across his handsome face, his long hair falling across his forehead, partially covering his left eye.

Riley blushed and said, "Nothing much, just trying to change the world over here!"

Evan chuckled. "Okay good, for a moment I thought something important was going on." He stood next to Eve and looked into her mug, "Looks like I missed the Hot Cocoa Summit."

As everyone laughed, Riley felt her phone vibrate, a welcome distraction since she felt silly for having a crush on her friend's older brother. She tapped her phone, the message read, *Loser.*

Riley put her phone away and stood abruptly. Who would send me that? she thought. She turned to Eve's dad. "Well, thanks for your time, Mr. Rycroft. We'll have to put a plan together. And thanks for the cocoa, Eve, it was great. Can we help you clean up?"

"No thanks, I'll wash up," Eve said. "Are you two headed home?" she asked, obviously a little confused by Riley's sudden need to depart.

Riley looked at Finn, "Yeah, I just got a text and have to get going," Riley said, hoping Finn would understand. "Plus, we've got work to do. Your dad is right, we need to get started on this while it's still fresh."

They were barely out the door when Finn asked, "What's up?" with a look of confusion on his face.

"Let's ride over to the park, I have to show you something."

CHAPTER SEVENTEEN

A Comforting Voice

Sloan Street Park wasn't far from Eve's house and Riley and Finn biked over to it in a matter of minutes.

"What's going on?" Finn asked once they were settled on a bench along the perimeter of the park. It was a small, neighborhood park with grass in the middle and a brick walkway around it with a few benches. A swing set was on one side of the park and a jungle gym on the other. Riley and Finn were on a bench at one end of the long narrow park, next to an arbor. Looking at the dormant brown grass, Riley longed for warmer weather and green grass.

"I got a weird text last night after I got off the phone with you," Riley said as she pulled out her phone. "I didn't think anything of it because it didn't make sense and I figured it was a wrong number." Riley handed her phone to Finn. "Then I got another one while we were at Eve's house."

Finn took the phone and looked at the screen. "Blocked number. That's weird." He read the messages and then repeated them aloud back to Riley. "'We win. Haha' and 'Loser.'"

"Weird, huh?" Riley said, looking at Finn for help.

"Yeah. You'd think if it was a wrong number and you didn't reply after the first message that they wouldn't text you again." Finn thought for a moment. "Why don't you write back?"

107

Riley thought about it. "I guess it would make sense if I wrote back and said something like, 'Sorry, wrong number.'"

"Yeah, do that and see what happens. It may just be that someone has a wrong number and they are texting you instead of someone who just lost a soccer game or something."

Riley felt better after hearing Finn's interpretation. "Yeah, I guess it could be something silly like that. It was just weird, and with everything else going on, I just got this weird feeling. I got the first message after the news about Mr. Clinton's sentencing, then I got the next message when we were talking with Mr. Rycroft about the case and stronger laws."

"Okay, well now you're sounding a little paranoid." Finn grinned at his friend. "It's probably just a wrong number."

Riley wasn't so sure. "It's a blocked number, though."

"Just text back that they've got the wrong number and see what happens," Finn said. He looked around. "By the way, why did you want to come here."

Riley looked up from her phone and smiled sheepishly. "I've kinda missed Mister Oscar and I think this is the spot where he first started hanging around with us." Riley thought back to the summer day when they were here in the park, the day that Eve later told them she saw Mister Oscar, a ghost who was a slave in Roswell. Riley felt honored that Mister Oscar had chosen to protect them, even if she didn't know why. She just wanted him to know that she appreciated him and liked having him around.

Finn grinned at Riley. "Is it too cold for an EVP session?"

Riley finished her text and put her phone back in her pocket. "Normally, I'd say yes, but...I kinda want to see if he's around."

Finn reached into the inner pocket of his jacket and pulled

out his digital recorder. "I'll let you start."

Riley swallowed hard. "Mister Oscar, if you're here, can you let us know?"

After a pause, Finn added, "If you're here, I want to thank you for looking after us in the caves."

Riley felt a lump in her throat, but she pushed it back so she could speak to Mister Oscar—if he was around. Getting the news about Mr. Clinton's sentence made Riley feel heavy, and she longed for the comfort and protection Mister Oscar had offered her before. "We really appreciate you keeping us safe. Is there anything you would like to talk to us about?"

Finn waited longer this time before speaking up. Then he added as an afterthought, "Mister Oscar, do you know who Arnie is?"

Riley didn't have any more questions. "I miss you, Mister Oscar. Thanks for taking care of us on our crazy adventures!"

Finn smiled and switched off the recorder. "It'll be interesting to see if we got anything."

"I kinda hope we do. It's nice knowing he's out there," Riley said as they walked over to their bikes to head home. "Let's go right home and listen."

They went straight to Finn's house and headed to the basement, Molly following them downstairs, her tail wagging. As Finn set everything up and transferred the recording to his laptop, Riley was content to sit with Molly on the floor. She stroked the beautiful German shepherd along her back as the two sat side by side. "I'm so glad we found you," Riley said to Molly as she petted her. "You're such a sweet girl." Molly licked Riley on her forearm, which made her smile.

Within minutes, Finn was already listening to the audio file, now saved to his computer. Riley could hear mouse clicks and keyboard strokes as Finn worked, and though she was anxious to hear the results, she was equally patient in letting Finn do his work, especially with Molly to keep her company. Dogs always made her feel more relaxed and she enjoyed this quiet moment. It wasn't long before Finn said, "Okay, this is crazy, but I think we've got something interesting."

Riley hopped up to join Finn on the sofa and Molly moved to the space between them. Finn had a smile on his face as he handed Riley his headphones. After she slipped them on, Finn played the short recording and Riley's face softened and a smile spread across it as she listened. Then she heard something that set her on edge. "Play it again," she said, closing her eyes to concentrate.

After another listen, Riley took the headphones off, equally concerned and amazed.

She grabbed her notepad as Finn did the same. "Crazy, huh?" he said as he started scribbling.

Riley nodded as she wrote down her notes and then they exchanged them. The results were nearly identical.

"Let's start with the first one," Finn said looking at the words they had both written.

'I'm here, chil.'

Riley smiled. "It's his accent, 'I'm here, child.' He's responding to me!" Riley was so excited that the spirit that seemed to be her guardian angel was indeed still around and had answered her.

"Let's look at the next line," Finn said, as both kids grew

serious. They had both written, 'Girl, danger.'

"It's the same thing the voice in the tunnel said."

Riley inhaled sharply, then exhaled. "I know, but the voice in the tunnel wasn't Mr. Oscar. It almost sounded...younger. It's like I recognize Mr. Oscar's low, deep voice and his accent. The one in the tunnel was different."

"I agree," Finn said. "But how weird they said the same thing?"

Riley shuddered as miniature bumps crept up her arms. "It's kinda scary. Do you think it's me?"

Finn shook his head. "I don't know, I'm really not sure. I don't know if Mister Oscar would call you girl...but he said it after you asked if there was anything he needed to tell us. He didn't say anything after I thanked him."

Riley could see that Finn was concerned as she searched for an explanation. "Maybe he's trying to tell us about someone else? Someone we're supposed to help?"

Finn thought for a moment then said, "Baby Girl! Mister Oscar knows how much we care about dogs. After all, he was with us in the caves, he must want us to help find Baby Girl!"

Finn's interpretation of the words, correct or not, made Riley feel a lot better. "Then what about the voice we heard in the Public House tunnel? It sounded more like Arnie's voice, so why would he be telling us the same thing?"

"I don't know..." Finn said, his voice trailing off. He seemed unsure and his brow furrowed. "Maybe it's not Baby Girl. We'll just be extra careful."

Riley agreed, there was nothing she could do, except be careful. There was still one more line to review. "The last line is confusing," she said, "-and we came up with something a little different." Riley looked at what she had written, *key sun* and what Finn had written, *keysun*. She was confused about what the words, or word, meant.

"Yours makes more sense than mine," Finn concluded.

Riley's eyes lit up as she realized what it meant. "The key! He was answering you about Arnie—when you asked, 'Do you know who Arnie is?'"

"Do you think he was telling us that Arnie left the key for us?" Finn asked.

Riley grabbed her pad and pencil and wrote, *Key, son*. "I think so! We were thinking of the sun, not how someone might refer to a boy, to you."

"That's awesome!" Finn said, excited. "He calls you 'chil" and me 'son,' that's pretty cool!"

"Okay, so if Mister Oscar is right, then Arnie left us the key...but why?"

"I have no idea," Finn said, "but maybe we'll figure it out, or maybe Mr. Wood can help us figure it out."

"I wonder what it's for..." Riley said, her mind wandering. "Why he gave it to *us*?"

Finn grew serious, "Maybe it has something to do with them both telling us about the girl in danger?"

At Finn's words, Riley felt unsettled again and Molly turned from Finn and rested her chin on Riley's knees, Riley petted her head. "Maybe, but why in the world would we need an old key?"

"I have no idea," Finn said. "It was clearly left for us for a reason, now we just have to figure out why."

Riley felt they were getting answers, but still couldn't make sense of it all. She was so glad that Mister Oscar was still hanging around, that made her feel happy and special. Riley wished she could figure out why this spirit had taken to her and her best friend. She may not ever know the reason but felt comfort in knowing that he had protected them.

CHAPTER EIGHTEEN

Here Comes Corey

The next day was bright, sunny, and warm for a winter day so Riley decided to take advantage of the nice weather and take Buster into the front yard to do some training. She might even see if Hawk could come out and help.

Riley filled a treat pouch with liver treats that Buster really seemed to enjoy and clipped it to the waistband of her jeans. She grabbed the leash and called Buster over, squatting down with a treat in her hand. Buster gently took the treat and Riley clipped the leash to his collar and gave him another one. "Good boy," she said and petted him on top of his head. She stood up and turned around as Hailey came into the room.

"Nice fanny pack," Hailey teased. She sauntered past Riley, plopped onto the sofa, and grabbed the remote control.

Riley looked down at the black treat pouch, her blood pressure rising. "It's a treat pouch. I'm taking Buster out to do some training."

"Well, I hope no one calls the fashion police," Hailey said over her shoulder.

Riley took a deep breath to calm her nerves as she slipped on her sneakers. Buster jumped up on her legs lightly scratching her shins with his tiny nails. Riley looked down at Buster and noticed a smile on his face, his tongue sticking out. She couldn't help but smile and picked him up, giving him a cuddle. She turned on her heel and walked out of the room without a word to her sister. Sometimes Hailey's teasing really hurt.

Buster had been doing so well with training in the back yard that he'd gotten used to the grass and how it felt under his paws. He had seen squirrels and birds and heard cars from the street, but today she would expose him to more activity in the front yard. He would see the road, the cars driving by, and potentially people out and about. Since it was a nice day, Riley actually hoped that they would see people so she could work with him. When she walked him before, it had been cold and quiet so he hadn't seen much activity and she knew more activity would mean more training opportunities. She sent Finn a quick text to see if he could swing by.

Buster found a good scent to pee over on a utility box and Riley gave him a treat. "Good boy!" She said in a high, sweet voice.

Buster wagged his little black tail at her and took the treat gently. Just then, a bike came up from behind her. "Your dog gets treats for peeing? How lame!"

Riley didn't have to look over her shoulder to recognize the voice, but she did anyway. "Corey, leave us alone." She said as she walked away from him and into her yard. "Why are you here anyway?"

Corey smacked a piece of chewing gum. "I'm going to see Seth, now that he lives in your neighborhood, I guess you'll be seeing more of me."

Riley's stomach churned. The last thing she wanted to see was more of Corey Thornton. She tried to ignore him, hoping he'd go away. She sat down with Buster and petted him to help calm her nerves. Riley wasn't paying Corey any attention, but she could feel he was still there.

All of a sudden a high pitched squeal went off and Buster lost it. He spun in a circle and pulled mightily on his leash, trying to find a way to escape. Riley was so glad she had a tight grip on his leash, but it nearly slipped out of her grasp. Buster was crouched on the ground, scared and shaking. Riley picked him up to comfort him and was about to lay into Corey when she saw someone else beat her to it.

Tim Harrington came flying toward them on his skateboard and saw what Corey had done. He slid to a stop right next to Corey and grabbed him by the shirt. "What do you think you're doing?" Tim was in Corey's face, he pushed Corey backward and he fell on Riley's front lawn with his bike still between his legs. Tim stood over Corey and turned to Riley. "Are you guys okay?"

Buster was still shaking and Riley was too, she held him tight. "Yeah, I think so."

Tim took a deep breath, looked at Corey and hissed, "You're lucky I don't want to scare that dog any more. Get out of here!"

"Give me a break," Corey said as he got his feet under himself and brushed off his jeans. "It was just a firework."

Tim's face was two inches from Corey's and Riley could tell he was holding back from yelling. "You just shot a firework at someone and her dog. Don't you know how dangerous that is? Don't you realize how that can scar a dog for life? That dog doesn't understand what a firework is!"

"It's just a dog," Corey said as he pushed past Tim.

Tim stopped him. "It's not just a dog. If I ever see you do

that to an animal again, you won't be so lucky."

Corey acted like he wasn't scared, but Riley could tell he was. He jerked his bike from Tim's grasp and headed in the direction of Seth's house.

Riley was holding Buster close, petting him as her own nerves calmed down. "Thanks," she said to Tim. "Buster is one of the mill dogs we rescued and I was out here trying to work on training him. Bad timing."

"Aw, man. I'm sorry. That kid is such a jerk," Tim said. "He shot that firework right at you two. I saw it from the top of the street and just went nuts."

"I can't stand him," Riley said. "I hope this doesn't traumatize Buster any more than he already is. He's been through so much and is already scared of men. I should probably take him inside."

"Wait," Tim said. "Can I give him some treats so he's not scared of me? I saw a trainer on TV say that you should always end a training session with a positive."

"You know, you're right. I've heard that, too." Riley freed her right hand and dug some treats out of her pouch and handed them to Tim. She set Buster down and she and Tim sat in the grass with him. Buster was sticking right by Riley's side.

"Buster, here you go." Tim made his voice high and sweet.

Riley stroked Buster's back, "It's okay."

Tim held his palm out and showed Buster the three treats awaiting him if he became brave enough to get them. "Here Buster."

Buster's nose wiggled from side to side and he took two tentative steps toward Tim, sniffing the treats. Then he took two more steps and stretched his body as far as he could so he could reach the treats without having to move any closer. Buster quickly grabbed the treats and trotted right back to Riley's side.

"Good boy!" Riley and Tim said in unison as Riley petted Buster. She looked at Tim, "Thanks again, I can't believe Corey did that. I don't know what his deal is."

"I'm glad I was passing by," Tim said. "I can't believe how cruel he is."

Riley smiled, "Yet you're the one who gets detention."

Tim laughed and looked at the grass, a sheepish look on his face. "I do silly things and get in trouble, Corey does mean things and doesn't. Go figure."

Riley saw Finn heading their way on his bike. "Come over slowly," she told him as he reached the driveway. "We just had an altercation with Corey."

"And be prepared to give Buster treats," Tim said. "We're doing damage control."

Finn looked perplexed but did as they said. Buster recognized him and was less tentative around him than Tim. Plus, Buster hadn't ever seen Finn almost beat someone up.

CHAPTER NINETEEN

A Visit With Mrs. Willnow

Riley was sad when holiday break was over. She had made great progress with Buster and didn't like being away from him for so long. The school day was only halfway over and she couldn't wait to get home to see him! Finn, on the other hand, couldn't wait to go ask Mrs. Willnow about the journals she got at an estate sale. First, they had to find Eve.

Riley and Finn scanned the lunch room. "There she is," Riley said, pointing to the back left side of the room.

Eve had grabbed an empty table by the back. "Hey guys," she said as Riley and Finn joined her. "Glad to be back?"

Riley was standing across from where Eve was sitting. "No. I miss Buster and now we've got these projects to do."

Finn smiled, "I'm kinda excited about the project, in fact, we're going to go see Mrs. Willnow. Do you want to come with us and see if she'll let us eat lunch with her?"

"Of course!" Eve said as she quickly packed up her lunch.

As they headed to the library, Eve said, "Well, at least we get to pick our own topic about the Civil War, do you guys get to do the same?"

"Yeah, I'm writing about the mill workers being forced out of Roswell," Riley said.

"Ooh, that's a great topic!" Eve said.

"I'm still trying to decide what to write about," Finn said. "But I think Mrs. Willnow might be able to help me." Finn could hardly contain his excitement.

When they got into the library, they found Mrs. Willnow in her office in the back. "Well, hello you three! Welcome back!"

"Hi, Mrs. Willnow!" They said in unison, then laughed at this.

"Do you mind if we eat in here today?" Finn asked, confident that Mrs. Willnow wouldn't say no.

"Of course not! Have a seat." Mrs. Willnow gestured to the table in front of her office.

"Did you have a nice break?" Riley asked.

Mrs. Willnow had a big smile on her face, her eyes were twinkling. "I did! You know I just love Christmas! It's my favorite holiday. Of course I spent the better part of the weekend un-decorating the house, but it was awesome!"

"How are Maggie and Nikki?" Finn asked, referring to the two Yorkies that Mrs. Willnow adopted from the puppy mill, some of the first to be adopted.

"Oh, they are just great! They got lots of toys and treats for Christmas!"

Riley pulled out her phone and scrolled to a picture of Buster. She held her phone out for Mrs. Willnow to see.

"Who is *that* sweet baby?" Mrs. Willnow asked as she grabbed the phone to get a closer look.

Riley was grinning from ear to ear. "His name is Buster, he's from the mill too!"

"Buster! I love it!"

Riley loved how enthusiastic Mrs. Willnow was. She

explained, "I thought of that name because I busted him out of the mill!"

"Oh, that is too cute!" Mrs. Willnow said as a mischievous look appeared on her face. "Guess what?"

"What?" Riley asked and could tell their librarian had something exciting to tell them.

"I adopted a third dog from the mill!"

"What?" Finn's eyes lit up as he sat on the edge of his seat.

Mrs. Willnow took out her phone and tapped the screen a few times, showing the kids a photo of her third mill dog rescue. "We've named him Harley, and he's just the sweetest!"

"Aww! He's so cute!" Riley said as she looked at the little beige Chihuahua with large pointy ears.

"What happened to his eye?" Eve asked, her face one of concern.

Mrs. Willnow inhaled sharply then exhaled, "It's awful. Apparently, sometimes puppy millers will just pressure wash the dogs' cages...with the dogs still inside. Harley lost his eye when this was done to him."

Riley gritted her teeth and she felt anger well up inside her. "That's horrible!"

"Disgusting," Finn said.

"It's criminal if you ask me," Mrs. Willnow said trying to stifle her anger. She moved to a happier topic about her new dog. "He's just a wonderful little soul and he fits right in with Maggie and Nikki. Those girls love to snuggle with him, and he loves it too!"

"That's awesome," Eve said. "He's lucky to have you."

"We're lucky to have him," Mrs. Willnow said as she put

her phone away and looked at Riley. "How's Buster adjusting?"

"He's good, we've made some great progress with him. He's almost always going to the bathroom outside, that came quickest, thank goodness, otherwise my mom might have been a mess. He still has accidents, but I can tell he's getting the hang of it."

"Does he play with toys?" Mrs. Willnow asked.

"Not really. I don't think he understands what he's supposed to do with them."

"Aww, that's okay, he'll get the hang of it."

"How about your dogs?" Riley asked.

"Of course I've had Maggie and Nikki a bit longer than you've had Buster, but we're still working on the potty training. I think if I had a dog around that already knew the ropes, it would be easier, but they're getting better at it. They love to play, though. They certainly picked that up quicker! Harley's the newest so he's learning from the girls and doing really well. Still skittish, but I can see him relaxing more and more each day."

"That's so great," Eve said.

"We'll have to get them together sometime," Riley said.

"That would be nice!" Mrs. Willnow's face grew serious. "You heard about Mr. Clinton, right."

"Yeah, it makes me so mad that he's getting off so easy!" Riley said as frustration welled inside her.

Mrs. Willnow agreed, "I know, I'm sure it has to do with Mr. Thornton representing him, that and our animal cruelty laws just aren't as strong as they need to be."

"If only the judge had been *in* the mill," Riley said. "The video doesn't give the full picture - it was gruesome!"

"Not to mention we don't know how many dogs died under his *care*." Finn used air quotes with his fingers when he said that last word. They had seen first-hand that those poor dogs received almost no care at all.

"At least he's getting some kind of punishment," Mrs. Willnow looked like she was trying to temper her emotions again and changed the subject. "So, how's your first day back been?"

"So far so good," Finn said. "We all have to write reports on the Civil War, so we need to work on that."

"And give oral presentations," Riley said with dread evident in her voice.

"Oh, you'll do fine," Mrs. Willnow said. "You gotta get used to getting up in front of people some day, so we may as well start you early!"

Riley tucked her hair behind her ear. "I know, I just like to blend into the background and do my work."

"Oh, it's not that bad. The more you do it, the better you'll get. So what are you thinking of writing about?"

"Riley's thinking of writing about the mill workers and I'm not sure what to write about. I bet like half the class will write about Sherman's march to the sea, so I want to do something different," Finn said. Riley could tell he was trying to find the right moment to ask about the journals.

Eve said, "I want to write about what happened at Fort Sumter, the Andersonville prisoner-of-war camp."

"That's a good idea," Riley said. "Some pretty bad stuff happened there, right?"

"Yeah," Eve said, "Tens of thousands of men died because the conditions were so bad."

"It was horrendous," Mrs. Willnow agreed, "I think you'll have a lot to write about."

"That's awful," Finn said. He looked at Mrs. Willnow, "Do you know anything about any tunnels that run under Roswell and may have been used during the war?"

Mrs. Willnow gave Finn a serious look. "Are you looking for more adventure, mister?"

Finn laughed, "No, Riley and I found a tunnel off the cellar of the Public House when we were helping my mom with an event there and I think there might be a system of tunnels that may have been used during the Civil War. If so, it could be a cool thing to write about that no one else would think of."

Riley looked at Mrs. Willnow and said, "He just has to be different!"

This made everyone including Mrs. Willnow chuckle. "I don't know about the tunnels, but if there were any, the Roswell Historical Society is the only place I could think of that would have information."

"Great, we'll have to check it out!" Finn said. "I'm sure Riley could find some good information there too. Oh, and I wanted to ask you about those journals you showed us."

Riley chimed in, "The ones you picked up at an estate sale?"

Mrs. Willnow thought for a moment, "Yeah, the ones that you girls were going through when you were here for detention."

Riley smiled thinking about how lucky they were to get to spend their detention with Mrs. Willnow, because it was the start of their friendship. She and Eve had gotten detention from a stuffy old teacher who saw Riley kick Corey Thornton while trying to save the cat he was tormenting. When Eve tried to defend Riley, she got detention too. "Yeah, those! Do you still have them?"

Mrs. Willnow nodded. "I do. I can't put them into the system and I think they were in a box of books that I purchased as a lot. Why do you ask?"

Finn said, "Well, we think they might belong to our friend Mrs. Powell. We think they might be her husband's journals and we thought it would be nice to get them back to her."

Riley fiddled with the strap on her backpack. "Mr. Powell died and she sold some of his things, but we're not sure she meant to sell the journals. We can pay you for them if you want."

Mrs. Willnow looked at the kids and smiled, "No need to do that. It's very sweet of you to want to return those personal items to your friend. I hardly paid much for the lot of books, so I'm not worried about that." She stood up. "They're in my office, I'll go grab them for you."

Riley looked at Finn and smiled. "Mrs. Powell will be so happy, though I'm not sure she knows they are missing."

Finn said, "Yeah, and I can't wait to see if there's anything else about the tunnels in them!"

Mrs. Willnow came back from her office with the two black journals in hand. "Here you go! Let Mrs. Powell know how I got them, okay?"

"We will, Mrs. Willnow, thanks!" Riley said as she took the journals from the librarian.

"Have a great day," Mrs. Willnow said. "Now go learn something!"

"Thanks for your help," Finn said. "I'll let you know what we find out about the tunnels!"

Mrs. Willnow gave Finn a stern look and said, "Researching them is fine, but don't you get any ideas about exploring anything. After what happened in those caves, you don't need to be going underground anywhere, mister!"

Finn laughed, "I told you I wasn't planning on it, Mrs. Willnow!" He headed after Riley and Eve and said so only they could hear, "But if they're worth exploring...that's another story. After all, I have to do my research!"

CHAPTER TWENTY

Learning From Mrs. Powell

When Finn met Riley at the front doors of the school, she had just put her phone away. "We're going on a detour before we go home."

Finn looked at Riley quizzically, "What's up?"

"Well, I didn't feel right going through the journals without permission, so I thought I'd see if Mrs. Powell was okay with it. I explained to her that we had looked through these journals before, with Mrs. Willnow's permission, but that if they were Mr. Powell's, I wanted her blessing."

Finn looked concerned. "What did she say?"

Riley smiled. "She said we had her permission to look through them, and if we had time, we can bring them over now and look at them with her. She said she'd love the company and she may have some insight into Mr. Powell's research."

Now Finn looked relieved. "That's awesome! Let's go see Mrs. Powell then!"

When Riley and Finn walked up the steps to Mrs. Powell's front porch, they could hear Lily barking inside. Mrs. Powell opened the front door before they could knock. "My little security system let me know someone was here! Come on in," Mrs. Powell said.

Riley and Finn gave the older lady hugs as they entered her

home. She brought them into the sitting room and had hot tea and cookies ready for them. "You didn't have to go to any trouble!" Riley said.

"Oh, it's no trouble at all, dear. I knew you would want something to warm you up and it's fun for me to do. I don't get many visitors, so it's my pleasure to do this for you."

Riley's heart swelled at hearing this. It made her happy to give Mrs. Powell company and joy. As they sat on the settee, Lily jumped up in between Riley and Finn, getting attention from both of them, and giving them kisses in return. Riley pulled the journals out of her backpack and handed them to Mrs. Powell. "When we saw one of Mr. Powell's journals on Christmas Eve, we noticed the handwriting and drawings looked to be by the same hand."

Mrs. Powell smiled and her eyes seemed to twinkle. "James loved to write and research." She opened the first journal and her smile grew larger, her shoulders softened. "Yes, this is his. He loved history and was always writing about the area, stories he heard, and of course, drawing the natural beauty he saw around here." She flipped through the pages, stopping at a drawing of a brown thrasher. "He always loved birds."

Riley smiled, "He was very talented at drawing them. There's a really pretty picture of a cardinal in there, too."

"Those may have been his favorite. He always said it was a symbol of a loved one who had passed coming back to visit."

"That's what my mom says, too," Riley said. "It's neat to think it could be true." Riley often thought of Sammy when she saw cardinals.

Finn petted Lily who snuggled up next to his thigh. "In

the journal in your library, it seems that Mr. Powell did some research on tunnels under Roswell. Do you know more about that? If they were connected to the Civil War, like he said in the other journal, I might be able to write about them for my research project."

Mrs. Powell set the journal in her lap. "He was fascinated with those stories! He did find tunnels that ran from the old cotton mill up to the Company Store, which is now the Public House." Riley and Finn looked at each other, their eyes wide as Mrs. Powell continued. "He said there were two tunnels that led from the mill, but one was blocked off. He had a theory that there were more tunnels, but if there were, he couldn't get to them."

"Where did he think they were?" Finn asked.

"He wasn't really sure, but what he saw underground led him to believe there were more."

"Do you mind if we look through these journals to see what else he has to say about them?" Finn asked. "In the other journal, he does mention that he thinks that they used the tunnels to move supplies from the mill to the Company Store, and that perhaps it was used to move things secretly during the war."

"I don't mind at all," Mrs. Powell said as she handed the journals to Finn. "Here, feel free to have a look as we chat, and you're welcome to take them with you as you work on your project. I'll get the other one from the library, too."

As Mrs. Powell left the room, Riley said, "That's so sweet of her."

"I know," Finn said, "She's so nice."

Mrs. Powell came back in and handed the third journal to

Finn. "James would be so happy to know that his notes and research could be helpful to you."

Riley thought for a moment, then said, "You know, his journals were already helpful."

Mrs. Powell cocked her head, "What do you mean?"

"Well, thanks to what we found in the journals that our librarian had, we were able to locate the Cherokee Caves." Riley and Finn looked at Mrs. Powell, unsure of how she would react.

The old lady giggled heartily. "You're kidding! That's how you found the caves?"

"Yep," Riley said. "There are some drawings in one of them that really helped us figure out where we needed to look."

Mrs. Powell laughed loudly now. "How wonderful! James would be so thrilled!"

"It's so great that he kept all these records," Finn said as he looked up from the journal he was perusing. "Otherwise, this stuff would have been lost to history."

"He would really appreciate that, Finn."

"So," Riley said, "we've heard that your families are related to the founders of Roswell, but that's all we've heard. How did your families come to settle here?"

Mrs. Powell's eyes twinkled. "Sometimes when you're old and you've lived in a town like this all your life, people make you out to be more interesting than you really are. We have so many residents here who aren't originally from here, that people take an interest to old folks like me whose roots go deep here."

"I think it's really cool," Riley said. "Everyone seems to be from somewhere else, and Roswell is one town around Atlanta that still has some history left, and I think that's what interests people so much."

"When Roswell King encouraged folks from coastal Georgia to come up here and settle this town, our families came as well. Our families weren't fancy, rich banking families, just average folks who wanted opportunity. The incentive to settle here came in the form of land and work to do. Plus, the climate was much milder than that of the coast."

"So, this property that we're on, it was Mr. Powell's family's?" Riley asked as Finn paused to listen.

"Yes, they were given this land and initially built a small, one room home on it, more like a cabin."

"Wow!" Riley said.

"They worked hard and were able to build this home once they got on their feet and established themselves and their business here. They were by no means like the Kings, Smiths, Dunwodys, or Bullochs, but they did well with lots of hard work."

"That's really cool," Finn said.

Mrs. Powell nodded in agreement, "Remember, hard work and faith will get you very far, further than your mind could ever imagine."

"What kind of work did your family do?" Riley asked.

Mrs. Powell smiled proudly. "The church. My great-great grandfather was a minister and came here to start a church for the founders."

"Wow, I bet you both have lots of interesting stories that were passed down," Riley said.

"Oh yes, but James did a much better job of preserving the town's history. He told me that when he was a boy, he would jot down the stories his grandparents, great aunts, and uncles would tell him. He just loved history and genealogy!"

Finn pointed to a page in the journal. "It says here that his family was close with the Smith family."

"Yes, I believe they were. If I recall correctly, his family did business with the Smith family and the two families became close."

"Mr. Powell definitely has a lot of research in this one journal about the tunnels and what they might have been used for. Do you know much about them?" Finn had been scanning the pages as he listened to Riley and Mrs. Powell.

"I remember hearing as a young girl, younger than you, that there were tunnels used during the Civil War." Mrs. Powell's tone grew conspiratorial. "There were stories that if the tunnels hadn't existed, the town would have been taken much quicker. Some even say that tunnels were used to move Confederate money out of town."

"Wow, really?" Riley asked, her blue eyes wide.

Mrs. Powell nodded. "Those were the stories we heard. Who knows if they are really true, but after the war, there were all kinds of stories that Confederates around the South hid money to use when the South rose again." She laughed as she said this. "I guess they're still waiting."

Finn was clearly intrigued, his eyes wide. "What did Mr. Powell think about that?"

"Like I've told you, James loved adventures and legends. He was always a kid at heart and I think he really wanted to believe in some of these things. I don't think he would have spent as much time on them had he not. Whether or not the tunnels were used for secretly moving money, or just as a convenience for moving goods is another story."

"What do you think?" Riley asked.

"I know James found tunnels from the mill and that makes sense so they could move goods, especially if they needed to move them under the noses of the Union Army, but Confederate money? I'm not sure, but it's certainly possible. It's been a while since I've looked at these, but I'm not sure how much help they will be for your project."

Riley could tell Finn was disappointed to hear this. "I'll go through them to be sure. It makes sense that tunnel is connected to the Civil War and if I can find evidence, that would be awesome!"

"You're welcome to take those with you," Mrs. Powell said. "James would love to know they are being put to good use and teaching others."

"Thanks Mrs. Powell!" Finn said as he gently closed the journal.

"Thank you so much for having us over, Mrs. Powell. This was really fun," Riley said as she stood up, waking Lily who had fallen asleep between her and Finn.

"Oh, any time, dear. I love the company and reminiscing about the past."

"I'm so glad you're here to tell us all this cool stuff!" Finn said as he put the journals in his backpack. "It's really neat to hear all these stories, and I'll let you know what I find in Mr. Powell's journals."

"That sounds lovely," Mrs. Powell said as she walked the kids to the door. "You two come over anytime. Lily and I so enjoy seeing you."

As Riley and Finn headed home, Finn couldn't contain his excitement. "I'm going to read through these tonight and see what else I can find. There has to be more than what Mrs. Powell remembers, after all, Mr. Powell's journals helped us find the caves! Maybe there's an entrance to the tunnels outside of the Public House that we can still access?"

"And if not," Riley said, "we can go to the Roswell Historical Society. I'll go on their website tonight to see if they have a database I can search. I need to start doing my own research too."

Finn stopped and looked at Riley. "What do you think about what Mrs. Powell said about the Confederates smuggling their money through the tunnels?"

Riley grinned at Finn. "First Cherokee gold, now Confederate money? I don't know, Finn. Maybe Mr. Powell was one of those treasure hunters who keeps looking for things that don't exist."

"But the caves existed!"

Riley laughed. "But the gold didn't!"

"That's because we weren't the first people to find the caves! That gold was long gone by the time we found the caves."

Riley conceded. "Okay, you're right, there may have been gold in the caves that was long gone, but with all the history we know about our town, don't you'd think we'd have heard about tunnels underneath Roswell?"

Finn grinned and Riley knew it was because he loved to banter with her. "Well, I'll go through the journals and let you know what Mr. Powell seemed to think!"

CHAPTER TWENTY-ONE

Eureka!

When the weekend arrived, Riley and Finn headed to the Roswell Historical Society to do some research. The Historical Society was located near city hall in the Roswell Cultural Arts Center. Since it wasn't far from their neighborhood, they set off on their bikes and headed toward Canton Street.

Once inside the arts center, they followed the signs to the offices for the Historical Society on the second floor and checked in with the volunteer. The nice lady asked what they were looking for and when they explained their projects were about the Civil War, she took several books out of a wood and glass case and set them on the table in front of it. "These contain records of Roswell during the Civil War; I think they'll help."

The two friends worked quietly for a long time as they read through the books and each made notes. "Remember, jot down anything that matches your topic, or that mentions the tunnels," Finn reminded Riley. She could tell he was eager for answers.

"I'm finding tons of information on the mill." Riley said after they had been working for nearly an hour. "There are some great old photographs of it and the mill workers that I can use when I do my presentation."

"Anything on the tunnels?" Finn had his hand on his

forehead, his hair pushed up as he continued searching for seemingly elusive information.

"No, nothing," Riley said. She felt bad that Finn was coming up empty and offered an alternative. "I've made some notes on other things you might want to cover, just in case the tunnels are a dead end."

"Thanks," Finn said. "I'll take it, because I'm beginning to think these tunnels don't exist at all. I mean there's absolutely nothing in here."

"But what about what you found in Mr. Powell's journals? Did it seem like it was a fictional story, or that he was writing about something real?" Riley held her place in the book with her hand as she looked across the table at Finn.

Finn exhaled, tilted his head back, and looked at the ceiling. "It sounded like it was in the same voice as the stuff we read about the caves. It sounded like they were real."

Riley thought for a moment. "Didn't you say that based on what you found in the journals, you had a pretty good idea where we should look?"

"Yeah, I just wanted to get more information. I figured there had to be records—I mean, why would this information be hidden?"

"Good point," Riley said as she considered Finn's suggestion. "We thought the caves were just a legend, but this is something there should be a record of."

"Exactly, so why can't we find anything?"

"It's weird, I'll give you that," Riley agreed. "They have so much info on the city and the Civil War in this town, do you think maybe the tunnels don't exist?"

"What about the one we found at the Public House, though?"

"Maybe it's just a small tunnel that doesn't lead anywhere." Riley hated to think that her friend would have to pick another topic and start from scratch. "I mean, we didn't get to find out where it went, maybe it's just an extension of the cellar?"

"Maybe," Finn said, but didn't look convinced. "Or maybe the city doesn't want anyone knowing about them."

***

Even if the Historical Society didn't have any information on the tunnels, Finn told Riley he still wanted to test his theory. The two friends met at Riley's house the next day and headed to a location where Finn thought they might find a tunnel entrance: Smith Plantation.

"I think it's a good idea that we left our bikes locked up at the park on Canton Street," Riley said as they headed down the familiar crushed granite path. "Who knows where this entrance might be, and we can't just park our bikes in front of it."

"Yeah, that was a good thought on your part," Finn said.

"And I'm glad you reminded me to bring my gloves and hat. It's not freezing today, but if we do find the tunnels, they might be pretty cold. I even wore two pairs of socks!"

Finn grinned and said, "I have hand warmers in a pocket just in case." He patted the left pocket of his cargo pants.

Riley slipped a small, black nylon backpack off her shoulder and looked inside. "I want to make sure I brought my real flashlight along with my copy of the map you drew. I have water and granola bars too...just in case."

"I'm starting to rub off on you, huh?" Finn laughed, then suddenly grew serious. "We really shouldn't have kept going in the caves," he said solemnly. "I should have backed off."

Riley and Finn hadn't talked much about her near-death experience in the caves, but she didn't fault Finn. They both wanted to explore the caves and the legend that boobie traps had been built into the caves proved to be true. Riley was so prepared today because of the fact that they weren't prepared when they went into the cave system. She had to admit, that her fall into the cave pit was something she still had nightmares about. If not for Finn grabbing her hand and super-human strength that he got to pull her out, she wouldn't have survived.

Riley didn't want to think about it anymore and tried to lighten the moment. "First of all, it was those bats. If they hadn't come screeching past my head, we wouldn't have fallen down the chute. After that, it was just bad luck. Let's face it, those caves were built to keep the wrong people out, and I don't think either of us were prepared for what we faced."

They approached the pretty white house and Finn was keen to think about something other than that frightening moment in the caves. "Okay, let's look at the map I drew. Based on what Mr. Powell wrote, I think there's an entrance somewhere on the grounds of Smith Plantation. I have a few ideas where it could be."

Riley pulled a copy of Finn's hand-drawn map out of her back pocket.

"Wait," Finn said looking at Riley in confusion. "Didn't you say your map was in your backpack?"

Riley smiled. "I have one in my backpack and one in my back pocket, you never can be too prepared. What happens if one gets wet?"

Finn laughed at this, "Next time you'll have them laminated."

"Ooh, good idea!" They were both laughing now.

"Let's get our bearings," Finn suggested as he and Riley took out their maps. "Okay, let's see." Finn was holding his map and turning, looking at the various white buildings along the property. "I think we should start with the cook house."

Riley looked at the map and agreed. "Yeah, it can't be the corn crib because that's elevated off the ground. The barn is out too, because it's got a modern lock and the sign said it is used for storage. Even if the tunnel entrance was there, we couldn't get into it."

Finn looked over at the carriage house, the doors were wide open so tourists could see the items inside. There was an old carriage, pitch forks, saws, all sorts of tools and old boxes. "They've got the carriage house open, so let's go see if the cook house is open too."

Riley and Finn strolled along the brick walkway that led to the cook house. They walked up five steps and into the old building. It had wood floors, a cabinet displaying old cooking utensils, and a large fireplace. Finn headed over to inspect the fireplace while Riley looked along the floor.

The building was small and Riley easily found a section of wood flooring in the back corner that looked odd. Upon closer inspection, she realized it might be a trap door. It blended so well with the floorboards and had metal pots around it, so she knew it could easily be missed if one wasn't looking.

"Finn, I think I've found something," Riley said is a whisper. "Look at the floor here." Riley moved the pots so they could get a better look.

Finn crouched next to Riley and rubbed his hand over the well-worn wooden floor boards. He looked at Riley, grinning. "I think you're right, I think this is a trap door!"

"Well, let's check it out," Riley offered. She looked out the windows that faced the main house. "It looks quiet outside, I think now's as good a time as any."

Finn reached into his pocket and pulled out a small multi-tool. He opened a piece that looked like a metal file and used it to pry up the door. The wood was strong, but he was able to move it enough to get his fingers underneath it and pry it open the rest of the way...with a loud squeak. Finn froze as Riley looked back outside.

"Coast is still clear, no one's out here," Riley said. "Wait a minute and we'll make sure no one comes this way." Riley pretended she was looking at the artifacts in the cook house in the event anyone came up, luckily no one did.

Finn peered into the square hole and grabbed the flashlight that was clipped to his waistband. It was a small but powerful light that lit up the space below him. "There's a drop," he said quietly. "Looks to be about three feet down."

"I hope it opens up, because I don't want to be on my hands and knees down there," Riley said. She was already feeling claustrophobic.

"I'll jump down and check it out, wait up here and signal me if anyone comes by." Finn didn't wait for a response. He dangled his feet over the edge and hopped down.

Riley went over to the hole and shined her flashlight into it. "You okay?"

"Affirmative," Finn said as he looked up at Riley from within the tunnel, his eyes shining with excitement.

"What do you see?"

Finn ducked his head, turned ninety degrees, and shined his light ahead of him. "Not much, it's really dark down here. Dirt floor, low ceiling." He was in a crouching position. "I'm going to crawl through here to see if it opens up. I can't imagine tunnels being very useful at only three feet high."

"Okay, be careful," Riley said, and she thought of the words they had heard on an EVP they captured by Vickery Creek. Words that turned out to be from Mister Oscar as he kept watch over them. Riley said in a whisper, "Mister Oscar, if you're around today, please keep us safe."

She looked down into the hole and saw a green light below her. "Glow stick," she said to herself. "He's still more prepared than I am." Riley looked over her shoulder and then back to the tunnel, beginning to get nervous that someone might catch them. Her stomach was starting to feel uneasy. I never did like hide-and-seek, she thought to herself.

After several minutes—that felt like forever—Riley started to hear scratching noises from below. Finn was crawling back on the dirt floor to where he had left the glow stick. When he got to the opening, he had dirt smudges on his face, but a huge grin and sparkling eyes.

"There are definitely tunnels under Roswell! Come on, let me show you!"

CHAPTER TWENTY-TWO

Exploring Again

As Riley hopped down into the hole, Finn said, "Don't worry, you only have to crawl about eight feet, then it becomes a real tunnel, with stone walls and everything! I left a glow stick where it gets larger and I'll leave this one here so we know when we're back at the hatch in the floor."

Riley squatted and got on her hands and knees so she could fit in the three-foot-tall space. "It's really dark in here, hang on," she said as she slid her backpack off and pulled out a powerful flashlight. She could hear Finn close the hatch with a loud squeak and it got even darker. She crawled forward to give him room to join her.

Riley took a deep breath. "You know, this feels awfully familiar. Are you sure this is a good idea?"

She could hear Finn scraping along behind her on his hands and knees. "Yeah, I went a good distance trying to see if our map looks right. It's kinda hard to tell since it's a little disorienting down here. We'll go as far as you want."

Riley thought about the tunnels and how they might have been used during the Civil War. "Wouldn't it be neat if we found some sort of Civil War artifact?"

"It sure would! I think that would help my report because I could pass it around. Even cooler if we found hidden

Confederate gold and silver!"

"Yeah, if we find Confederate treasure, you're definitely not bringing that to class!" Riley laughed. Just ahead she saw the glow stick, and as Finn had promised, the tunnel opened up.

The tunnel had a dirt floor with stone walls and ceilings that were probably six feet high, so at least they could stand and walk normally. The tunnel was also now wide enough for them to walk side by side. Finn pulled out his map. "Our map shows that it should go straight for a little while, then there's a fork. I think one path heads South which would take us by City Hall, I think the other path should take us like...Southwest." Finn turned the map and then said, "Yeah, Southwest, but mostly West, toward Mimosa, I think."

"So not only is there a tunnel under Roswell, but it might go right near our neighborhood? That's pretty cool!"

"I know! Let's do a little ghost hunting while we explore. You man the flashlight, we can do an EVP session and I'll have my EMF detector out, too."

"Wait," Riley said as she grabbed Finn's arm. "I'm going to set the pedometer on my phone so we can track how far we go, then maybe we can figure out where this tunnel goes."

"Good idea," Finn said. "I'll keep an eye on my compass to see if we change direction."

After walking a little way down the tunnel Finn paused to start an EVP session. "Is there anyone in this tunnel with us?"

Riley waited for a response, then said, "If there's someone here, can you tell us your name?"

After a pause, Finn said, "We mean you no harm, we just want to say hi." He watched his EMF detector and it was steady green. "Let's keep walking. I'll stop recording but keep this out just in case." He held up his EMF detector and turned off the recorder which he had hanging around his neck.

"What do you think they used these tunnels for?" Riley asked as they continued on.

"Well, like Hawk said, it would be a good way to move people and supplies around during the war. There should be a section that leads from the mill and maybe that one joins with the one in the cellar of the Public House? They probably used it to get fabric for the Confederate soldiers' uniforms up to the Company Store where they could distribute it without the Union troops knowing."

"That makes sense since the Company Store was in the building where the Public House is now. Do you think slaves used these tunnels to try to escape?" Riley asked.

"I don't know, maybe."

"I wonder if Mister Oscar knew about these tunnels?" Riley thought aloud. She wondered what he was like in real life and hoped that he had a decent life all things considered. "Let's record while we're down here, just in case." Finn smiled at Riley and pressed the record button on his digital recorder.

When they got to the anticipated fork in the tunnel, Riley said, "This is more of an intersection than a fork."

Finn agreed and took out his compass to check it under Riley's light. "Okay so if we want to go toward City Hall and the mill, we need to just keep going straight." He pointed straight ahead. "This other tunnel looks like it goes West," Finn said as he shined his light down the tunnel to their right. "If we're going to find any artifacts, I think we need to keep going straight."

"Works for me," Riley said, taking the lead and continuing straight ahead. "It seems more likely since this one looks like it might connect to the mill and the old Company Store."

They had walked a little while when Finn said, "Too bad we haven't seen any artifacts yet."

"I know. It would even be cool to find an old button or something." Riley thought of the key they had found. "I guess we can't be too disappointed, after all, we found that cool old key in the cellar of the Public House."

"Yeah, even if it did freak us out!" Finn laughed as he said it.

"I'm positive it wasn't there when we got down there," Riley said. "You know I tend to look at the ground when I walk."

"True, even if you aren't looking for snakes."

"Ugh, why did you have to remind me," Riley said. She shined her flashlight around the tunnel walls.

Finn laughed. "Don't worry, I don't think there are good nesting places for snakes down here."

"Nesting places?" Riley shuddered involuntarily. "I don't even want to think of a nest of snakes!"

Finn laughed then stopped abruptly and spoke quietly. "Do you hear that?"

Riley stopped and tilted her head to listen. At first she didn't hear anything, then swore she heard voices. "I think so," she whispered. "What's your EMF detector showing?"

Finn held it up. "Solid green."

Riley got nervous. "Do you think people are down here?"

"I don't know," Finn whispered. "Let's move quietly and see if we can hear any more as we go forward.

The friends moved quietly down the tunnel listening intently and after a few moments, they heard voices more clearly.

"I'm not sure she's going to work out," a gravelly male voice said. "Do we give her time?"

After a pause, they heard another male voice. "Yeah, let's give her a little more time. If we don't see an improvement, let her go."

"Terminate her?" the gravelly voice said with a laugh.

"Just let her go," the man who spoke with authority said.

Finn montioned above them where an old pipe was situated in the wall, near the ceiling. He nodded for Riley to follow him down the tunnel.

Once the got a fair distance from the pipe, Riley said, "That was weird."

Finn said, "Yeah, it sounds like someone's getting fired."

"Or worse," Riley said.

Finn laughed, "You have the wildest imagination!"

Riley laughed with her friend, "At least we know there's an air shaft."

Finn said, "Let's do a quick EVP session, then get out of here. I'm not seeing any artifacts." Riley nodded, still listening closely for any voices. Finn started. "Is anyone here with us?"

Riley left time for a response, then said, "Can you tell us your name?" She was speaking quietly in case someone else *was* down here.

Finn said, "We mean no harm. We're looking for Civil War artifacts."

After a pause, Riley said, "Were these tunnels used by the Confederates during the war?"

Finn was just about to speak when he and Riley heard a

low moan from far down the tunnel. "Did you hear that?" Finn asked.

Riley nodded, then started to feel sick. "Finn, I don't feel so good."

Finn looked at Riley's worried expression and said, "Are you okay?"

Riley took a deep breath. "Yeah, I'm just not feeling so great down here all of a sudden."

Finn shined his light down the tunnel where the moan came from, then looked at Riley. "Let's get out of here. We might not be getting enough fresh air. That pipe was the only one I've seen since we've been down here."

Riley was quick to turn and head back the way they came, walking at a brisk pace.

"You sure you're okay?" Finn asked as he jogged to catch up to Riley who was keen to get out.

Riley slowed her pace and smiled at her friend. "Yeah, I just need some fresh air."

When they got to the point where the ceiling got low, Finn picked up the glow stick he had left there and whispered, "Let's make sure not to talk in case there are tourists in the cook house."

Riley gave Finn a thumb's up and watched as he got on all fours and headed toward the glow stick that marked the entrance at the hatch. As Riley crawled in behind Finn at the hatch, she swore she felt a draft behind her, but it was still so dark, she knew the hatch couldn't be open.

As they made it to the area below the hatch, she saw that it was definitely closed and Finn was listening for voices in the cook house above them. After a full minute of listening, he nodded to Riley and she nodded back in confirmation. It sounded like the coast was clear.

Finn had to open the hatch with a bit of pressure. After all, it was made to blend into the floor so well that it was tight to begin with, the boards had probably warped some over time. He opened it a crack and Riley's stomach was nervous, she hoped it was still early enough that there weren't a lot of visitors yet. She could see Finn peering out, trying to see as much as he could. He slowly released his hands from the hatch and held his finger up to his lips, then he looked at his watch.

Riley hoped they wouldn't get caught; she hated getting in trouble.

After a full minute, Finn pushed up on the hatch door and peered around as best he could. He gave Riley a thumb's up and opened it all the way, its hidden hinges squeaking loudly again. Finn pulled himself out of the hatch and Riley followed quickly behind him. Finn shut the hatch tightly and Riley again marveled at how well it blended in with the floorboards of the old cook house. They moved the pot that had been sitting on top of it back in place and just as they turned around, a family came in to look around. Phew, that was close, Riley thought to herself. She and Finn pretended to look around and admire some of the old cooking utensils on their way out the door.

Riley was so relieved about not getting caught, but that relief lasted briefly when she thought about how she had felt in the tunnel and what they had experienced.

CHAPTER TWENTY-THREE

Canine Play Date

The following Saturday as she was finishing her cereal, Riley thought about the weird feeling she had gotten in the tunnel the previous weekend. She was relieved when Finn had called her that night to say that they hadn't actually captured anything when they were in the tunnel, but she had definitely had an unsettling feeling. As her mom flipped through a tabloid magazine in the family room, a local news channel was on the television. "We have sad news from Roswell this morning..."

Riley looked up at the television as the reporter said, "...a five-year-old boy was playing outside when a neighbor's dog attacked and seriously injured the child."

Riley gasped and her mom dropped her magazine into her lap, "Oh that's awful!"

The reporter continued. "The child had played with this dog before and was unsupervised at the time of the attack so unfortunately, we don't know what sparked it. The dog was a pit bull. The family prefers to remain anonymous at this time."

"You know, those pit bulls make me nervous," Riley's mom said. "I know Hawk's new dog is a pit mix, but I just don't trust those dogs."

Riley felt frustration rise. "Mom, it's not about the breed. I used to be scared of pit bulls too, but Lennox is the sweetest dog. And he's a trained service dog. They don't allow dogs with any sort of aggression or issues become service dogs."

"But you hear stories like this and it's *always* a pit bull. And this child played with this dog before, so what happened to make it snap? Why did it turn on the child?"

"Mom, unfortunately, we don't know what happened because the boy wasn't being supervised."

Riley could tell this set her mom off. "Honey, you can't blame the parents. They must be devastated! Besides, must I remind you that you could have gotten yourself killed in those caves? Should I keep you trapped in this house so nothing bad can ever happen to you?"

Riley saw her mom's point. "I get it, Mom, and I didn't mean it that way. What I meant was, since no one was there, we can't be sure that the kid didn't do something to provoke the dog. I'm always seeing videos online where parents think it's really cute that their kid is jumping on their dog, or pulling its ears or tail...you can see the dogs are stressed, but people don't read the dog's body language. Dogs usually give several signs before they bite. People are more concerned with capturing a cool video that might go viral, they don't stop to actually see what's happening."

"But this dog seriously hurt a child, Roo. That's pretty aggressive behavior, and it always seems to involve pit bulls."

"Actually, the statistics are interesting," Riley said, recalling some of her research from her own curiosity of this issue. "Before people worried about pit bulls, it was Rottweilers, and before them it was German shepherds. I'm not saying this dog didn't have issues, maybe it did, but the owner and the parents should never have let the child around it unsupervised. It's so sad."

"And you always side with the dogs. Honey, not all dogs are good."

Riley took a deep breath. "Not all people are good either!" Riley said thinking of Mr. Clinton. "There are some pretty bad people out there, but it's not because of their race or how they look. The same goes with pit bulls, it's more than just the breed, mom. I hope you know how terrible I think this situation is."

"I do, honey. But I just get scared of those dogs because of what I hear."

"I know, but a lot of that is because the media reports those cases then sensationalizes them. I promise, if you meet Lennox, you'll see what I mean. He's a sweetheart." Riley paused. "Have you ever even met a pit bull?"

Her mom thought for a moment then sheepishly replied, "Well...no, I haven't."

"Why don't you come to Hawk's with me and meet Lennox. You can see for yourself."

"You're right, I should make an educated decision. I can't say all pit bulls are bad, but then let you go hang out with one," her mom said, laughing at her own hypocrisy. "The news does tend to sensationalize, like you said," she added, smiling at Riley.

Riley felt relieved at her mom's reaction and was glad she had listened. She knew that, like people, all dogs are not perfect and was glad she could help her mom keep an open mind. Riley could use the time with Lennox and her mom this morning. It had been a long week at school with extra homework, plus work on her Civil War project, so she and Finn hadn't had any more time to explore. Riley spent her free time in the evenings after her homework was done, with Buster and was still worried about Baby Girl. It had been nearly a month since the dog had disappeared and Riley's heart wrenched every time she thought about it. A morning with Mom, Buster, Hawk, and Lennox was just what she needed! She texted Hawk to let him know they were on their way, then Finn to see if he and Molly could join them.

***

"Hey Hawk!" Riley said walking up with her mom, Buster trotting along beside her on his leash. So far, so good, she thought, proud of Buster for being so brave. He had improved over the past couple weeks and didn't seem nervous, but Riley knew that could change in an instant. In fact, at the moment, her mom looked more nervous than Buster.

Hawk waved back at Riley and her mom, and Lennox waved too, with his long black tail. The sturdy dog grinned at them, his tongue sticking out, a broad smile from ear to ear.

"See, mom," Riley said quietly. "Look how he's smiling, his tail is relaxed and wagging, and his body isn't tense."

As they approached, Buster slowed a bit, his nose going a mile a minute. "How are you doing today?" Riley asked Hawk, mindful that he probably still had good days and bad days, even if he did have a service dog now.

"Pretty good, thanks," Hawk said, and a slight smile appeared from underneath his thick beard. "Lennox here is helping me a lot. It's nice to have him around."

"His coat is so shiny!" Riley's mom said.

"I feed him well," Hawk said.

As if knowing she was talking about him, Lennox walked up to Riley's mom and sat perfectly before her, his tail was wagging along the ground.

"Let him sniff your hand, Mom."

Riley's mom leaned down a bit so Lennox could meet her. He sniffed her hand, then licked it, still grinning at her. "Good boy!" she said and Riley could tell her mom was only a little nervous.

At that moment, Lennox flopped over onto his back, exposing his belly. "He's being submissive to you!" Riley said. "Go on, give him a belly rub, he won't hurt you."

Riley could see from her mom's face that she was anxious, but she smiled and rubbed Lennox's chest, he was still smiling and that made his tongue hang out the side of his mouth and onto the grass. "You are a good boy, Lennox!"

"See, mom, like I told you, he's a real sweetheart."

"He sure is!"

"I'm glad he's helping you," Riley said to Hawk. She knew how important love from a dog could be. She looked down at Buster who was now trying to sniff underneath Lennox. Buster moved slowly and sniffed behind Lennox and the stocky black dog allowed Buster to get to know him.

Riley blushed. "Isn't it weird how dogs do that?" She noticed her mom looked a little grossed-out.

Hawk chuckled. "Yeah, they say it's their way of shaking hands. I prefer just shaking hands."

Riley laughed at Hawk. "They also say they can smell if the other dog is sick, what he's eaten, and stuff like that. It's kinda cool...in a weird way."

"Buster seems pretty relaxed around Lennox," Riley's mom said. "I wasn't sure because..."

"Because he's a pit?" Hawk said, but without judgment.

"Honestly, that did worry me a little bit. I don't mean to be rude, but they do have a reputation." Riley was glad her mom didn't mention the child who had just been seriously hurt by the same breed. "It's just that you hear so many bad things, you start to wonder." Riley could tell her mom felt bad saying it, but she was being honest.

"I understand," Hawk said. "People judge me all the time because of how I look and because I was a special forces guy. It's like some people expect me to lose it at any moment and others think I'm some kind of superhero, neither of which are true. But Lennox here, he's a good dude. I've been out around town with him and I haven't seen one ounce of aggression in him. He's a big baby to tell you the truth."

Lennox was now sniffing Buster and while Buster was a little stiff, he was doing fine. Just then, Lennox made a quick move and had his head and arms low and his bottom and tail in the air. He barked and shook his head from side to side. Buster jumped in Lennox's direction and imitated his posture, they were both making a play-bow, a signal to play.

"Looks like they like each other!" Riley said with a big smile.

The two dogs wrestled with each other, as much as a five-pound and fifty-pound dog could. Riley and Hawk were both smiling now, and laughing.

Riley's mom said, "Yep, I think they like each other!"

Finn walked up with Molly and said, "I guess I missed the

introductions!"

Lennox was barking like crazy, wagging his tail and chasing Buster around, as much as they could on leash. The leashes kept getting tangled up. Meanwhile, Molly let out a whine as her tail wagged and her front paws tapped from side to side. "I think Molly is anxious to join in!" Riley said.

"Let's take them in the back yard so they can play off leash," Hawk said.

Hawk, Riley, and Finn walked the dogs around back while Riley's mom headed home.

In the back yard, Buster was more interested in sniffing around the yard, while Lennox and Molly were meeting each other. Once they all agreed all three dogs were comfortable with one another, they took the leashes off and let them play. Lennox started hopping sideways, barking at Buster trying to get him to play while Molly tried to get either of them to chase her. Buster found a place to relieve himself, and mark the yard, and then ran after Lennox and Molly. The little dog had to take multiple steps for every one step the other dogs took. Lennox would bolt through the yard and Buster and Molly would chase, then they would reverse.

"It's like Lennox and Molly know how much faster they are so they don't chase at full speed," Riley said.

"Yeah, like they enjoy the chase and realize they would run right over Buster if they went too fast."

Hawk was standing with his arms crossed and a huge smile across his face. "This is really good for Lennox and Buster."

Riley smiled. She could tell it was good for Hawk too.

Finn was smiling too. "And Molly is happy to have new

friends!"

When Buster started to slow down, Lennox kept barking at him, trying to get him to chase and wrestle, but Riley could tell Buster was losing steam. As she stood to get Buster, she spotted their neighbor, Mr. Felton, on his deck. Riley waved, but the man didn't wave back. She saw Hawk look to where she waved and his face hardened.

He turned to the dogs, softening. "Buster looks like he's done. Do you want to take them inside to get some water?"

Riley noticed Hawk's jaw was flexing. "Yeah, I think you're right, he looks pooped. I think they could all use some water."

Hawk opened the back door which led to the basement and whistled for Lennox who darted to Hawk and ran in the door, Molly following closely behind. Buster followed at a much slower pace, his little pink tongue hanging out of his mouth. They walked through the media room and toward the stairs. Lennox and Molly were halfway up the stairs when Lennox turned in anticipation, barking to Buster.

Riley laughed. "Buster hasn't figured out stairs yet, boy," she said to Lennox who cocked his head to one side as if trying to understand.

Lennox now barked from the top of the steps, calling his new friend to join him and Buster responded with a slight whine.

"Lennox is trying to call him to follow!" Finn said, clearly impressed at how the dog was trying to communicate.

"Maybe if Buster watches Lennox, he'll try going up?" Hawk suggested. He called Lennox down and Lennox came running and sat in front of Hawk. Molly waited patiently at the top of the steps, watching her crazy new friends.

"Let's give it a try," Riley said.

Hawk told Lennox to go up and Lennox raced all the way up the stairs then turned around facing them all. He barked three times, tail wagging. He ran half-way back down the stairs and barked again. Buster sat at the bottom, panting, but grinning.

"I don't know," Riley said. "He doesn't look like he knows what to do." She walked over to Buster and Lennox came bounding all the way down again. He jumped up and licked Riley on the face and ran up to the middle of the stairs. Molly barked once from the top of the stairs. Riley went to pick up Buster and to her surprise, Buster hopped up three stairs before she could grab him.

"Good boy!" Riley said. Lennox seemed to agree and barked some more. Buster hopped up three more stairs and watched Lennox sprint to the top. Buster went as fast as he could and joined Lennox and Molly at the top.

Riley patted her hip and said, "Oh no, I left his treat pouch at home!

"I've got some!" Hawk said as he easily took the stairs two at a time with his long legs and was getting treats out of a jar and handed one to Riley as soon as she entered the kitchen. "Just in case he doesn't want to take one from me."

Riley grabbed the treat and gave it to Buster. "You're such a good boy!" She petted him as he scarfed down his treat. Lennox came over and nearly toppled her over, he was so excited.

"Lennox, here," Hawk said. Lennox went over to Hawk and took his treat gently, then went to his bowl to lap up some water. Molly sat politely in front of Hawk who grinned and gave her a treat.

Riley watched in awe as Buster slowly walked up to Lennox's water bowl and stood next to him. Lennox moved to his left to give Buster room and Buster tentatively approached the bowl and lapped up water with Lennox.

"Now that's cool," Finn said.

"Totally," Riley agreed.

"Well, I think this was a success," Hawk said. "I think these three are going to be good buddies." The smile appeared beneath his beard again.

"Thanks for having us over," Riley said to Hawk as Lennox appeared in front of her, the dog's tail wagging slowly back and forth. Riley knelt and scratched Lennox behind the ears and above his tail. "Thanks for teaching Buster the stairs, I'm glad he has new friends." Lennox just sat there smiling, tongue hanging out, totally eating up the attention and scratches. Molly joined them and Riley relished in petting both dogs. Then, she picked Buster up and gave him some love too. "You've got new friends!" She turned to Hawk and said, "Do you want to try to give him a treat?"

Hawk smiled. "Of course." He grabbed three small, soft treats and walked over to Riley and Buster and held out his open hand. "Here you go, Buster," Hawk said in a higher pitch than was normal for him.

Buster looked up at Hawk wide-eyed. Riley gave him a moment. He slowly sniffed the edge of Hawk's hand. "Good boy," Riley said sweetly.

It was as if she could see the confidence in her little dog growing. Buster tentatively moved his face to the center of Hawk's palm and took the treats quickly.

"Good boy," all three of them said with excitement.

Riley kissed Buster on the side of his face. "Such a good boy!" Lennox and Molly looked at Riley with anticipation. "Oh, do you need a treat too?" Riley giggled then asked the dogs to sit, which they promptly did. "Good!" Riley said as she gave each of them a treat.

"Thanks for having us over, Hawk," Finn said.

"Any time. We need to do this more often. It looks like the dogs love it."

"Sounds like a plan!" Finn said.

As they walked down the driveway to go to Riley's house, her heart felt full. Not only had Buster made huge progress today, but she was so happy to see how good Lennox was for Hawk. Riley saw Mr. Felton at his mailbox and waved again. This time he waved back.

She said so only Finn could hear, "That was weird."

"Mr. Felton?" Finn said.

"Yeah, you noticed that too?"

"Yep, he ignored you before."

"And Hawk looked irritated when he saw who I waved to," Riley added.

"I saw that too."

Riley wondered what had gone on between Hawk and Mr. Felton. Her family had always thought Mr. Felton could act odd, but he hadn't ever been so downright rude.

CHAPTER TWENTY-FOUR

A Proposed Law

The following week Riley and Finn spent time with their dogs and Lennox at Hawk's house as often as they could. When they couldn't get together with the dogs, they spent time at either Finn's or Riley's house working on their projects, talking about the tunnel and the strange feeling Riley had, or wondering about Baby Girl. As they headed toward Riley's house from Finn's, Riley said, "I can't believe we haven't spotted Baby Girl and that she hasn't been found yet. There seem to be less and less posts about her."

"Yeah," Finn said as he let Molly sniff a utility box two houses up from Riley's house. "Remember at first, a dog like her was spotted, but they couldn't ever catch her, then we didn't hear much else. My mom said they may not be sharing details of the sightings because they don't want people to scare her off."

"I still want to help find her if we can. It's amazing how many dogs look like her, but turn out not to be her," Riley said as they continued walking. Dogs had been spotted or brought in that looked just like Baby Girl, but none of them turned out to be her. "I watch posts on a lost and found pets site and I've seen a couple of dogs that look like her, but when I compare the found dog to Baby Girl, there's always some sort of different markings or coloring. I bet her family is so sad."

"I know," Finn said. "Just not knowing if she's safe and warm...or who has her. I think it would drive me crazy."

"Totally," Riley said as Finn pulled out his phone and scrolled through. She knew he would be checking to see if he could find anything new on Baby Girl.

"Oh no!" Finn said.

"What, is it Baby Girl?"

"No," Finn's tone was somber as he turned his phone so Riley could read.

Riley swallowed hard and read the heading of the news article aloud. "After Child Was Mauled, BSL on the Table for the City of Roswell." She put her hand to her mouth. "No, please don't tell me Roswell is going to do that!"

"BSL, what does that stand for? Big Stinking Losers?" Corey Thornton had biked up and Riley could have kicked herself for not noticing. She figured he was on his way to Seth's.

"I'm glad at least you think you're funny," Riley said, "because no one else does." She just wanted him to go away and was so mad that Roswell was considering BSL.

"It's Breed-Specific Legislation, Corey. It's an unfair law that bans certain breeds of dogs," Finn said, his back to Corey.

"Specifically, pit bulls," Riley said. "Why am I even bothering to explain this to you," she wondered aloud.

"So? Those dogs are jerks," Corey said. "Why do you care?"

Riley's blood was boiling. She knew she should just ignore him and go inside, but she felt so passionately, she knew she had to speak up. It was in keeping silent that innocent dogs would be hurt. "Some people are jerks, too," she said. "Maybe we should just ban them from Roswell?"

It took a moment for her comment to register with Corey, but when it did he said, "You're just jealous because my dad is more successful than yours."

Riley's dad worked with Corey's dad so she knew she had to be careful about what she said. Plus, everyone knew that Corey's dad, Hadrian Thornton, was powerful in town—his family had been here for generations. "Yeah, Corey, that's right," she said. "I'm just jealous of your dad." Her voice dripped with sarcasm.

"It's not for good reason, my dad is running for the open City Council position and no one is opposing him," Corey said. "So, I guess he'll have a vote on that BSF or whatever it is." He biked off laughing before Riley could respond, her heart sank. She felt completely defeated and hoped that Corey wouldn't influence his dad on BSL because of their disagreement and shared dislike for each other. She didn't even correct him on his incorrect acronym.

Finn looked at her with a sympathetic smile. She could tell he was thinking the same thing, "How were we supposed to know?" Riley decided they would have to avoid Corey at all costs, there's no sense poking a snake.

Riley heard noise across the street and said to Finn, "We can't let this bill pass."

Finn followed Riley's gaze and Hawk waved to them. They smiled, waved back, and headed across the street to say hello.

Finn said, "You're right, you don't think they'll make owners give up their dogs, do you?"

Riley steeled herself. "They better not. Lennox isn't a threat to anyone. If anything, he's a huge support for Hawk. We can't let this happen."

As they approached Hawk and Lennox, they put smiles on their faces and tried to act like they hadn't just heard news that could devastate their neighbor. Maybe he hadn't heard yet. They had to figure out what they could do to make sure BSL didn't pass in Roswell.

CHAPTER TWENTY-FIVE

Bad News

Word of the proposed breed-specific legislation spread fast around Roswell and the rest of the world. Sometimes Riley thought she was the only one who cared so much about issues related to dogs, but she quickly found out she wasn't alone. Pit bull advocacy groups from across the country and world were raising their voices on social media and local groups were putting a plan in place to fight the proposal. Despite the uproar from so many people, the BSL proposal would go to the Mayor and City Council for either approval or denial. A decision was due any day now.

Riley couldn't believe that the city would even consider BSL, especially after all the petitioning that had been done so far. She was having dinner with her family and feeling helpless. Her parents had the TV on in the family room and Riley was keeping an eye on it for news that was supposed to come soon.

"What's the matter, Roo?" Her dad asked as he cut his steak.

"I've just been thinking about this BSL proposal and feel so helpless. I'm just a kid, what can I do to try to stop it?"

Hailey sighed and tossed her hair over her shoulder, "Why are you so serious and dramatic all the time? This isn't your problem, don't stress over it."

"Now Hailey," their dad said. "What if John F. Kennedy

turned a blind eye because he didn't think civil rights were 'his problem?' If we all stopped fighting for what's right just because it's not *our* problem, imagine how different this world would be."

"Yeah, but we don't even have a pit bull," Hailey said. "It's not going to affect us."

Riley's mom chimed in. "Honey, we can't just ignore a problem because it doesn't affect us. Do we not support issues for the poor because we're not poor? Riley's concerned because she wants to do what's right."

Hailey was clearly getting irritated. She was always seen as the smart one and in this case, Riley thought she sounded very stupid. "Mom, I thought you didn't like pit bulls. You were mad that Hawk's service dog is a pit bull and you told me not to tell Riley." Hailey gave Riley a smug look and was clearly trying to make Riley mad...but she didn't realize what happened when their mom met Lennox.

Their mom smiled and said, "Yep, I said that, and it was very ignorant of me."

Hailey's jaw dropped.

"Riley and I had a discussion about pit bulls and she made her case, so I went over to meet Lennox. He is the sweetest, most lovable dog. He and Buster played together like they were old pals. And look, we all came back in one piece."

Riley felt proud. Not only had she made her case with her mom, but she helped change her mom's perspective and was thrilled.

Their dad said, "Riley, you sound like your old man, pleading your case to your mom and winning!"

They all laughed, except Hailey. While she was really pretty, when she was upset, she had a face that looked like she had just sucked on a lemon and it wasn't attractive.

Riley felt better now, but it wouldn't be for long. She noticed her dad look up at the television with a serious face. Riley looked to her right to see the television. There was a red banner with white text that read, "Breaking News."

Riley hopped up from the table and grabbed the remote control to turn up the volume.

"—Thanks, Maria," the reporter in the field said. "We're here live in Roswell and have just heard the news that the Mayor and City Council have passed a bill to ban pit bulls and pit bull mixes in their city. We have some details on the law."

Tears welled up in Riley's eyes and her dad joined her in the family room.

"Residents who currently have a pit bull or pit bull-type dog will have to register their dog with the city and pay a $150 registration fee yearly. Additionally, all breeds that fall under this ban will be required to be muzzled at all times when outdoors."

Riley gasped and thought of poor Lennox being muzzled any time he wasn't inside. Her dad hugged her around the shoulders.

The reporter continued and looked at a piece of paper in her hand, "Breeds affected include American Staffordshire terriers, Staffordshire bull terriers, American pit bull terriers, any mixed breed dogs that have any one of those breeds, or any dog with similar physical characteristics. Maria, back to you."

The anchor had a follow-up question. "Is there anything else in the bill that residents need to be aware of? Will the city be taking any of their dogs?"

"Good question, Maria." The reporter's face was grave. "As if the bill isn't controversial enough, there is a piece stating that if the owner of an existing pit bull-type dog dies, the dog will be euthanized."

"Wow," Maria said. "I'm sure this won't be the last of this story. Thanks, Trish."

"Any dog with similar physical characteristics? That's so vague! Euthanized when the owner dies?" Riley couldn't stop the tears from falling onto her cheeks. "So that's it? It's done?"

"Honey, they make the laws," her dad explained. "I know you and many others voiced your feelings on this issue, but the Mayor and City Council Members get to decide. I guess there were more citizens for it than against it."

"But people just don't understand! If we just had time to show them dogs like Lennox, they would understand. We have to educate people because they just believe whatever they hear on TV."

Riley's dad hugged her. "I know, Roo. Sometimes it's hard to educate people and tough to get people to care about issues that are so important to us."

After she settled down some, Riley returned to the dinner table and forced herself to finish the rest of her meal. It was hard to eat when she was so upset. She worried about Lennox and Hawk, and any other families that might be affected by this law.

Hailey looked at her and said, "It's like you only care about the dogs. Don't you care about the kid that was mauled? What about that family?"

Riley's fork fell to the table and she could feel her heart

start racing.

Their mom looked at Hailey and said, "Not now, Hailey."

Riley couldn't help the tears and anger, they came swiftly. "Of course I care, Hailey! It's awful what happened to that child! Just because I care so much about dogs, doesn't mean I don't care about people, that's ridiculous!" Riley's face was flushed and tears streamed down her cheeks. Buster appeared at her side and scratched at her legs, trying to get her attention from under the table. "Just because one dog who happens to be a certain breed did this, doesn't mean we should ban all dogs like that! What about Lennox, what about what he does for Hawk? What about all the families who have pit bull type dogs who have never hurt a fly? If one person of a certain race kills someone, do we blame the whole race? No, we don't, that would be stupid!" Buster was starting to whine, so Riley picked him up and he licked at her tears.

Riley's mom stood up and put her arm around Riley's shoulders, "Go on upstairs with Buster, we'll clean up."

Riley wiped her nose on the back of her hand and stood up, cradling Buster in her right arm. She went up to her room and after she settled down, she washed her face while Buster waited for her on her bed, watching her the whole time. Riley had to call Finn and see what he thought. She laid on the bed and dialed his number while Buster snuggled up next to her and rested his little head on her hip.

Finn answered on the first ring and said, "I was about to call you."

Riley inhaled deeply, trying not to cry again. "I can't believe it passed. It's like they didn't even listen to what our side had to say."

"I know, my mom is on the phone with her network of supporters, trying to see what we can do. She thinks we can try to petition them to repeal the ban, but it's going to take a lot of work."

"I hope we can get them to repeal it. Once your mom figures out what we can do, let me know what I can do to help."

Even though Mrs. Murphy seemed to think they could petition a repeal, Riley still went to bed feeling defeated. She tossed and turned all night, seeing Lennox and Hawk in her mind, praying that no dogs would be killed just because of their genetics. Riley didn't understand how some grown-ups could be so stupid.

She heard her phone buzz and looked at the text message from a blocked number that read, *Still winning!*

CHAPTER TWENTY-SIX

Figuring It Out

Riley woke up exhausted after a restless night's sleep. She thought about the text message she received last night, and in a moment of clarity, felt dumb for not thinking about it sooner. When Finn arrived she showed him the message and said, "I think I know who has been texting me."

"I think I know too," Finn said.

"Corey Thornton," they said in unison.

Riley shook her head from side to side. "I mean, it still bothers me, but at least it's not someone random and scary."

"Yeah, as much of a pain as he is, I think he's all talk." A silly grin formed on Finn's face, "Maybe, like your mom said when you got detention, Corey has a crush on you?"

"Gross! That's not even funny!" Riley laughed at her best friend.

Finn was laughing too, "At least I got you to laugh. After everything going on, I figure you can use a laugh or two."

Riley smiled. "So, we have to work on our projects and you have to figure out if you're going to write about the tunnels or something else. Your mom will kill you if you wait 'til the last minute. Besides, that's usually my job."

Finn chuckled and said, "I just really want to write about the tunnels, but if there's nothing there that ties them to the

Civil War, I'm going to have to pick something else...and soon."

***

Thankfully, the school day went quickly and without an encounter with Corey and his friends. Eve joined Riley and Finn after school at Finn's house to work on their research projects on the Civil War. They were sitting at Finn's kitchen table enjoying a snack when Mrs. Murphy came home. Molly hopped up to greet her when she heard the garage door open.

"Hey guys, how are your projects going?" Mrs. Murphy asked as she set two bags of groceries down on the kitchen island.

"Fine," Riley said with dread.

"Still nervous about speaking in front of the class?" Mrs. Murphy asked with sympathetic eyes.

Finn answered, "Her presentation is really good, I think everyone will enjoy it. I still have some research to do."

"You better get going on that, Mister," Mrs. Murphy said and gave Finn a serious look.

"I know, I might have to change my topic, but I've made a lot of notes so I won't be scrambling."

"I wish I could just record a video and show that instead of having to get up in front of everyone," Riley said.

"I'm not looking forward to it either," Eve said, "but everyone has to do it, so I'm sure we're not the only nervous ones."

Mrs. Murphy smiled at the kids. "So of the three of you, Finn's the only one looking forward to presenting, but he's not even set on his topic?"

"Pretty much," Riley said with a giggle.

Finn was grinning, "You know I'll get it done, and it'll be awesome!"

"I just like that I'm not the one lagging behind...I just don't want to get up in front of everyone." Riley sounded pained at the idea.

"When you read your presentation to Eve and me, you sounded great," Finn said. "You'll do fine."

Eve smiled, "At least we'll know everyone in the room."

Riley said, "Maybe I'll just pretend I'm giving my presentation to you guys...or a room full of dogs." This made everyone laugh.

Mrs. Murphy had finished putting her groceries away and said, "I have some calls to make to some of the anti-BSL folks, but you guys keep working." Before heading out of the kitchen, she looked at Finn and said with a smile, "Especially you, mister!"

Finn smiled but Riley could tell his thoughts were far away. "Earth to Finn," Riley said as she waved a hand in front of his face.

"Sorry," he said, his eyes focusing back on the present and his voice low. "I've just been thinking about my report and I want to get back into those tunnels to see if I can get any evidence that they were used during the Civil War."

"Can't you write your paper without writing about the tunnels?" Riley asked.

"Yeah, I could...I've already written about Roswell during the War and what happened to the families here. There's just nothing riveting about my report. I don't want it to be boring."

"I'm sure it won't be boring," Eve said. "You're a great story teller!"

Riley wasn't used to Finn lacking confidence in his decisions. "I think you do a really good job talking about what life was like for everyone. From those who went to fight, to those who stayed back and what they went through."

"You don't think it's boring?" Finn asked.

"No, and I don't know that we should tell everyone about the tunnels, you know? Do we really want everyone else knowing about them?" Riley said as Eve nodded.

"Yeah, I guess you're right. If the city wanted everyone knowing about them, they'd probably do a tour of them like they do the houses...or the Ghost Tour—" Finn stopped abruptly. "I can't believe I didn't think of this sooner!"

"What?" Riley and Eve said in unison.

Finn was smiling now. "I can talk about Catherine and Michael, that's riveting!"

"Great idea! Their story is from the Civil War and it's tragically beautiful. Plus, it's a story you already know a lot about, so you could easily write about them. You can still talk about what life was like in Roswell during the war, they can be the feature of your story."

"And people can actually go to the Public House themselves...the place where the spirits of Catherine and Michael haunt! Thanks for talking this through with me, I've got to add this to my report!"

"Hey, no problem. You're the one who thought of it after all."

Finn spoke quietly again, "I do want to go back to that

tunnel. We left so quickly last time, I just want to see if we can find anything at all that would tie them to the war."

Riley thought back to the unsettling feeling she got in the tunnel. "I'm kind of glad we didn't capture anything else when we were down there. Maybe I felt sick because I needed fresh air?"

"That might have been it," Finn said. "I would think that if something or someone was down there, we would have captured evidence of it." He looked at Riley. "Let's go back to the tunnels this weekend and see if we can find any evidence of them being used for the Civil War. If not, I'll just write about Roswell during the war and highlight Catherine and Michael's story."

"Okay," Riley said. She thought it would be so cool to tie the tunnels to the Civil War, even if she was apprehensive about going there again. She hoped they didn't experience anything weird like they did last time.

***

That evening, Riley was hanging out in the family room with her dad. She had been following the social media posts about the child who was mauled by the dog and the sides were clearly divided. On the one hand were people who had pit bulls themselves and they talked about how wonderful their dogs were. On the other were people who were so outraged that they demanded all pit bulls or pit bull-type dogs be banned... or worse.

Her dad was reading a book and she decided to get his input. "Dad, how can people be so opposed on one issue?"

Her dad put down his book and cocked his head, "What do you mean, sweetheart?"

"I'm reading all these comments about pit bulls and people either love them dearly or want them banned. How come they can have such different views?"

Her dad put a bookmark in his book and set it aside. "Well, Roo, the people who love the dogs dearly are probably those who have pit bulls themselves and that's where the love comes from. I would think that those who are so scared that they want them banned have mostly never had experiences with the dogs. Some of them may have had bad experiences, but I would guess most of them just hear the news and form their opinions."

"So, you're saying that people just believe what they hear and don't try to find out for themselves?"

Riley's dad smiled, "Yeah, I guess that's what I'm saying... and when you put it like that, it sounds really crazy, doesn't it?"

"It's stupid! How can you make a decision based on what you hear and not do any research?"

Her dad leaned forward, "Stupid may be too harsh a word, I would say it's ignorance."

"What do you mean?" Riley asked as Buster hopped up onto the sofa with her.

"Ignorance is a lack of knowledge or education. Someone who says that all pit bulls should be banned may be a very smart person who simply doesn't have any knowledge or information on the topic of pit bulls. They aren't dumb, they just don't know about that subject. Does that make sense?"

"Yeah." Riley was irritated that people wouldn't do their own research before making such bold statements. "If the news makes them scared, then it makes things worse."

Riley's dad joined her on the couch. "That's the thing, Roo, sometimes people make decisions based on fear, and it's often fear of the unknown. Sadly, it can take a lot of work to educate them. Fear is a powerful emotion."

"I need to figure out a way to educate people, then."

"What about your shirts?" Riley's dad asked referring to the shirts with Riley's design about puppy mills.

"Do you really think I can sell them?"

"Of course you can! Your mom and I can help you, and I'm sure you can design one about this issue too."

Riley smiled, "Thanks, dad, that's a great idea!" Riley picked Buster up and headed upstairs with him. She turned back in the hallway and said, "Dad! Buster didn't get up when you sat down!"

Her dad smiled broadly, "I know, I didn't want to say anything and jinx it!"

Riley felt better. Buster was making strides and she had an idea she could work on to help educate people about pit bulls. She couldn't just sit around feeling helpless, she had to do something.

CHAPTER TWENTY-SEVEN

A Careless Oversight

Riley was so glad when the weekend arrived and to see how happy Hawk was on this sunny Saturday morning. She thought he was the best she'd ever seen him. Buster, Molly, and Lennox had a blast playing and Riley was careful not to over exert Buster. He was so much smaller than Molly and Lennox, he had to run a lot more to keep up with them. She took Buster back home while Hawk, Finn, and their dogs kept playing on leash in the front yard. Riley neared her porch steps, turned around, and said, "Watch this!"

As they approached the steps, Buster climbed right up them and Riley pulled a treat from the pouch on her waistband. She didn't care if Hailey made fun of her, or if she looked like a dork, she knew she had to be diligent with Buster's training and it helped to have treats ready.

Hawk and Finn hooped and hollered which made Riley giggle as she opened the door and took Buster inside. She could hear Lennox barking at the excitement from Hawk and Finn. She loved how exuberant he was. After she got Buster some fresh water and put the treat pouch away, she grabbed her backpack and headed back to Hawk's.

At the top of her street, Riley saw Tim Harrington coming their way on his skateboard, passing Corey who was presumably on the way to see Seth. She was glad she had just missed Corey. Across the street, Mister Felton was starting his morning walk, his hiking stick in hand and ball cap on his head. Lennox and Molly were still frolicking, but a bit less vigorously than they had been. Just as Mr. Felton passed Hawk's house, Tim came flying by on his skateboard, the wheels making a loud whirring and clacking noise as they rolled fast on the pavement.

Riley saw Molly cower and bark loudly three times. She couldn't tell if it was Mr. Felton or Tim, but one of them spooked her. Upon hearing her barks, Lennox began barking and jumping at Mr. Felton. Hawk had a hold of the leash and quickly used the command for Lennox to settle and sit next to him.

Riley could hear Mr. Felton say, "Keep that dog away from me! It should have a muzzle on!"

Riley's pulse quickened, she hated confrontation. She jogged across the street, her eyes wide. "Who was he talking to?" Then it dawned on her. The muzzle. He was talking about Lennox and that stupid law.

Hawk's jaw muscles flexed and Lennox put his paws up on Hawk's hips, searching for attention. "He's complained about Lennox's barking twice already and has been rude ever since I got him. And with that new law, he's right, Lennox should be muzzled. It's my bad, I forgot."

"He has to be muzzled, even in your front yard?" Finn asked.

"Unfortunately, yes." Hawk scratched Lennox behind his ears.

"That's ridiculous, that entire law is stupid," Riley said.

"Besides, it's not like Lennox is out here barking all the time," Riley said. "I only hear him bark when he's playing."

"He only barks when he's playing or excited. Still, I should have had that stupid muzzle on him." Hawk said as he squatted to pet Lennox, the dog's arms now on Hawk's shoulders, like they were hugging. Lennox's tail wagged as he licked Hawk on the face. "He can tell I'm frustrated," Hawk said, "and he's trying to calm me down." Hawk started to laugh as he fell into a seated position, "Okay, I'm fine, enough kisses."

Riley smiled softly, "Looks like he's doing a good job."

"Sorry, Hawk," Finn said. "I think Molly was startled by Mr. Felton. She's still nervous around men with hats and he had that stick, so who knows if that set her off."

Riley thought back to when she had "seen" what Molly had gone through before ending up in a shelter. They knew Molly's first owner wore a hat and abused her, so they were trying to help her with that issue.

"He's a grumpy old man," Hawk said, "Molly probably read his energy, too. Didn'tcha, girl." He used his left hand to pet Molly on her chest. She was fine now and licked Hawk's forearm as he stroked her fur. "I need to be careful now that they've passed BSL here. I have to get into the habit of putting that muzzle on. His life may depend on it."

Riley saw sadness wash into Hawk's eyes. She didn't know what to say.

"We know Lennox is harmless and a great dog," Finn said. "If anything ever happens, we'll help you."

"He's a service dog," Riley added. "Surely there are exceptions for dogs like Lennox. He's better behaved than most dogs!" Lennox seemed like he knew what Riley had just said and sat pretty in front of her, his tail sweeping the grass back and forth. Riley smiled looking at the huge goofy grin on Lennox's face. "I mean look at him. How can anyone be afraid of that face?"

CHAPTER TWENTY-EIGHT

Another Exploration

Riley and Finn were on their way to Smith Plantation to explore the tunnels again. As they walked their bikes down Riley's driveway, Riley tucked her hair behind her ear and took a deep breath. "So, I don't want this to sound weird but..."

Finn, ever casual, looked at Riley and said, "What's up?"

Riley fidgeted with the strap of her backpack. "Well, I mean, we don't have to, but Eve told me that she asked Tim Harrington to the Sadie Hawkins dance and doesn't want to go alone, so she asked who I was taking."

Finn smiled and said, "Oh cool! Who are you taking?"

Riley laughed at his devilish grin. She appreciated that he used humor when he could tell she felt uncomfortable. "No one. You know me, I don't like dressing up...or dancing, but I would hate for Eve to feel uncomfortable and since neither of us went to the Fall dance, this would be our first middle school dance..."

Finn wasn't going to let her off easy. "Yeah...?"

"Oh come on, are you going to make me ask you?"

Finn smiled triumphantly and said, "It's the Sadie Hawkins dance, the girls have to ask the boys!"

Riley shook her head and rolled her eyes, smiling brightly. "Finn Murphy, will you go to the Sadie Hawkins dance with me?"

Finn paused. "Let's see what day is that again? I might have plans." He pulled out his phone and pretended to search his calendar.

Riley wasn't going to let him win. "No worries, I can find someone else to ask if you're busy." She really was kind of nervous that he would say no.

Finn glanced at his calendar, "Nothing like asking me less than a week before the dance..."

Oh no, maybe someone else has already asked him, Riley thought.

Finn laughed. "I would love to go to the Sadie Hawkins dance with you, Riley Carson."

"Awesome," Riley said, she was glad that was over. "Are you cool with me wearing sneakers?"

Finn chuckled. "Why should the Sadie Hawkins dance be any different than a normal day? Your mom might have something to say about that though..."

"Oh yeah," Riley said, a little down-trodden at the idea of her mom forcing her into some silly, frilly dress. Riley thought back to how excited her mom got when they had to find a dress for her to wear to tea with Mrs. Powell after they had first met her. Then it dawned on her. "Mrs. Powell!"

Finn furrowed his brow in confusion. "What? What does Mrs. Powell have to do with the dance?"

"Dressing up, but that's not it. I just thought of Mrs. Powell and realized that we should see if she can help us overturn BSL!"

"I'm not sure how you thought of it, but that's a great idea!

She has a lot of influence in this town."

Riley was excited and hopeful. "I'll call her and see if we can pay her a visit. Oh, I hope she has enough influence to help us! She may be key to fixing this!" With renewed optimism, they rode their bikes down Mimosa Street toward Canton Street.

***

Like they had done the last time, Riley and Finn locked up their bikes at the Heart of Roswell Park, crossed the street, and headed down the crushed granite path. Finn checked his watch. "They should have opened ten minutes ago," he said. "Hopefully that means the first tour is going on inside and no one's touring the grounds yet."

"Yeah, I hope we can make it in and out without being seen," Riley said as they neared the cook house.

They walked up the brick steps and into an empty cook house. They took advantage and quickly got the hatch open, its hinges squeaking loudly just like before. They paused and made sure no one had been around to hear it and then Finn hopped into the tunnel. He opened his bag and pulled out a small can, spraying it on the hinges.

Riley laughed. "Seriously, you thought to bring something to lubricate the hinges?"

Finn had a wry grin on his face. "Of course! I know how you don't like getting in trouble and I wanted to be sure we can make a quiet exit."

Riley grinned and shook her head then hopped down into the tunnel with Finn. He closed the hatch, which didn't squeak this time, and cracked a glo-stick to mark the location. Then, they crawled on all fours the short distance to the main tunnel.

From the moment they got to the area where the tunnel opened up, Finn and Riley scanned the ground and walls for anything that could indicate these tunnels were used during the Civil War. So far, all they saw was dirt on the ground and stacked stone walls.

"I think I should invest in a metal detector," Finn said, clearly frustrated that they were coming up empty.

"Now, that would be cool!" Riley said. "Someone had to drop something in here at some point." She really hoped they would find something too. She loved history and would be so excited if they could even find an old piece of hardware, something dating back to the 1800's.

"This is about where we thought we heard voices last time," Finn said. "Let's wait here and just listen."

"Okay," Riley agreed. "I can't believe we didn't capture them on your recorder."

"I know," Finn said. They both stopped to just listen...to see if they might hear something again.

Riley was getting cold since they had stopped walking and thought about how long it felt when you just sat there waiting for something to happen. Underground, in a tunnel that might be haunted, no less. Just as she was about to ask Finn how much longer he wanted to wait, she heard something to her right, further down the tunnel where they had not yet explored. "Finn!" She whispered. "Did you hear something?"

"Yeah," he whispered back as they both headed silently toward the noise. A faint whimper was audible and Riley grabbed

Finn's arm. They both froze in place, listening intently. Their flashlights shone down the tunnel and they watched, but they saw nothing, so they continued on.

Finn pulled out his EMF meter as they walked. "I'm not sure if someone is down here, or if we're hearing paranormal activity," he whispered.

Riley involuntarily shuddered, a chill cascading up her spine. "Maybe Mister Oscar will hang out and keep us safe."

Finn held up the EMF meter which had gone from green to red, "Maybe!"

Riley loved how excited Finn got about hauntings and ghosts. She enjoyed it as well, but not as much as her friend. She had just started to relax when she heard a low growl and stopped dead in her tracks. Finn stopped too. They listened and waited. After a few seconds, the growling stopped and then they heard a high pitched whimper.

"A dog!" Riley whispered as she started ahead.

Finn grabbed her arm, "We still need to be careful. It could be rabid, mean, or just scared. We have to keep our wits about us."

"You're right. Let's go."

They set off at a brisk pace, but cautious about running into whatever lay ahead. They hadn't heard anything for several minutes and stopped again to listen. As they stood there, Riley grabbed the wall with her right hand and bent forward. "Finn, I don't feel so good all of a sudden."

"What's wrong?"

Riley clutched her stomach, and then her head. "Oww! My head is killing me and I feel like I'm going to throw up."

"Do you want to head back?"

There was another whimper somewhere a head of them. "No, that definitely sounds like a dog, let's keep going."

Finn shined the light so he could see Riley's face. "You're pale," he said. "Are you sure?"

"Yeah, I'm fine," Riley said, trying to ignore the pain. "Let's go."

They continued on and Riley didn't feel any better, in fact she was starting to feel dizzy and faint, she braced herself against the wall when suddenly it felt like a wall of frigid air had descended on them. "Do you feel that?"

Finn nodded and held up his EMF meter which was solid red. "Yeah, this is weird." He remembered his recorder was on and said, "Is anyone here with us."

As they waited through the pause, they heard a low growl but it didn't sound like a dog, it sounded menacing. Riley could see Finn's face in the dim light and she had never seen him so terrified. All he could say was, "Let's get out of here!"

They turned and ran back the way they came as fast as they could, not stopping until they were almost back to the inter-secting tunnels. Riley was starting to feel better, physically and mentally. Her head felt better and she no longer felt dizzy or nauseated. She took a bottle of water out of her backpack and had a long sip.

"Feeling better?" Finn asked.

"Yeah, much." Riley took another long sip and looked at Finn. "What do you think that was?"

"I don't know." Finn was panting and wiped his hair off his forehead, the color had returned to his face which was now rosy from exertion. "It felt evil."

"What about the dog?" Riley hated to think a dog was stuck down here.

"What if there wasn't a dog?" Finn suggested. "What if we were being lured down the tunnel?"

Riley shuddered. "Like an evil spirit?"

"I don't know, but what I do know is that we don't need to be messing with whatever that was." Finn looked as serious as Riley had ever seen him. He never missed an opportunity to capture paranormal activity, but if he thought what they heard was something evil, she didn't want to go after it either.

***

When they got back to the hatch, they were both exhausted. They crawled along the dirt floor and Finn picked up the glo-stick, pocketing it in his cargo pants. He slightly pushed up the door and peered through the small opening. Having seen no one, he pushed the door up all the way and all of a sudden a stern-faced older woman was looking down at them. Finn hadn't seen her when he cracked open the door, but there she was, and Riley's stomach flipped again.

"Did you have fun down there, you two?" The woman snapped.

"We just—" Finn started. He really didn't know what to say.

"Get on out of there, now," the woman said.

They hesitated.

"Come on, up you go," she pushed.

Finn lifted himself out of the hatch, followed by Riley

who did the same. They stood almost eye to eye with the small woman.

"What are your names?"

"Riley Carson ma'am, and this is Finn Murphy." Riley was scared to death, hoping this little woman hadn't called the police...and that she wouldn't call their parents.

"What on earth were you doing down there?"

"Well, we thought—" Riley started, but Finn interrupted. Riley realized he had an idea.

"We thought it would be cool to see if there were any artifacts in the root cellar. We know we should have asked permission, but we're working on a project for school and when we were looking around the out-buildings, we thought there might still be artifacts that you all hadn't found yet."

Riley could tell the woman was surprised that they knew there was a root cellar in the cook house.

"Of course we would have brought them to you since they are property of the city as is this land." Riley felt that came off sounding way too goody-goody. She realized that Finn didn't want to say anything about the tunnels in case this woman didn't know they existed.

The woman moved past them and looked into the hatch before closing it. After it was closed tight, she tilted her head as she looked at the floor. "Hmph."

"We're really sorry," Riley said. "We should have asked for permission first."

"I noticed the pot that sits over here had been moved. I called into the cellar, why didn't you answer?"

Oops, Riley thought.

Finn pulled a pair of ear buds out of his jacket pocket. "Sorry, we were listening to music while we looked. We're really sorry."

The woman flashed glances between Riley and Finn as if to assess the honesty of their story. "I suppose no harm was done, and since it was for a school project, I'm not going to call your parents. But if you're telling the truth, there's no reason to be down in that hatch again, which will be padlocked by the end of the day, mind you," she added. "If you need help with a project, please just come to the office building over there." She pointed to a white building across the way. "We're more than happy to help students with projects."

Riley was so relieved. "Finn and I have to write about the Civil War in Georgia and give an oral presentation. Do you have any information that will help with that?" She hoped that changing the subject would help convince her she made a good decision to let them off with a warning, but also back up their story about the projects, which was at least half true, Riley realized.

A small smile appeared on the woman's face. "Why yes, a book of letters written by members of the Smith family was compiled and we sell copies. It's called, The Death of a Confederate. Would you be interested in one?"

How could she refuse. "Yes, I'd love to buy one!" Riley wasn't lying. She loved to read and figured it would be cool to read real letters from the family during the war. She followed the woman out of the cook house and Finn shook his head at her, a grin on his face. Riley shrugged and smiled sweetly. Finn wasn't the only one who could think fast.

After Riley bought the book, she handed it to Finn and smiled. "Here, this will probably help you with your project." They headed back to their bikes and turned their conversation back to what happened in the tunnel.

"That was crazy," Finn said.

"You felt it this time, too, huh?"

"Yep. Something has to be haunting that tunnel," Finn said.

"I don't want to disappoint you, but if she does get that hatch locked up, I won't be that upset," Riley said. She knew Finn would want to figure out what was going on in the tunnel, but wasn't keen on going back.

"We'll see," Finn said. "For now, we've gotta go listen to see if we captured anything!"

Riley felt her stomach flutter. For the first time, she wasn't sure if she wanted to listen to one of their recordings.

CHAPTER TWENTY-NINE

E.V.P. Results

Once at Finn's house, Riley hung out upstairs with Finn's mom who made them sandwiches while Finn went to the basement to load the recording onto his computer to see what they got. Molly followed her boy down the stairs and Riley smiled. "I love how Molly follows him everywhere. I'm so glad y'all adopted her; I knew she was special when I met her."

"Me too," Mrs. Murphy said with a sweet smile. "She's the perfect dog and we know she's just as grateful as we are. That's the cool thing about rescue dogs, they seem so appreciative because many times they've experienced unhappy things."

"Yeah," Buster is making good progress and seems very content. He may still like to sleep under the coffee table, but I can see the worry leaving him," Riley said.

"I'm glad he's doing well. I know you've been working hard with him to get him used to this great, big world. He's lucky to have you guys."

"Thanks." Riley was proud to receive such a compliment from Mrs. Murphy. "Finn and I have been looking for Baby Girl, but the sightings have gone down, and I'm worried her family will never find her."

Mrs. Murphy plated the two sandwiches. "I know you want to help, but the family has tracking dogs and they've set traps with food. As much as you want to help, in cases of a missing dog who is skittish like Baby Girl, you can actually do more harm than good if you go searching on your own."

"How do you mean?" Riley asked.

Mrs. Murphy set a sandwich in front of Riley who was perched on a stool at the breakfast bar. "Dogs who are skittish are likely going to be afraid of strangers, so if you go looking in the area where there have been sightings, you might actually be pushing her out of that area because you are a stranger to her."

"Oh gosh, I didn't realize that." Riley said feeling bad that they might be doing more harm than good.

Mrs. Murphy smiled gently at Riley. "Don't worry too much, honey. They'll find her."

Riley enjoyed a bite of her sandwich, then said, "Mrs. Murphy? Do you think we'll be able to get BSL overturned?"

Finn's mom looked pained. "I sure hope so, Riley. We really need to educate the folks in charge and help them understand. We've got lots of groups working with us to fight it, we just need to get to the right people to help."

Riley knew she had to go see Mrs. Powell. She was the only person Riley knew who might have enough power to help get BSL overturned.

Riley heard Finn's footsteps pounding up the stairs. "Okay, come listen and let me know what you think," he said, his expression not giving away his own thoughts.

Riley noted he wasn't as excited as he normally was when they captured an EVP, and she thought back to how bad she had felt in the tunnel earlier. She hopped off the stool and grabbed her plate and Finn's. "Thanks Mrs. Murphy," she said. As she followed Finn toward the stairs, handing him his plate, a twinge of dread crept into her stomach.

When they got downstairs, Finn said, "The good news is, I don't think there was an actual person down there with us—"

Riley finished his thought. "The bad news is it's an evil spirit."

"Uh, yeah, that's what I'm thinking," Finn said and Riley could tell he was nervous.

"For real?" Riley asked. "What about a dog? Did it sound like there was a real dog down there?"

Finn handed Riley the headphones. "I don't know. Let me know what you think."

Riley felt anxious and took the headphones, she listened intently to where Finn had cued up the recording. She heard footsteps, hers and Finn's, and their voices debating whether they heard a dog or not. As she continued listening, she heard a low growl, then their footsteps stop. Next she heard the high pitched whimper and her voice exclaim, "A dog!" She heard Finn stop her and tell her to be cautious, then heard their footsteps pick up the pace. Riley's eyes grew wide as she heard a deep, low groan immediately followed by her own voice saying, "Finn, I don't feel so good all of a sudden." She heard Finn ask her what was wrong. Then, Riley heard a low gravelly voice say, "Go away!"

Next she heard herself complain that her head hurt, saying she may throw up, and reliving it all through the recording made her anxious. She heard Finn ask if she wanted to go back and then heard another whimper. "Was it a dog, or something else?" She thought to herself as she strained to hear. She heard Finn's and her own voice when they agreed to move ahead. Then Riley heard herself say, "Do you feel that?" That was when she felt like they walked into a blast of icy air. She heard Finn say yes, and then ask, "Is anyone here with us?"

Riley was nervous as she awaited a response. A low voice said, "Yesssss." Then the voice got louder and meaner, "Now, go!" Next Riley heard her best friend's voice and it sounded so scared, "Let's get out of here!" Riley slipped the headphones off and felt her pulse racing.

Finn's eyes were wide and expression serious. After Riley took off the headphones he said, "Pretty crazy, huh?"

"Uh, yeah!" Riley's mind was reeling. "Whoever that was didn't want us there." Her thoughts went to the whimper. "Do you think a dog was down there?"

Finn drew in a breath then exhaled. "I don't know. It was so hard to tell if that was a dog, or maybe another spirit."

"Could it be a spirit of a dog?" Riley wondered.

"I suppose it could," Finn said. "Remember when Eve saw the spirit of the mill dog we found?" Finn thought for a moment, "And, there are stories of ghost dogs that haunt places. We'll have to do some research on that."

"Or," Riley offered, "Like you said when we were in the tunnel, it could be something trying to lure us. It might not be a dog at all."

CHAPTER THIRTY

Searching

As Riley was getting ready for the dance, she thought about how glad she was when she and Finn saw that the docent at Smith Plantation had made good on her promise and locked up the hatch. She loved exploring, but was glad they wouldn't be able to get back into the tunnels. They hadn't found any Civil War artifacts and had experienced something truly frightening. She was glad they wouldn't be able to get back in because she didn't want Finn going on his own.

As Riley finished fixing her hair, she laughed to herself because Finn was right - her mom was not about to let *her* daughter wear sneakers to the Sadie Hawkins dance. After what had felt like the longest evening of shopping ever, they had found the perfect outfit the night before and both Riley and her mom were happy. Riley thought she was happiest because the shopping was over.

Riley stood in her bedroom, looked at her reflection in the full-length mirror on the back of her door, and smiled. She twirled in the mirror and her skirt spun around her. Since this dance was the most casual one of the year, she was able to negotiate a more comfortable option and wore a fuzzy white, short-sleeved sweater with a sparkly black skirt that made her feel like a ballerina. Her hair was in a simple ponytail, tied with a black satin ribbon and she wore black ballet flats. Riley went to her dresser and opened the top drawer. She pulled out a black satin ribbon with a key hanging from it, the key they found at the Public House. Riley thought it would be a cool addition to her outfit.

When she walked downstairs Riley's parents were waiting for her. She swore her mom had tears in her eyes. "Oh, you look absolutely beautiful!" Her mom grabbed her hands and held them out, then twirled Riley around. "Sweetie, you should dress up more often, you are gorgeous!" Her mom paused and tilted her head, "What's this?" She held the old key in her hand to inspect it.

"It's an old key we found at the Public House. Remember that mannequin we saw at the mall that had all those necklaces? One of them had a key on it and I thought about this thing," Riley said as she held it in her hand and looked at it, wondering why it had been left for them. "It's cool, I like it."

"Well, I was thinking you could wear my pearls, but this looks cute...and you look so pretty!" Her mom beamed at her.

Riley felt embarrassed. She always thought it was silly to worry so much about someone's exterior beauty. She smiled, though and said, "Thanks, mom. Thanks for getting this outfit for me." She stuck her hands into pockets in the skirt. "I just love that it has pockets!"

"I know, it's so cute, and you can put your lip gloss in your pocket."

"And my phone," Riley said with a smile. "What else do I need?"

Her dad gave her a kiss on her forehead and said, "My little girl is growing up, and I'm not sure I like it!" He chuckled as her mom reapplied lipstick before Finn and his parents came over. "You look beautiful, Roo, but you always do. Inside and out."

"Thanks, dad. I'm just glad mom and I agreed on something," Riley laughed and smiled at her mom.

Her mom turned from the foyer mirror and said, "I was beginning to think we weren't!"

Riley smoothed her hands over her skirt and went to tuck her hair behind her ear, a nervous habit that she realized when her hair was tied up. "I'm so glad it's comfortable."

"And pretty!" Her mom said as she fixed her own hair in the mirror. She turned and said, "So, your dad will take you and Finn to the dance and you're meeting Eve and Tim there?"

"Yeah," Riley said. "Tim's dad is taking him over to pick up Eve and we'll just meet them at the dance."

The doorbell rang and Riley went to answer it. She was taking her best friend to the dance but for some reason, she felt nervous. Her pulse quickened and she felt stupid for being anxious around her best friend. Riley opened the door and Finn was standing there with a crooked grin on his face, looking sharp in a pair of chinos and a light blue button down with a dark brown vest over it. His parents were behind him on the porch. Riley smiled and said, "Well, you clean up nice."

Finn laughed. "I was about to say the same thing! Seriously, though, you look really nice."

"Thanks," Riley said. She no longer felt nervous, just happy to have her best friend by her side. "Come in."

Finn had a clear plastic box in his hands and it had a simple white rose wrist corsage with two sprigs of purple heather.

"Your mom helped me with this."

He opened the box and Riley's mom said, "Wait, wait! We have to get a picture!" She and Mrs. Murphy grabbed their phones and took pictures as Finn slipped the accessory on Riley's delicate wrist.

Riley held her wrist up to look at it. "It's so pretty, thank you! And that's why this matches." She grabbed a similar box from the table in the foyer and opened it up. She turned to her mom. "I may need some help with this."

Her mom smiled. "Just pretend like you're putting it on for a picture, then I'll do it."

Riley felt so awkward posing for these pictures, but she obliged.

"Let me get a couple of shots of the two of you," her dad said. "Let's go in here." They all followed him into the formal living room which they rarely used. In fact, Sammy had seemed to use it the most. It got lots of sunlight and he would sit and watch the neighborhood, making sure to alert the family if anyone was walking by.

After they took their pictures, Riley grabbed her bag and they got ready to head out with Finn and her dad.

"What do you need your bag for?" Riley's mom asked.

"Just in case we leave early and decide to go bowling or something," Riley said.

Her dad chuckled and they headed to the garage, her mom still fussing over her. "You just look so pretty, honey, and Finn, you look dashing! I hope you two have fun tonight!"

"Thanks, Mrs. Carson!" Finn said.

"Thanks, Mom, see you later! Bye, Mr. & Mrs. Murphy!"

They buckled up in Riley's dad's SUV and he turned around and said, "You have sneakers in that bag, don't you?"

Riley looked surprised, then smiled. "I'm that predictable, huh?"

"I was wondering..." Finn said.

Riley pulled out a pair of black, sparkly sneakers. "Half the reason I got this outfit was because it matched these sneakers! They're like my special occasion sneakers."

Riley's dad and Finn laughed. "I'm glad that's what I have to worry about," her dad said. "Most dads would love to have this problem!" He reversed out of the garage and headed toward the school.

Riley looked at Finn. "You don't mind do you?"

Finn cocked his head. "Of course not!"

Riley smiled. She was so lucky to have such a good friend who accepted her 100% for who she was.

CHAPTER THIRTY-ONE

Sadie Hawkins Dance

When they got to the dance, Riley and Finn spotted Eve and Tim, already waiting for them in the lobby in front of the doors to the gym. Eve was wearing a pretty red dress and Riley could see that Tim had gotten her a red corsage to match. Tim had on khaki pants with a white button down, red tie, and flip-flops.

"Hey guys!" Finn said as they approached. He looked at Tim's feet. "Flip-flops in January?"

Tim smiled, it was a friendly grin that showed the little space between his front teeth. "Flip-flops all the time. Whenever I can, anyway!"

Riley laughed and said, "I know what you mean!" She looked at her own feet and modeled her black, sparkly sneakers.

"Skater shoes, too. Nice!" Tim said as he held up a hand to give Riley "five."

Riley smiled, "Slip-on sneakers are my favorite."

"Eve, I love your dress," Riley said.

"Thanks," Eve said sweetly. "My poor dad had to go shopping with me."

Riley felt bad. Again she was reminded that even though she and her mom didn't always see eye to eye, she was lucky to have her. Riley smiled and said, "I'm sure he enjoyed it!" She meant it too; she knew from the short time that they knew Eve and her family that her dad loved her very much.

"Well, let's go in and check this thing out," Finn said.

As they entered the gym, they saw it was decorated with pretty white decorations with a winter theme. White paper snowflakes were fluttering from strings and a disco ball made silver sparkles all around the room. A deejay was playing music from the stage and there was a punch bowl and snacks on the left side of the room. It looked like half of the students were dancing, and the other half of them were sitting in the bleachers on the right side of the room.

"It looks like most people came to the dance, even if they don't have dates," Eve said as they noticed a group of girls sitting together on the bleachers.

"Yeah, that's cool," Tim said. An upbeat song was playing and Tim turned to Eve, "Wanna go dance?"

Eve's face lit up, "Yeah, let's go!"

Riley had a moment of panic when she realized she might actually have to dance at the dance, and apparently her horror was evident.

Finn smiled. "Don't worry, we don't have to dance. Remember, I know you better than anyone in this room."

Riley exhaled. "I couldn't ask you to a dance and not dance with you, but let's hang out for a bit first. I feel so uncoordinated when I dance." She nodded to the dance floor. "Look at Eve and Tim, they look like they are having so much fun, and they don't even look ridiculous dancing."

"You won't look ridiculous either, but I'm sure you won't look as carefree as they are." Finn laughed which made Riley laugh, too. "Come, on, let's go check out the food," Finn said.

They crossed over to the food table and grabbed some of the little desserts and punch then headed over to the bleachers. A slow song came on and Eve and Tim joined them.

"That looked like fun!" Riley said.

Eve was beaming. "It was! Tim's a good dancer."

Tim was smiling, "Thanks, you are too!" He was facing the doors into the gym and said, "Well, looks like Corey brought Brad and Seth as his dates."

Riley, Finn, and Eve all looked over and tried to suppress their laughter.

Riley and Finn were sharing their snacks with Eve and Tim when a look of pure disgust washed across Tim's face. Riley turned to look and she saw Corey and his friends behind a girl named Amy who used a walker because she had cerebral palsy. Corey was waving his arms in jerking motions and standing with his legs crooked. Poor Amy didn't notice, but Tim certainly had and now Riley had seen it too.

"Be right back," Tim said as he stood and headed down the bleachers. Corey and his friends were snickering on their way to the food table and Tim stopped to talk to Amy, who thankfully still seemed oblivious to what had just happened behind her. Riley told Finn and Eve what she and Tim had seen and, of course, they were just as upset.

Tears pricked Riley's eyes as she saw Tim hold out his hands and move Amy's walker to the side. Amy held on to Tim's forearms and they swayed to the slow song that was still playing, smiling and talking as they danced.

Finn and Eve noticed too and Eve grabbed Riley's arm. "Oh my gosh, that is so sweet!"

Riley smiled and blinked a tear out of her eye. "So sweet," she said.

Finn had a lopsided grin on his face as he watched Tim and Amy and said, "You know, for a kid who gets in trouble so much, he's really very kind."

"It's like I've said, he just can't help but get himself into trouble," Riley said.

The song ended and Tim slid the walker back over to Amy. They chatted briefly and Tim walked over to the food table where he said something to Corey and his buddies. Corey was stuffing his face, so even if he had something to say, he couldn't have done so easily. Riley could tell Tim was still angry but trying not to make a scene.

When he walked back to the bleachers, Eve said, "That was really sweet of you."

Tim smiled as his anger seemed to subside. "I can't believe that kid. He's such a jerk."

"I can't believe you didn't just knock him out." Finn paused, "Not that I'm advocating violence."

"Believe me, I wanted to, but if I had, Amy would have known what happened and that would have been worse."

Riley's shoulders softened. "Wow, who knew you were so nice?" She wasn't sure how Tim would react if she were sappy, so she went with funny.

Tim grinned. "I try to keep that under wraps."

"Seriously, though, that was really nice of you," Riley said.

"It was," Eve said. She looked at Riley and Finn and said, "Have there been any sightings of Baby Girl?"

"Unfortunately, the search page for her has been pretty

quiet," Riley said.

"That stinks," Tim said. "I've been keeping an eye out for her when I'm out, but haven't seen her."

"Same here," Finn said. "I'm starting to wonder if someone kept her as their own pet and doesn't realize her family is missing her."

"Yeah, between trying to find her and fight BSL, it's been kinda crazy," Riley said.

"I can't believe Roswell passed that," Tim said. "It made me so mad."

"Us too," Riley said and Finn and Eve nodded. "Finn and I are going to talk to Mrs. Powell about it. She has such influence in town, we're hoping she can help."

"That would be awesome!" Tim said.

Riley really hoped Mrs. Powell could help. She felt like she was their only hope at this point.

CHAPTER THIRTY-TWO

An Unexpected Visitor

Monday morning raced by and though she panicked in the beginning, stumbling over her words just a bit, overall Riley felt she had done a decent job with her oral presentation. Mostly, she was just glad she was done with it. She had spent hours the night before rehearsing with her dad who, as usual, in his casual way built her up and gave her the confidence she needed to succeed.

As she met Finn for their walk home from school he confirmed her own assessment, "You did a great job with your presentation!"

Riley smiled. "Thanks, Finn. You did great too!" she said. "But honestly, I've been really distracted with BSL."

"Me too," Finn said. "I really hope Mrs. Powell can help."

"And there haven't been any sightings of Baby Girl..." Riley felt so sad for her family.

"It's like she's just disappeared," Finn said. "That's why I think someone must have taken her in. Otherwise, you'd think someone would find her."

"I know," Riley said. When they turned up their street, Riley noticed a boxy, white truck parked in Hawk's driveway. As they got closer, she read the side, *Fulton County Animal Control.*

"Oh no!" she cried out, and dashed off, Finn on her heels.

They reached Hawk's yard, panting, to see a man in a uniform in the truck, pulling out of the driveway. Hawk stood in his doorway with a grim look on his face.

Riley panicked. "Hawk, what's going on?" she said, jogging up the porch to greet him.

Hawk took a deep breath. "Someone reported Lennox." His jaw flexed after he said this.

"Reported him, for what?" Riley could feel her pulse quicken.

Hawk's overall appearance was stoic; he showed very little emotion and his demeanor worried Riley. "Apparently he was reported for being aggressive."

"What?" Finn exclaimed. "That's ridiculous!"

"Yeah," Riley said. "Do they know he plays with kids, small dogs, and big dogs? All without any trouble?"

Hawk exhaled sharply. "I told him all of that. The man who just left saw Lennox and will let me know what the city decides. For now, Lennox is still inside."

Riley's heart sank. "So Lennox's fate is determined by one guy?"

"Apparently," Hawk said.

Riley didn't know what to say, she could tell Hawk was devastated, internalizing his frustration. She didn't know whether they should politely leave or stay to try to cheer him up. She figured the right thing to do was just ask. "Do you want us to stay, or do you just want to be alone right now?"

Hawk smiled slightly at her kindness. "Why don't you come in and see Lennox; I know he would love to see you guys."

Riley was relieved and she and Finn followed Hawk inside

where Lennox was immediately at Hawk's feet. He put his paws on Hawk's hips and licked his hands. Hawk scratched Lennox behind his ears and said, "Go on, say hello to your friends."

As if Lennox knew exactly what Hawk meant, he ran over to greet Riley and Finn, getting pets from each of them before heading back to Hawk. Riley noticed Lennox was glued to Hawk, more so than usual. As they all sat down, Lennox rubbed his head against Hawk's leg, then rested his chin on his thigh so Hawk could pet him. Riley knew Lennox was sensing Hawk's anxiety and trying to help him settle and focus.

"I reached out to Mrs. Powell when we heard that BSL passed and asked her if she could help us," Riley said. "She has a lot of influence in Roswell, so hopefully she can help. I'll call her tonight and fill her in if you're okay with that."

"That would be great," Hawk said as he looked down at Lennox's wide grin, the sweet dog oblivious to the grave situation they were facing. "We need all the help we can get."

Riley knew Hawk was right, and didn't want to even think about what would happen if Lennox was taken from him.

CHAPTER THIRTY-THREE

A Horrible Morning

Riley was on pins and needles ever since seeing the Animal Control truck outside of Hawk's house on Monday afternoon. On Thursday morning, Finn was waiting on Riley's porch for their walk to school. "I'm glad Mrs. Powell wants to meet with us this weekend," Finn said as they headed down Riley's front steps. "I sure hope she can help."

"Me too," Riley said as she nervously twisted the strap on her backpack. "She sounded positive, so hopefully that means she has a way to help. It's so frustrating being a kid and not having the power to do more," Riley said. "I just wish—"

"Oh no!" Finn cried out, grabbing Riley's arm and pointing. Heading up their street was a large white truck with an enclosed back for cages—Animal Control was back. Riley felt her pulse quicken and could feel her blood pounding through her heart. She and Finn froze in their tracks as the vehicle passed them and pulled into Hawk's driveway.

"I'm calling my mom," Finn said. As he dialed and spoke to his mom, he and Riley walked back to Riley's driveway to watch. Mrs. Murphy joined them in minutes and the three observed as the man from Monday got out of the truck and knocked on Hawk's door.

"Hawk looks upset," Riley said as she tucked her hair behind her ear.

"Mom, they can't take Lennox away, can they?"

Mrs. Murphy ran her hand through Finn's hair. "Now that they've passed that law, they can if they have reason, and you said Hawk forgot to muzzle Lennox when he was outside, so..." Her voice trailed off as if she didn't know what to say next.

The next thing they knew, Lennox was on a leash led outside by Hawk. Poor Lennox had no clue what was happening. His tail wagged like crazy, that huge grin on his face. Hawk squatted down and gave Lennox kisses, scratching him behind his ears, talking to him, and before she knew it, Riley had tears streaming down her face. Lennox jumped up and put his paws on Hawk's shoulders and nuzzled against his neck. Riley couldn't help but let out a small cry. Mrs. Murphy put her arm around Riley's shoulder, her other around Finn's. Hawk hugged Lennox and then allowed the man from Animal Control to load him into the truck. Riley noticed Hawk's shoulders slump forward as he walked to the porch and through his front door. He couldn't look back and Riley knew he was devastated.

"They can't just take him away," Riley said between quiet sobs.

Mrs. Murphy removed her arms from the kids' shoulders and marched across the street. She walked up to the man before he could get in his truck and said something that Riley couldn't hear.

When she crossed back to where Riley and Finn stood, Finn asked, "What did you say?"

Mrs. Murphy had a look of determination on her face. "I asked him why Lennox was being taken away. He told me that there had been a complaint and that Lennox was deemed to be a danger to the community."

"What? There's no way!" Riley said. "They don't know Lennox. They don't know how he acts around people and pets!"

"Don't they know that he's a service dog?" Finn demanded.

Riley thought Finn's mom looked so mad that she could spit nails. "I informed him that my nephew's organization had trained Lennox to be a service dog for Hawk. He seemed a bit surprised, but it didn't change anything. He said it's the new protocol and that they would do an in-depth evaluation at Animal Control to see if the dog is safe to live in the community. I asked if I could be involved, or speak to someone at Animal Control, with little response."

"Why don't they ask people like us?" Riley could feel her heart beating fast, she had to take a deep breath.

Finn looked up at his mom with a fear in his eyes that Riley didn't see often. "Mom, what are we going to do? We have to get Lennox back."

Riley couldn't stop the tears. "We have to, Mrs. Murphy. Lennox is so important to Hawk. I'm afraid what will happen if we don't get him back."

Mrs. Murphy hugged Riley with one arm and Finn with the other. "Me too, Riley. We need to be there for Hawk, now more than ever."

Riley could hear the fear in Mrs. Murphy's voice and it scared her.

CHAPTER THIRTY-FOUR

Don't Discriminate

Riley was useless throughout the day and through to Saturday. She couldn't focus in any of her classes and was so sad about Hawk and Lennox. Mrs. Murphy had taken her and Finn to school before going back to Hawk's house to check in on him. Riley and Finn had dragged through all of their classes.

Saturday morning, Riley met Finn at his house to research other instances of BSL and dogs that had been taken away from their families—and she was more determined than ever. They would be heading to Mrs. Powell's house around two-o'clock so they wanted to get as much done beforehand as possible. Eve was heading to Atlanta with Tim and her family for a service project, but she had sent them a spreadsheet she created with anti-BSL groups they could contact for advice and support. She even found some veteran's groups that might be able to advise them or help Hawk.

Riley and Finn were in the media room, each with a laptop on their laps. "Oh, I want to show you something," Riley said as she clicked a few things on her computer and turned it for Finn to see. "When Mrs. Willnow said to use our talents to do what we could to help, my dad said the same thing. So, I thought of this."

Riley saw Finn look at the image on the screen of a smiling

pit bull, like Lennox, inside a circle. Written around the top of the circle it said, *No Hate* and below the circle it said, *Don't Discriminate.*

A smile spread across Finn's face, "I love it! You are so talented!"

"I was trying to think of what I could do and I came up with this. I just think so many people have these ideas that pit bulls are all mean dogs and that's so untrue. Lennox is one of the sweetest dogs I know and if this is what I can do to help people realize they can't judge a dog by its breed, then this is what I'll do."

"Are you going to make stickers?" Finn asked.

"Yeah, I've already ordered stickers and it would be cool to get t-shirts that we can wear around town. Do you think your parents will want shirts?"

"Definitely," Finn said. "Let's get some ordered right away. I'll wear mine every single day to school if I have to."

Riley focused back on the task at hand. "Okay, so I'm going to contact people who have been through this kind of situation before and reach out to them for advice. We can use Eve's list to start emailing people who we think can help."

"Yeah, and I'll research the legislative side," Finn said. "What people have done to get laws like this overturned." He looked at the clock on his computer. "We have a solid three hours before we need to leave, so let's get started."

Riley and Finn worked in silence as they were determined to find a way to help Hawk and Lennox and the three hours came and went fast. Riley closed her laptop and said, "Why isn't school work this easy to do?"

Finn grinned. "Because this is important and potentially life-altering for Hawk and Lennox...and so many other families."

"Yeah, and we're trying to right a wrong, nothing that we do in school is this serious."

"Come on, let's get going." Finn said.

As they got to the top of the stairs, Finn held his arm out for Riley to stop. She heard his parents talking, and for some reason Finn wanted to stop and listen.

"—worried about Hawk," Mr. Murphy said.

"What did he say when you went over there?" Finn's mom asked.

"He said it's been tough without Lennox. Really tough."

"Do you think he's going to be okay?" Mrs. Murphy asked.

There was a pause. "I don't know. He doesn't look well, and he told me he's had to take sleeping pills. I can tell he's not taking care of himself, or his house."

Riley and Finn exchanged shocked glances.

"What can we do to help?" Mrs. Murphy asked.

"I don't know, but—"

The Carson's were interrupted by the sound of the doorbell, and Riley knew it was her mom coming to pick them up. The plan was for Riley's mom to take her and Finn to Mrs. Powell's house. She had been wanting to stop in and check on her, and thought this would be a good opportunity.

"Come on," Finn said and Riley followed him up, but she couldn't get Mr. Murphy's grim tone out of her mind. She knew they needed to do whatever they could to help Hawk...and fast. They needed Mrs. Powell's help now more than ever.

Neither Riley nor Finn could believe what they had heard.

When they got upstairs, they acted like they hadn't heard anything and Finn's parents stopped talking. Riley knew it wasn't right to eavesdrop, but they couldn't help it. They really cared about Hawk.

"Bye mom, dad," Finn said as he put on a rain jacket.

Mrs. Murphy had greeted Riley's mom at the door when Finn approached, gave him a kiss on top of his head. She was definitely emotional and Riley knew why. "Okay, let's hope Mrs. Powell has some good ideas. You let her know that I've been working with Angels Among Us and a few animal behaviorists to weigh in on this. You have the list of City Council Members, I've called and emailed all of them. Let her know I will do *anything* I can to help get Lennox back."

Riley's mom looked sympathetic. "We will. This is just awful. That sweet dog isn't a threat."

Riley knew this situation pained all of them. Surely together they could fix this. She slid on her rain jacket and then put her backpack over her right shoulder as they headed outside. "This weather matches my mood," Riley said as the cold drizzle fell on them.

"Mine too. I hope Hawk is going to be okay."

"I know, if he's this bad after only a couple of days without Lennox, I worry what he'll be like if this drags on."

"We need to share all of this with Mrs. Powell, we have to let her know it's not just about a dog's life, it's about Hawk's life too."

Once they were buckled up in the toasty car, Riley's mom said, "All set?"

"Yeah, thanks for taking us, mom."

"Of course. It's too nasty out there for you two to be walking." She stopped and looked at Riley and Finn. "You okay?"

Riley exhaled. She didn't want to tell her mom what they had overheard before she got there. "We're just really hoping Mrs. Powell can help us with Hawk's situation."

"If anyone can, I'm sure it's Mrs. Powell." Riley's mom had an encouraging smile on her face. "Remember, she may be a little old lady, but she has a lot of power in this town. She understands what a good dog Lennox is, and how important he is to Hawk. I know she'll find a way to help."

Riley was glad her mom could be so positive, of course they hadn't told her about what they had just overheard. Riley managed a smile, "Thanks, mom."

Her mom smiled back, "You know how much Mrs. Powell loves dogs and Hawk. You said she had a plan, so let's go see what she says."

CHAPTER THIRTY-FIVE

A Visit With Mrs. Powell

Since Mrs. Powell lived a short distance down Mimosa, they got to her house in minutes. Riley's mom pulled into the driveway and Riley gazed up at the beautiful antebellum home. "This house is so pretty."

Riley's mom put the car in park and turned off the engine, she looked at Riley and smiled, "I just want to say hello and see how she's doing."

Riley smiled softly, "Of course, mom." She knew it meant a lot to her mom to be able to chat with Mrs. Powell.

Riley's mom got out an umbrella and walked the kids up to the front door, setting down the umbrella once they were under cover of the porch. Finn gazed up at the tall white columns at the front of the porch and Riley rang the doorbell.

Lily was barking loudly inside, announcing their arrival and Riley heard the lock click and the large wooden door swung open. Mrs. Powell was wearing a thick sweater and a pair of jeans, a sweet smile on her face. "Hi Riley, Priscilla, and Finn. Do come in."

They walked into the foyer and Riley's mom said, "I'm not staying but just wanted to say hello and thank you for offering to help us out."

Lily was running in circles around Mrs. Powell, which

Riley thought was strange. She hadn't seen the little dog do that before. In fact, she expected Lily to be more interested in seeing her and Finn.

Mrs. Powell said, "Riley has told me a bit about the situation, and I do think I can help…"

Riley looked at Mrs. Powell. Something wasn't right, her eyes looked confused and dull. Lily was still running around her in circles, jumping up as if wanting attention.

Mrs. Powell blinked heavily and reached out toward Riley's mom. Right before she collapsed, Riley's mom grabbed both of Mrs. Powell's forearms, catching her.

Riley felt queasy, her vision was fuzzy. What's happening, she thought.

She heard her mom's voice. "Riley, call 9-1-1! Finn, help me get Mrs. Powell on the sofa!"

Finn helped Riley's mom put Mrs. Powell on the settee while Riley called for an ambulance. Her heart was racing, her fingers trembling. "Yes," she said into the phone. "We need an ambulance at 251 Mimosa Street."

"What's your emergency?" the dispatcher asked.

"Our friend collapsed. Mrs. Powell is an elderly lady and she just collapsed!"

"Okay, an ambulance is on the way. Does she have a pulse?"

Riley was frantic, "Mom, does she have a pulse?"

Riley could see her mom and Finn attending to Mrs. Powell, each with two fingers on either side of Mrs. Powell's neck. "Yes, she has a pulse!" Finn said.

Riley told the dispatcher who gave her a few more instructions and then told her to wait on the phone until the paramedics arrived. Within moments, Riley heard sirens. Her heart still raced, her thoughts a blur as she silently prayed for Mrs. Powell to be okay.

Riley hated the way she felt when someone got sick. In situations like that, she froze in fear and felt all fuzzy in the head. She was so glad that her mom had come to the door, so glad that Finn was there too.

The paramedics arrived and worked on Mrs. Powell who had regained consciousness for which Riley was thankful. Mrs. Powell was really weak, but was able to ask Riley to please take care of Lily for her. After the paramedics had gone, Riley sat on the staircase and cried, partly from nerves and partly from worry. Lily immediately came to her side and hopped into her lap.

"Honey, it's okay, Mrs. Powell is going to be just fine." Her mom sat down next to her on the wide staircase and stroked her back.

"We don't know that," Riley sobbed. "We don't know she's going to be okay. Did you see her face when she started to fall? It was so scary!"

Riley's mom hugged her around her shoulders and tucked Riley's head under her chin. "I know, sweetie, it was really scary, but thank God we were here. If Mrs. Powell had been alone, it could have been much worse. They'll take good care of her and she'll get better."

Riley had been so scared, emotions now poured from her. Her mom sat with her until she had settled down. Finn busied himself in the kitchen locating Lily's things.

Riley's mom got up and got to work. She found a set of

house keys hanging on a hook in the kitchen and she found bags in the pantry and loaded them up with Lily's food, treats, and toys that Finn had gathered.

Riley was still on the stairs and buried her face in Lily's soft, white coat. "It's okay, Lily, we'll take care of you until your mama is better." Lily gave Riley a kiss on her cheek where tears had fallen.

"Here," Finn said as he held out Lily's pink leash.

"Thanks," Riley said as she clipped the leash to Lily's collar and set her on the wide-plank hardwood floors. "Sorry about that, I don't do well when people are sick."

"I know that, remember when Daphne Pilato fainted in class and you said you almost fainted too?"

Riley stood up and smiled, "Yeah, I just froze and the poor girl tipped over in her chair."

"It's okay, just don't plan on becoming a doctor or nurse," Finn said.

"Don't worry, I won't." Riley was so glad Finn was here, he always made her feel better, even when things were going really badly.

Riley's mom came from the kitchen and Finn grabbed the two bags she was carrying. "The back door is locked and I have Mrs. Powell's keys. I think we're all set to head out."

Riley felt weird leaving Mrs. Powell's house, not knowing when the sweet lady would be well enough to return. "What do you think happened to her?" She asked her mom as they turned off the lights.

"I don't know, honey," her mom said as she hugged her shoulders. "They'll run some tests and we should know more in the morning. Once I get you two home, I'm going to head over to the hospital to see how she's doing. She doesn't have anyone here, so I'll make sure she's okay."

They headed out of the house and Riley's mom locked the front door. Riley let Lily sniff around the yard to relieve herself before they got in the car. Lily had settled down a little and sat on Riley's lap looking out the car window as they headed back home.

As they were turning into their neighborhood, Riley said to Finn, "What are we going to do now?"

Finn looked at Riley and then at Lily who was seated in her lap. "I don't know. But I just got an idea of something that might help...even if just a little."

CHAPTER THIRTY-SIX

Helping Hawk

When they arrived at the Carson's house, Finn's parents were waiting inside with Riley's dad. Finn had texted them from the car. He looked at Riley and her mom and said, "I had an idea."

Riley let Lily off her leash and Buster came right up to meet her. "Buster, it looks like Lily is going to be staying with us for a while," Riley said.

Riley's dad looked at his wife quizzically. "Is everything okay?"

Riley's mom explained to her husband and the Murphys about what had just happened to Mrs. Powell. "Based on her vitals, they wanted to take her to the hospital. I'm going to head over there to be with her."

Finn's mom looked at him, "So, what's your idea?"

"I think we should take Lily over to Hawk's house," Finn said smiling proudly.

Finn's dad looked at Riley's mom, "Do you think she would be okay with that?"

Riley's mom said, "She asked us to take care of Lily, but she is quite fond of Hawk."

"And Lily loves Hawk," Riley said. "She seems to sense when he's tense. I saw it on Christmas Eve," Riley said.

Finn looked at his parents and said, "Hawk could really use having Lily around."

"Yeah, we're really worried about him," Riley said.

Riley's dad looked at Finn's parents, "Is Hawk okay?"

Mr. and Mrs. Murphy exchanged pained expressions and Mrs. Murphy said, "Hawk has been having a tough time since Lennox was taken away..."

Finn's dad glanced at Finn and Riley then looked at Riley's dad, "Really tough."

Riley could see her dad was thinking, he ran his hand through his brown hair, his blue eyes looked troubled.

Riley's mom said, "Why on earth would they take a man's service dog away, anyway? I was scared of Lennox at first since he's a pit bull, but he's the sweetest dog. He even plays well with Buster and if he wanted to, he could eat Buster!"

Buster was back under the coffee table and his head popped up. Riley was proud of him for staying in here with two men and lots of people. She was glad he was getting better, slowly but surely. She saw Lily had made herself comfortable on Buster's dog bed...the one he never slept on.

"Aside from the fact that it's a discriminatory law," Riley's dad said. "They left no provision for a service animal and that's a big problem."

"You can say that again," Mr. Murphy said.

"Any idea when Lennox will be able to come home?" Riley's mom asked.

"They are evaluating him to see if he's aggressive." Finn's mom said. "I hope they are done soon and he gets Lennox back quickly."

"Do you think he'll get him back?" Riley's dad asked.

"There isn't a bad bone in that dog's body," Mrs. Murphy said. "Hawk should get him back soon, in fact, it's ridiculous he was even taken away."

"This is why we think we should take Lily over to Hawk," Finn said. "It will only be a little while, and Hawk needs someone."

"Yeah," Riley said as Buster walked over to where she was sitting on the floor and cuddled next to her leg, "I hate to think of him all alone." She didn't want to admit to eavesdropping on the Murphys, but she knew Hawk really needed company.

Riley's mom looked at her husband and said, "I think Mrs. Powell would want us to do this, Jack. What do you think?"

"Absolutely," he said. "And if she's well enough to talk to you tonight, you can ask her."

Finn looked at his parents and said, "Can we take her over there now? Since you and dad know Hawk best, that's why I wanted you to come over."

"I think that's a good idea," Riley's mom said. "I'm going to head over to the hospital so Mrs. Powell knows she's not alone."

With that settled, Riley, Finn, and his parents headed over to Hawk's house with Lily in tow.

When they rang the bell, it took a few moments for Hawk to answer. When he did, Riley noticed the lines on his face seemed deeper and he had dark circles under his eyes.

"Hey guys, what's going on?" Hawk asked as he looked down at Lily and squatted to greet her. Lily's white, furry tail was wagging furiously.

"Well," Riley said, "we were just at Mrs. Powell's house to

see if she could help us with Lennox's situation, and unfortunately, she fell ill and had to be taken to the hospital."

Hawk's face grew concerned. "Is she going to be okay?"

"We think so," Mrs. Murphy said. "Luckily, Priscilla had
taken Riley and Finn over and was there to help. She's heading
to the hospital now to see how she's doing and what her prog-
nosis is."

"It was so scary," Riley said. "She started to fall and was
really weak..." She hated even thinking about it. "We told Mrs.
Powell we would take care of Lily, but then, Finn thought you
might be able to help."

Finn said, "Well, we know it's been hard since Lennox was
taken away, so we thought you might be able to take care of Lily
for a bit. You know, until you get Lennox back."

Hawk's jaw tightened when he heard Lennox's name, but
he was still petting a very loving Lily. "Oh yeah?" He looked
from Finn to Lily, "Would you like that? Do you want to hang
with me for a bit?"

Lily seemed to know what Hawk was saying and placed her
front paws on Hawk's legs and licked him on the hand that was
petting her. Hawk looked up at Mr. and Mrs. Murphy. "Do you
think Mrs. Powell will be okay with this?"

"Yeah, Priscilla is going to ask her when she gets to the
hospital, but we know how fond of you Mrs. Powell is, I'm sure
she'll agree." Finn's mom said.

"It has been lonely around here. If she's cool with it, I'd love
to have her. She's a really sweet dog." Hawk stood up, "Come
on, let's bring her inside."

They went inside and Lily sniffed around and explored

Hawk's house.

Hawk gestured to the sofas in the family room, "Have a seat."

Finn gave Hawk the bags with all of Lily's things. "Here's all her stuff."

They all sat down and once they did, Lily came into the room prancing with a plush toy in her mouth. It was a plush duck toy and it was almost the same size as the little Maltese. She was practically dragging it along with her.

"Is it okay if she plays with Lennox's toy?" Riley asked hoping it would be okay with Hawk. "Otherwise, it's too late!"

"Oh yeah, Lennox won't mind." Hawk's face showed his emotions for a split second. Lily pranced over to him and laid her chin on Hawk's foot, the duck toy still in her mouth. A faint smile appeared on Hawk's face as he scratched Lily gently behind her ears.

Mrs. Murphy said, "Well, she knows whose house this is!"

Hawk was looking down at Lily, "She's so sweet...I just hope Mrs. Powell is okay."

"We do too," Riley said. "I'll let you know what my mom says when she gets back from the hospital."

Mr. Murphy looked at Hawk and said, "Have you heard anything?"

Hawk exhaled a deep breath and said, "No, they said the earliest I'd hear would be Tuesday."

Riley could tell Mrs. Murphy was trying to suppress her frustration. "I can't see why they wouldn't give him back. He's a trained service dog. He'll pass any temperament testing they throw at him."

"He wouldn't hurt a fly," Hawk said. "I can't believe I was stupid enough to forget that muzzle. I asked who reported him, but they won't tell me."

"It's not your fault," Finn said. "We were there, Lennox wasn't threatening at all. It's the stupid government's fault for passing such a ridiculous law."

Riley said, "You have our support and we'll all vouch for Lennox. Like Finn said, he and I were there, we know he wasn't causing any trouble. No more than any other dog in that situation."

Hawk smiled, "Thanks. It really helps having good neighbors like you."

"It's the least we can do," Mrs. Murphy said.

Lily scratched at Hawk's leg and he picked her up and put her in his lap. "I think we'll take a nice nap on this dreary day. What do you say, Lily?" As if completely understanding him, Lily curled up into a tight ball in Hawk's lap

Even though he didn't say it, that confirmed to Riley that he wasn't sleeping well without Lennox. While she was glad Lily was there to help, she knew they had to help Hawk get Lennox back, and the sooner the better.

CHAPTER THIRTY-SEVEN

Good News, Bad News

Tuesday came and went and Hawk still had no word about Lennox. The day had gone by painfully slow for Riley and she felt on edge all day, waiting for news. She couldn't imagine how Hawk must have felt.

Riley had received her "No Hate. Don't Discriminate" stickers in the mail and on Wednesday, she, Finn, Eve, and Tim had been handing them out all day. They got to the lunchroom early so they could pass out more.

"Don't Hate," Finn said to a group of seventh-grade girls. "Help us stop BSL."

"Don't Discriminate," Eve said to the next group of kids who walked through the doors as she handed each of them stickers.

Riley was handing a sticker to an eighth-grade boy who asked, "What's BSL?"

"Breed-Specific Legislation," Riley said. "They want to ban certain dog breeds in Roswell."

"Wow, that's not cool," the boy replied as he took a sticker.

"I'm going to need more stickers," Eve said. "I'm all out."

"Yeah, me too," Finn said showing Riley what he had left. "I'm almost out."

"That's awesome!" Riley said as she dug into her backpack.

"Here are some more." She handed each of her friends another stack of stickers.

"It's the least I can do," Eve said. "My dad is so strict, I feel like I'm not helping you guys as much as I want to."

"It's okay," Finn said as they headed to a table, passing out stickers to kids already seated. "You're helping where you can and we really appreciate it."

Riley felt her phone vibrate. There was a text from her mom, *Just saw on the news, Baby Girl was found!* She showed Finn and Eve her phone. "They found Baby Girl!"

"Wow, that's awesome!" Eve said.

I wonder where they found her?" Finn asked, then took a bite of his apple.

"My mom didn't say. I hope she's okay," Riley said. "She's been missing for a while now and if she's been loose this whole time, there's no telling what condition she's in."

"Maybe someone had her and was taking care of her, not knowing she was someone's dog," Eve said before taking a sip of bottled water.

"That's what Finn kept saying and would at least be better than just living on the street all that time. Let me see if there is any more information on the Help Find Baby Girl page." Riley tapped her phone a few times and slid her finger slowly along the screen. "It must be recent news because all it says on the page is that she's been found and they thank everyone for their hard work and support."

"I'm so glad they found her," Finn said, finishing his apple. "I was getting worried they wouldn't."

"Me, too," Riley said. "Now, we just need to get Lennox

back...and overturn BSL and everything will be right in the world!"

Finn smiled. "At least in our little world."

"And Mrs. Powell, we need her to get better," Riley added. "My mom has been in touch with the hospital and she's doing better, but still isn't well enough to be released."

"I'm glad she's getting better," Eve said. The kids were eating fast so they could hand out more stickers before the lunchroom cleared out.

"When she's well enough, I'm sure she'll help us get BSL overturned," Finn said, then turned to Eve. "What does your dad think?"

"He said that as far as these laws are concerned, the citizens have to speak up," Eve said. "We just have to keep talking to people about this issue."

"Well, for now, things are looking up. I'm so glad Baby Girl was found. Maybe this is a sign that our luck has turned." Riley said.

Eve was smiling, "I hope so!" She gathered the last of her trash and was about get up and to take it to the trash bins when she saw Corey, Seth, and Brad heading their way.

"I'm surprised you guys are so happy," Corey said with a smirk, Seth and Brad snickering behind him.

Riley rolled her eyes. "Why's that, Corey?" She was anticipating some kind of rude joke and wasn't prepared for his response.

"That stupid pit bull your neighbor has is getting put to sleep."

Riley felt like she was going to pass out and braced herself on the table.

"Corey, that's not even funny," Finn said, standing.

"Funny or not, it's true."

"Back off!" Eve said, standing up with Finn to defend her friend.

Riley had tunnel vision as she felt her phone vibrate again. She pulled it out of her pocket and slid her finger across the screen, then tapped it to view the text from her mom. *Call me ASAP.*

Riley felt her chin tremble as she got up and turned to walk out of the cafeteria. She would not give Corey the satisfaction of seeing her cry, her hands shook as she called her mom. Within moments Finn and Eve were by her side.

"Hi honey," Her mom's voice came through the speaker and Riley could tell by her tone that the news wasn't good.

Riley's throat tightened and she was only able to squeak out the words, "Mom, tell me it isn't true." She fidgeted with the key necklace she wore regularly now.

Mrs. Willnow came down the hall and stopped before the kids, clearly worried.

"I'm so sorry, honey, they made the decision to put Lennox down." The words echoed past Riley's ears as she saw Eve's hand go up to her mouth and felt Mrs. Willnow put an arm around her.

Riley heard Mrs. Willnow sniffle and found her voice. "What about Hawk, can you go check on him?"

"Finn's mom is already over there. Oh honey, I'm so sorry." Riley heard pain in her mom's voice. "I'm going to come and pick you up. Mrs. Murphy asked me to get Finn too. We can't expect you to stay at school and try to focus after hearing this. I'll be there soon."

Riley hung up the phone and felt a shiver run up her spine. She felt a strength that made her feel like she could fight an army one-handed. She looked at Finn with a red face full of tears. "We're *not* going to let this happen," she said, and she meant it.

CHAPTER THIRTY-EIGHT

Framed?

When Riley woke up the next morning, she hoped the news from yesterday had been a nightmare, but as her mind went from sleepy to awake, she knew it was her reality. She couldn't shake the funk she was in and after getting ready, headed downstairs for breakfast.

Her sister was already eating, looking as if today was just a normal day, chatting with their mom about some useless celebrity gossip.

"Good morning, Roo," her dad said as he gave her a kiss on her forehead.

"Morning, dad," Riley said as she went about her routine, pouring cereal, then milk, and then orange juice. As she joined her family at the table, she heard her phone chime. She read the text from Finn. *Call me. We've got trouble.*

Riley's dad noticed her eyes widen. "Everything okay?" he asked.

Riley looked up from her phone. "I don't know," she said exasperated. What more could be wrong? "Finn said to call him, there's some sort of trouble." She dialed Finn's number and he picked up on the first ring.

"Hey."

"Hey," Riley replied. "What's going on?"

"Someone vandalized City Hall last night!"

"Really? What did they do?" Riley was eating her raisin bran as they spoke so it didn't get soggy.

"There's graffiti all over that says, 'Save Lennox,' 'End BSL,' and...'No Hate. Don't Discriminate.' It kinda looks like your design."

Riley dropped her spoon into her bowl with a clang. "What? Where did you see this?"

"My dad went jogging this morning with Hawk, they went for a long run because Hawk was really upset last night. Their run took them by City Hall and my dad took some pictures, I'll send them to you. Hang on."

Riley waited and watched her phone. After several seconds, a text from Finn appeared with photos of the vandalism. "Oh my gosh!" She put her hand up to her mouth as her dad looked at her curiously. "It does look like my design." Her heart raced. "You know I didn't do this, right?"

"Of course," Finn said. "The question is, who did? And even more, why did they use your design?"

Riley hung up with Finn.

"Roo, what's the matter?" Her dad's brow was furrowed.

"Dad, someone vandalized City Hall, and they used *my* design." Riley handed her phone to her dad so he could see the pictures.

Her mom hurried over to the table to take a look. "Oh my goodness, Riley!"

Riley looked at her mom's startled face. "I know, I can't believe it either!" she said, and her panic rose seeing her mom so worried.

Hailey got up to take a look before taking her dishes into the kitchen. "Did you sneak out last night?" She asked with a haughty grin.

"Hailey!" Her dad admonished her. "Now's not the time!"

"You know I didn't do this, right?" Riley looked at her parents for confirmation.

"Of course we know that, Roo," her dad said. "But either someone saw your image and liked it enough to use it for this message, or someone's trying to set you up."

"Oh, Jack," Riley's mom said dismissing this last statement. "You don't really think someone would try to frame our daughter for vandalism, do you?"

"I don't know, but this is something we need to get cleared up right away. Surely they have security cameras and can take a look at the footage. I'll call one of my contacts over there and see what I can find out." Her dad hurried off to his home office.

Riley's mom sat down at the table grabbed her hand. "Honey, we know you wouldn't do this. Your dad will sort this out and everything will be okay."

"Do you think so, mom?"

"I do, now eat that cereal before it's totally mushy and get ready for school."

"Do I really have to go?"

"Yes, you go to school and your dad will take care of things. You didn't do anything wrong and we'll figure this out."

Riley's stomach hurt and she didn't feel much like eating. But she did what her mom asked and hoped she was right. Riley hoped that someone wasn't framing her, but she knew who her first guess would be...and she really didn't look forward to seeing him at school.

***

All Riley could think about was sleeping as she trudged down the hallway from her locker to the front of the school to meet Finn. The school day had dragged on and she couldn't wait to get home. She needed a nap, her homework could wait.

Finn was waiting for her by the front doors with a sympathetic smile on his face. "Hanging in there?"

"Barely." Riley tried to stifle her yawn, but couldn't. "I didn't sleep well last night and I've been worrying all day about the vandalism. Do you think someone is trying to set me up?"

Finn thought for a moment. "I don't know. You would think that there would be plenty of video cameras around City Hall. It might not be the best place to commit vandalism in the first place, let alone frame someone."

"I've been really vocal about this issue, though, and someone could totally be setting me up."

"Hey guys, wait up!" Eve was heading down the hallway with Tim Harrington. As they approached, Riley noticed Tim looked as tired as she felt. "Everything, okay?" She asked.

Tim shook his head. "I can't believe they are going to kill that dog. We were there when he lunged. He wasn't being aggressive, he wasn't going to hurt anyone."

"I know," Riley said. "I don't know what to do. I'm sure Eve told you that Mrs. Powell got sick the day we went to talk to her about BSL. She thought she could help, but now that she's been hospitalized, we're not sure she's strong enough to get involved."

Eve looked defeated. "Sometimes it really stinks being kids. I wish we had power to do something."

Riley looked at Eve and had a revelation. "But we do have power," she said with conviction. "Think about it. We have a voice—where Lennox does not. We have knowledge and information. We have a way to spread our message online. And we have a neighbor who we can appeal to."

Finn looked at Riley quizzically. "Who can we appeal to?"

"Mr. Felton," Riley said feeling the first glimmer of hope all day. "When Tim mentioned how we saw Lennox lunge and knew it wasn't aggressive, I remembered Mr. Felton. If he's the one who reported Hawk, then maybe we can appeal to him? He may not know why Hawk needs Lennox. He may be scared of Lennox just because of the way he looks. If we can ask him to plead to the city not to take Lennox's life, maybe we can at least save Lennox? Then we can work to get BSL overturned."

"Well, what are we waiting for?" Finn said. "Let's go talk to Mr. Felton!"

Riley followed her friend from school with a renewed sense of hope, even if ever so small.

CHAPTER THIRTY-NINE

Doppelganger

When they got to Mr. Felton's house, Riley felt a confidence she wasn't used to feeling. She led the way, marching up their neighbor's front steps and knocking on the front door with authority, absentmindedly fidgeting with her key necklace. Finn, Eve, and Tim came up behind her. After a few minutes, the retired man opened the front door.

"What are you selling today, kids?" Mr. Felton asked, smiling.

Riley stood up straighter. "We're not selling anything, Mr. Felton. We have something important we need to talk to you about."

"Oh, okay, then, let's hear it."

"We wanted to let you know that our neighbor, Mr. Hawkins is a good man, and so is his dog, Lennox. In fact, Hawk, Mr. Hawkins, is a veteran suffering with PTSD and Lennox is his service dog. We understand that you might be scared of Lennox because of the type of dog he is, but now he is scheduled to die and we can't just sit by and let that happen." Riley's heart beat fast, but she was proud of herself for not faltering as she got all her words out.

"I see..." Mr. Felton started, but Tim interrupted.

"Mr. Felton, we know Lennox scared you that day in front of Hawk's yard, but I think it was because I was skateboarding by, and he's an active young dog who was excited seeing a kid on a skateboard flying by. Do you think you would consider retracting your report and appealing for Lennox's life to be spared?"

Mr. Felton looked at Finn and Eve, "Do you two have anything to add?"

Finn thought for a moment, "I actually think it was my dog, Molly, who was scared. She doesn't like men with baseball caps and she started it. Lennox isn't a dangerous dog, he was probably feeding off of Molly's energy."

Mr. Felton looked at Eve expectantly.

"I think my friends have pretty much covered it," Eve said with a gentle smile. "Lennox is a great dog and we can't bear to see him killed for no reason."

"I agree," Mr. Felton said, "and I would be happy to testify on behalf of the dog and Mr. Hawkins, but I'm afraid I'm not the one who reported Lennox."

Riley was dumbfounded. "Wait, what? We thought you didn't like Lennox's barking and then that instance with the lunging. Soon after, Lennox was taken away."

"It's true that I don't like his barking and I know Mr. Hawkins was working on that, but I didn't report that dog. While I didn't realize he was a service dog, I do know that Mr. Hawkins is a veteran living by himself, so barking or not, I knew that Lennox was a good companion for him." He looked around his house. "I've been widowed for five years now so I know how lonely one can get. I would never want his dog taken away. It's clear Lennox isn't dangerous."

Riley was at a loss for words.

"Sorry to bother you," Tim said.

"Oh, it's no bother, I'm glad for the company. I'm just so sorry to hear about this."

Riley smiled politely and said, "Thank you for your time." She was about to follow her friends down the steps when she turned and said, "If we *are* able to appeal to the city, would you consider testifying about your experience with Lennox?"

"I'd be happy to," Mr. Felton said, smiling genuinely.

"Thank you, we'll let you know." Riley turned and walked down the steps, sad for lonely old Mr. Felton, but also sad he wasn't the one who had reported Lennox. "If he didn't do it, then who did?" she wondered.

"I'm going to walk Eve home," Tim said when they reached the street.

Riley thought Tim seemed preoccupied, but didn't have time to worry about that. "Okay," she said. "Thanks for coming along, you guys."

As Riley and Finn headed across the street, Finn asked, "If Mr. Felton didn't report Lennox, who do you think did?"

"That's what I'm wondering," Riley said. She looked up as they reached her driveway. "That's weird," she said. "I wonder why my dad is home." The garage door was up and both cars were inside.

When Riley and Finn walked inside, they saw her parents sitting at the kitchen table looking very serious.

"Is everything okay?" Riley asked, afraid to hear the answer.

"Not really," her dad said as he motioned for them to come over and sit down.

Riley felt her stomach tighten and she tucked her hair behind her ear as she sat, Finn finding a seat beside her.

"Eve's dad called us to give us a head's up. They reviewed the video from last night and they want to speak to you."

Riley couldn't believe what she'd heard. "Me? Why?" She felt her pulse race and her hands started to tremble. "This must be a mistake. You know I wouldn't do that."

Riley's mom reached for her hand, her eyes glossy with tears. "You've been so outspoken about BSL and Lennox, are you sure you didn't have a lapse in judgment when you were so upset?"

Riley jerked her hand away. "Mom! I can't believe you would even think that! No, I didn't have a lapse in judgment. I'm really angry they are going to kill an innocent dog, but I know that vandalism isn't going to solve anything."

"You know how Riley follows the rules and is afraid to get into trouble," Finn added. "She didn't do it."

Riley's dad studied her for a moment, his weary eyes searching. "The video quality isn't great and frankly, I think it looks like a young male, but he's wearing sneakers like yours. Slip-ons with a checkerboard pattern and a large hooded sweatshirt and jeans. We don't get a look of the person's face, mostly just from behind."

Riley's eyes pleaded with her dad. "Dad, you don't think I did it too, do you?"

Her dad exhaled. "No, I don't. Like Finn said, I know you are passionate, but I also know you do not like getting into trouble. I think we should go to the police station first thing in the morning and discuss it all with Detective Rycroft."

Riley's mom looked at her dad, her eyes wide. "Jack, do you think that's a good idea? You always say that the less a suspect talks, the better." Her mom unconsciously smoothed her hair with an elegant hand.

Riley felt sick to her stomach. "Suspect?" she managed say. "Am I really a suspect, Dad?"

"I'll do the talking, Roo, don't worry. I'll see what info I can get out of them, but we have to see if we can find out what else might make them think you're to blame."

Finn put a comforting hand on her shoulder. "Look, it'll be okay. We know you didn't do this and your dad will sort it all out."

Riley could tell that Finn didn't know what else to say, but she was certain of one thing—her friend believed her. She thought about the predicament she was in. "Dad, I've been passing out stickers at school with my design on it, so there are plenty of kids who know it's my design. It could have been anyone."

"Do you know anyone else who is as upset about this as you are? Someone who would vandalize City Hall to make a statement?"

Riley thought about what her dad had said. "There might be one person," she said. "Otherwise, it's a set-up."

CHAPTER FORTY

A True Friend

So much for the much-needed sleep. Riley had been up all night just like when she heard the news about Lennox. She was in the front seat of her dad's SUV as they made the short drive to the police headquarters next to City Hall. She checked her phone for what felt like the thirtieth time this morning, but still no response.

"Roo, don't worry," her dad said when they arrived. "Just let me do the talking and we'll figure it out. It'll be okay, I know you're not to blame."

Riley exhaled, her stomach felt horrible and her heart beat hard in her chest. She felt like she was going to explode from all angles but she managed a smile and said, "Thanks Dad, I'm glad you believe me."

Her dad leaned over and hugged her. "I know you didn't do this, we just need to figure out who did."

Once inside, the receptionist told them that Detective Rycroft was running late, but that his partner, Glen, would meet with them until he arrived. This didn't make Riley feel any better. They waited in the lobby for a few minutes until Glen joined them. He was average height and losing his hair, but seemed friendly enough. Riley reminded herself not to let her guard down. He might use kindness as a tactic to get her to say something she shouldn't...even though she wasn't guilty.

They went to a conference room down a hallway and Riley was glad to see there weren't any two-way mirrors, just a window that looked out into the parking lot. She followed her dad to the far side of the table with their backs to the window and sat down next to him.

Glen sat down at the head of the table. "Sorry that Detective Rycroft is running late. Something came up that he had to attend to. He's normally never late." He wiped a stray crumb off his tie as he said this.

"Detective Rycroft informed us that there is some resemblance between my daughter and the person who vandalized City Hall," Riley's dad said. "Can you tell me what that information is?"

Glen opened the folder and licked a finger to turn the pages. Riley hated when people did that. When he got to the page he was looking for, he said, "Well, it looks like the video evidence may or may not be your daughter, and..." He licked his finger again and turned to the next page, "...it looks like someone called in and told us that one of the graffiti designs looks just like one of her designs."

Riley swore she could hear her heart in her ears. "Someone called in?" Her dad put his hand on her knee under the table and she knew he was telling her to leave the talking to him.

Glen looked at the piece of paper. "Yeah, an anonymous tip."

Riley's dad leaned toward Glen. "Detective, my daughter has passed out stickers with that design at school, so plenty of kids know that's her design. As for the video, there's nothing on it to suggest it's my daughter."

Glen sat back in his chair, crossed his arms over his chest, and appraised Riley and her dad. He was about to say something when the conference room door opened.

Detective Rycroft was standing in the doorway with a familiar face—Tim Harrington. Tim's dad was standing behind him... and didn't look very happy.

Eve had come through.

"Glen, I'll take it from here," Eve's dad said.

After Glen left the room Detective Rycroft took his place. Tim's dad sat to his right and Tim sat next to his father. "It looks like we had a case of mistaken identity," Eve's dad said. "I know you and those sneakers, and when we got the call about the design, we had to start looking at you. That video was hard to make out, but you've clearly got a good friend here."

Riley smiled at Tim. "Thank you."

Tim smiled. "When Eve told me that you were a suspect, I couldn't let you take the fall. I did it, and I shouldn't have. I was just so mad about Lennox. They shouldn't be killing him. How did you know it was me?"

"The day that you were skateboarding by Hawk's house, I noticed you were wearing sneakers like mine instead of flip flops...which was smart since you were skateboarding. I was going to say something because they looked just like mine, but then Lennox and Molly got spooked..." Riley was sad just thinking about that day.

Tim's dad looked at him and said. "You will clean every speck of paint off of that building. I can't believe what you did." He looked at Detective Rycroft, his face red. "What happens next, will he get charged?"

Riley could tell that Tim's dad was upset, but it was also clear he loved his son a lot and was worried what the city would do. Tim just couldn't help from getting into trouble.

Detective Rycroft smiled. "Tim, you just keep getting in the way of yourself. You're a good kid, otherwise, I wouldn't let you near my daughter. In fact, maybe I shouldn't let you near her. I know you have a good heart; I saw it at the homeless shelter. I also know that you want to do good in this world. What makes you do this kind of thing?"

Tim looked at his hands as he picked at a cuticle. "I guess I was just so upset and felt like adults don't get it, so I would make them get it. Riley and all these other people have been working hard to educate people and these stupid laws still get passed. I thought it might make a statement and wake people up."

His dad put his hand on his shoulder. "Son, that's not the way to get people's attention. I didn't raise you to disrespect property like that. Sometimes we're dealt a really bad hand, but we have to roll with the punches."

"I can't roll with this. Killing a dog for no reason is wrong, and just because adults made the decision, doesn't mean it's right."

Riley agreed, but she didn't think tagging City Hall with graffiti would really do much either. She felt so stuck.

Detective Rycroft leaned his forearms on the table and interlaced his fingers. "I know you've got a wild streak, but you can't go doing things like this. I'll do what I can to recommend community service and since you're a minor, nothing will go on your record. But Tim, you have to think of other ways to reach people."

"Thanks, Mr. Rycroft." Tim said, and then hung his head.

"He will be cleaning every speck of paint off of that building," Tim's dad added, "whether it's part of his community service or not...and he won't be seeing Eve outside of school, he's going to be grounded for a long time."

"I'll make a note of that," Mr. Rycroft said with a smile.

Riley finally felt like she could breathe. She was so glad that Eve had gotten her message to Tim and that Tim stepped up to take responsibility for what he did. While she felt relieved, she hadn't forgotten that someone had called in an anonymous tip that could have landed her in lots of trouble. She wondered who it could have been.

CHAPTER FORTY-ONE

Much Needed Help

When Riley got home from school on Thursday afternoon, her mom was waiting for her with hot tea and shortbread cookies. Riley felt like a zombie. She had two nights of restless sleep and was hoping that she would be able to get her homework done and go to sleep early. The stress of everything that had happened in the last couple of days contributed to her exhaustion. Her feet felt like they had weights on them as she trudged over to the breakfast bar to sit on one of the stools. Her mom, as usual, looked perfect. Rested and beautiful.

"Honey, I'm so happy that Tim confessed to being the one who vandalized City Hall. When your dad called me I was so relieved!"

Riley sipped at her very hot tea and set it aside to cool as she grabbed a cookie. "I can't believe you thought I did it." Riley's feelings were still hurt. It was like her mom didn't even know her.

"Oh, Riley, I just know how passionate you are about this issue and...well, I thought maybe you had gotten so frustrated that you did something out of character." Her mom looked at her and rolled her glossed lips together, waiting for Riley's response.

"I would never do that, no matter how I feel about this

stupid law." Riley took a bite of her cookie and savored the buttery taste. "I wish I could break Lennox out of animal control. Now, that I might do, if I could figure out how."

Riley's mom looked at her in shock. "You wouldn't!"

Riley set her cookie down on the plate, her weary eyes focused on her mom. "Yeah, mom, I would. There is no reason for that dog to die and what's happening is ridiculous. I wish some of the grown-ups around here would stand up and do what's right. People just want to go about their own business until it's something that affects them." Riley felt like she might cry and knew it had to do with how tired she was. She knew she shouldn't have talked to her mom that way, but she was fed up with being a kid, not being able to do anything.

Riley's mom took in a deep breath then exhaled slowly. She leaned her forearms on the counter so she could look at Riley at eye level. "Please don't let this make you bitter. It's a tough lesson that I learned when I was much older than you, but life isn't fair and sometimes people in charge make some bad decisions."

"And we should stand up to them, show them that they are wrong. Who are we as citizens if we can't stand up for our neighbors?" Riley exhaled and closed her eyes tightly. "If the city council knew the whole story, Lennox wouldn't be scheduled to die."

Riley could see her mom thinking and after a few moments she said, "Sit tight and enjoy your snack, I have an idea."

Riley felt so defeated and tired as she sat there waiting for her tea to cool, she heard tiny scratches beneath her and saw that Buster had come out to say hello. She hopped off the stool and gently picked Buster up and scratched his little face. She was so glad Buster trusted her and would let her do this - it had taken a while. She also felt honored that she was the only one in the family that he was comfortable snuggling with. "Hey, buddy," she said as she nuzzled her face into his neck. She instantly felt better and Buster turned to kiss her on her face. She grabbed her tea in her other hand and carried Buster over to the sofa that faced out to the rest of the house. Riley sat on the sofa and grabbed the fluffy throw blanket off the corner and covered herself with it, gently placing Buster on top. Riley sipped at her tea while petting Buster. After a few moments, Buster had relaxed and curled up into a ball on her lap. Riley felt so peaceful at this moment, her eyes were getting heavy so she set her mug on the side table and rested.

Riley woke up to the phone ringing and when she opened her eyes, she noticed the sun was setting. She blinked, her sleepy eyes adjusting to the light in the kitchen, and heard her mom on the phone.

"Thank you so much! I'll get Riley." Her mom came over to hand her the phone. "It's Mrs. Powell."

Riley sat up and noticed Buster was still in her lap and this made her heart happy. She took the phone from her mom and tried to sound awake. "Hi, Mrs. Powell. How are you? Are you coming home soon?"

Riley heard her friend's voice, which sounded weaker than usual, but still filled with so much love. "Yes, dear, I hope to be home tomorrow and I'm feeling much better. I can't talk long because I'm supposed to be resting, and my nurse is a stickler, but I have some good news for you."

Riley was wide awake now. "Great, I could really use some good news today." She pressed the speaker phone button so her mom could hear.

The old lady spoke softly. "Your mom filled me in on what's been going on with this new law. She said that's why you wanted to see me the day I fell ill. I had no idea, but I'm sick about it. I wish I could do more, but I made some calls over to City Hall and used my influence as best I could."

Riley got excited. "Are they going to spare Lennox's life?"

"I wish I had that much influence, dear, but they have agreed to a special session to hear an appeal."

"That's great, who can speak on Lennox's behalf?" Riley asked, her mind running with ideas of who could help.

"They will only allow for one person to speak, and it can't be the dog's owner. I had to give them a name right then and there and told them you would be presenting the appeal."

Riley swore she could feel her stomach flip over yet again— it was becoming a regular occurrence. Buster hopped up and tilted his head to the left, trying to read her expression. "Me?" Her voice cracked as she spoke.

"I didn't know who else was involved and based on what your mom told me, you know more about this case than anyone. You are very passionate about it, and I'm not surprised about that at all."

"Do they know I'm just a kid?"

Riley could hear the smile in Mrs. Powell's voice. "They do, and they said you would need your parents to join you." Riley was silent and Mrs. Powell said, "You can do this, dear. You can make them see their mistake. Just speak from your heart and give them the facts. Your heart will give you courage."

Riley wasn't so sure, but she was so grateful that Mrs. Powell had gone out of her way, from her sick bed no less, to help. Finally, an adult had stepped up to do something. "Thanks, Mrs. Powell, thank you so much."

Mrs. Powell's voice had resolve and strength now. "You're giving a voice to one who has no voice of his own." She added, "Be courageous."

Riley felt stronger at her words. She could be the voice for Lennox. He couldn't speak, but she could speak for him. She needed to believe in herself like Mrs. Powell believed in her. She need not be scared, but courageous. "Thanks Mrs. Powell, I'll make you proud."

After they hung up, Riley's mom sat down next to her and tucked Riley's hair behind her ear and looked at her earnestly. "You can do this, Roo. I know you can."

Riley hugged her mom tightly, tears pricking at her eyes, two adults had come through for Lennox. "Thank you so much for calling Mrs. Powell. Thanks for doing something. I'm sorry I was rude earlier."

"Oh, honey, I know you're under a lot of stress. I didn't want you to lose faith in every adult. I knew Mrs. Powell was getting better so I took a chance and called her. I'm so glad she can help."

"Me too," Riley said, "but I'm so scared, though."

"I know you are, but think of how scared Lennox is right now. He's locked up in a shelter and has no idea why he's been taken from Hawk. Imagine how scared Hawk is too, knowing that Lennox..." She couldn't bear to finish the statement.

"You're right, mom," Riley said. "I shouldn't be scared. I should be brave. I might be shaking like a leaf when I stand up there, but I can do this, someone has to."

CHAPTER FORTY-TWO

Preparedness Is The Key

Riley spent the weekend researching and planning for her appeal on Monday. Finn's mom was able to help her with some very important information on the case, and Rhonda helped her with facts and statistics on dog bites and attacks. Riley hoped they could all work together to get BSL overturned, but this appeal was for Lennox's life, and it was an important step in the right direction.

The Carson house had been a flurry of activity with people over on Saturday to help with data and information. Hawk had come over to go over every detail of his time with Lennox and David had come up from Dog at Hand to give them information on the temperament testing and training they had done with Lennox. Nothing in any of the tests they had done showed any aggression. Riley felt confident that they had enough information to save Lennox's life. Mr. Felton even came over with a typed letter speaking on behalf of Lennox and was happy to help any way he could.

On Sunday, Riley's dad helped her with her presentation. Since he was a lawyer, he was able to show her how to structure her talking points so that they would flow together and make sense, and make the most impact for the appeal—kind of like how he had helped her with her presentation at school. Riley was now grateful to have had that experience and hoped she would be less scared since she had some practice speaking in front of her class. By Sunday night, Riley had gone through her talking points so many times she nearly had them memorized. After dinner, she would present the case to her parents as if she was presenting to the City Council.

As they were cleaning up after dinner, Hailey said, "Do you really think you'll make them change their minds?"

Riley was ready for yet another argument with her sister, but this time, she didn't let her sister get under her skin. "Actually, I do." Riley said calmly and with a smile.

"Cool," Hailey said handing Riley a pot that she had just washed. "I hope you can."

Riley was stunned. She dried the pot and wondered if perhaps her sister might be coming around. Maybe she was already changing minds?

After presenting her case to her parents a couple of times in her dad's study with a mock question and answer session, Riley's parents called it a night.

"I want you to go upstairs and take a hot bath, I'll bring up some chamomile tea," her mom said.

Riley looked at her parents anxiously, "Do you really think I'm prepared?"

Her dad put his hands on her shoulders and looked her square in the eyes, "Yes. You are more than prepared and you will do great. You are the best person to do this and we want you to get your rest so you are focused tomorrow. No more thinking about this or over-analyzing it - you've got this."

Riley smiled, "I don't know how I'll stop thinking about it, but I will go up and take that hot bath. I'm pretty tired." Riley opened the study door and found Buster lying right outside. She picked him up and took him upstairs with her. She nuzzled his fur and said, "Maybe you'll sleep with me tonight, I could use the comfort and company." When she got to her room, Riley set Buster on her bed and said, "I sure hope I can do this." Buster cocked his head to the left and opened his mouth, a smile appearing on his furry little face. "Well, if you have confidence in me, then I should too." She thought of Hawk and Lennox and how happy she would be to help them both.

CHAPTER FORTY-THREE

V for Valor

Riley didn't know what to expect when she got to City Hall. Her stomach was in knots, but her spirits soared when she saw what looked like hundreds of people lined up with signs that said, "Save Lennox," "End BSL," and the coolest thing - signs with her design, a pit bull with the phrase, "No Hate. Don't Discriminate."

"Look at all the support you have!" her mom said as they drove into the parking lot.

"Wow!" Riley said in awe.

They got out of the car and headed toward the supporters where, right in the middle, they found Finn and his parents along with Eve and her family. Finn had a huge smile on his face and Riley immediately felt better seeing him. The Murphys, Eve, and Evan all wore shirts with her design...she figured Eve's dad had to be impartial.

"My dad had shirts and signs made, and my mom and I spent yesterday getting the word out," Finn said. "We have people here from all around Atlanta, and some even drove from other states!"

Riley couldn't believe it. "This is amazing!" She looked around at all the people who had rallied to save Lennox and her heart felt full. She noticed Tim and his parents along with

Mr. Felton, all here to support her, Lennox, and Hawk.

Finn's mom gave her a hug, looked her right in the eyes and said, "You've got this. Go get 'em!"

Standing behind the Murphys and Rycrofts was Hawk, and Riley felt tears prick her eyes upon seeing him. Still, she quickly composed herself because she didn't want Hawk to feel uncomfortable, and she had to keep a level head with what she was about to endure. His face was serious and she could see the pain in his eyes. "Thank you, Riley," was all he said. And Riley knew it meant everything to him, just like it did her.

Riley smiled and nodded resolutely. "You're welcome," she said. She wanted to give him a big bear hug, but knew that would *really* make him uncomfortable. Seeing Hawk almost erased her fears because she knew she had to do a good job for him - and for Lennox. As far as she was concerned, two lives were at stake today. So, instead of a hug she looked up at him and said, "Rangers Lead The Way."

Hawk's face broke into a grin upon hearing the U.S. Army Rangers' creed and he headed up the steps with Riley and her family marching behind, the Murphys and Rycrofts bringing up the rear. City hall looked huge from the bottom of the steep steps and Riley felt so tiny, but all the supporters outside gave Riley a confidence she didn't imagine she had.

When they got into the council chambers, Riley felt the butterflies flutter—it felt real now. Her dad reached for her hand and walked with her to the table where she would be presenting. The wooden table had two chairs and a podium with a microphone and it faced a semi-circular platform that had nameplates for each council member and the mayor. In the center, behind where the mayor and council members would sit was an American flag. Riley was doing this for a patriot and seeing that flag made her feel better. She knew she was on the side of what was right.

Her mom hugged her and gave her a kiss on her forehead. "Hawk, Hailey, and I will be right behind you, you're going to do great."

Riley smiled at her mom. She looked perfect, as always, and Hailey had even softened a bit, smiled and said, "Good luck."

Finn was right next to Hailey and looked as confident as ever. "You're going to do great. I know you're nervous, but you know this case better than anyone."

The room was filling up and Riley noticed that Eve, Evan, and Detective Rycroft were a few rows back. Eve gave her a comforting smile while Evan and her dad gave her thumbs-up. Across the aisle in the second row was a big, broad man writing in a notebook and she wondered who he was. He wasn't a reporter—all of them were in a section together on the far side of the room. Whoever he was, he looked dead serious and made Riley's stomach flutter. Riley fidgeted with her key necklace and inhaled deeply to try to calm her nerves.

She turned to her dad who had her note cards and a glass of water ready. "Here," he said. "Take a sip. Once you start talking, you're going to get thirsty." Riley was so lucky to have such an awesome dad. She sat down so she could focus on the task at hand and mentally get her mind right. She smelled stale cigarette smoke and noticed the animal control officer who had taken Lennox pass behind her to speak with someone she didn't recognize. His glance caught hers and she felt a strange sensation of unease, probably because he felt like the enemy. Some of the city council members started to file in and Riley was ready to plead the case. She turned around to her right and gave Hawk a smile. He nodded, leaned forward, and held out his hand. "Here," he said, his deep voice low, almost a whisper. Riley reached out with her right palm facing up. Hawk put something in her hand and sat back, his eyes looked like steel as he focused on the council members, his jaw muscles flexing.

Riley turned around and opened her hand below the table. Hanging from a red ribbon with a blue stripe down the center was a bronze star. In the middle of the ribbon was the letter 'V'. Riley felt a pin clasp on the back of the ribbon. Her dad looked over and his eyes got wide. He looked back at Hawk who nodded. Riley felt her dad lean in and he whispered, "That's the Bronze Star Medal, it's for heroic achievement or service. The 'V' stands for valor." Riley swallowed hard and prepared to fight.

CHAPTER FORTY-FOUR

Speaking For The Voiceless

The mayor and remaining city council members filed into the chamber and Riley's heart skipped a beat. She had forgotten that Corey's dad, and her dad's colleague, had recently been elected to the city council. Hadrian Thornton was tall and proper; and, if his son was anything like him, Riley figured he wouldn't care much about what she had to say. Compassion was not something that one associated with Corey Thornton—quite the opposite.

After they were seated, the woman in the center of the semi-circular elevated desk spoke and Riley recognized her as the mayor.

"This is a special session to hear the appeal on behalf of resident Calvin Hawkins whose dog, Lennox, was recently confiscated and sentenced to be euthanized this Friday. Our Chief Animal Control Officer has evaluated Lennox and has made the determination that the dog be euthanized as he is a risk to our community. We will only hear from one party and at the request of Lucy Mae Powell, longtime resident and relative of a founding family of this city, Miss Riley Carson will speak on behalf of Mr. Hawkins."

Riley felt her pulse quicken. She squeezed the Bronze Star in her hand to give her confidence to begin.

"Miss Carson," the mayor said as she gave Riley a stern look.

Riley saw a few of the male council members, including Mr. Thornton, whisper to one another. Rather than shatter her nerves, their whispers gave her the resolve to knock their socks off with her presentation. Just because I'm a kid, doesn't mean I shouldn't be taken seriously, she thought to herself. Just as her dad was about to nudge her to begin, she stood up confidently.

She looked at her note cards, the Bronze Star still tucked in the palm of her right hand. "Thank you to the Mayor and City Council for allowing me to present my appeal on the case of Lennox and Calvin Hawkins." Her voice sounded small and quivered a bit, but she kept going, making sure to speak louder and with authority like her dad had told her.

Her hands trembled as she held her note cards. "I am lucky to call myself a friend and neighbor to Mr. Hawkins and his dog Lennox. If you aren't aware, Mr. Hawkins served our country as an Army Ranger and served several tours overseas fighting for our freedoms. He chose Roswell to put down roots after he left the service and I'm so glad that he moved in across the street from my family.

"Late last year, Mr. Hawkins received a service dog, Lennox, who was evaluated, trained, and certified by a non-profit group called Dog at Hand. This organization is run by a retired Army Ranger who trains dogs to be service dogs for returning veterans who need assistance. Lennox received more training than most dogs ever receive and is able to help Mr. Hawkins with his PTSD." She paused and looked up. "That's Post Traumatic Stress Disorder." She noticed the big broad man across the aisle was writing notes, his serious expression hadn't changed.

There were a couple of chuckles from the crowd, but Riley continued. "I got to know Lennox and found that he is a fun-loving, docile dog who is able to read Hawk's...um...Mr. Hawkins' mood and needs. This is very important for someone suffering with PTSD. Also, since Mr. Hawkins lives alone, Lennox provides companionship." Riley stopped and looked up at the council members like her dad told her to do. "Do any of you have pets?" About three-quarters of them nodded. "Then you know the importance of companionship from our pets. Now, imagine if you lived alone and suffered with Post Traumatic Stress Disorder. Wouldn't you feel so much better having a dog or cat with you? A living creature by your side?"

Riley noticed that a few council members were leaning forward on their elbows, and even Mr. Thornton appeared to be deep in thought, his left arm across his torso and his chin resting on his right hand as he surveyed the crowd.

"My family recently adopted a Yorkshire terrier named Buster. Lennox and Buster love to play together and this is a testament to both of their dispositions. Believe me, if Lennox were aggressive, he could take Buster like that." She snapped her fingers. "My friend, Finn, and I have played with Lennox and never once has he been aggressive. Again, this dog has been temperament tested. Service animals cannot be aggressive, they have to be calm in all kinds of situations and not get flustered. This is a very well-behaved and balanced dog who is safe to be in our city."

Riley's dad stood up. "My dad is going to give you all the records from Lennox's testing and training, testimonials from Mr. Hawkins' neighbors, and some statistics to review about dog bites and attacks. There is also a brief history on pit bulls. At one time, German Shepherds were the most feared dogs, then it was Rottweilers, and now it's pit bulls. The problem is not about the breed, it's about the dog. Any dog can bite, and dogs that are raised to be aggressive will be aggressive, no matter what breed they are. The problem isn't a dog problem, it's a people problem." Riley paused to let that statement sink in and the man across the aisle caught her eye again. This last comment had gotten his attention and he locked eyes with Riley; she thought he might be considering what she had just said.

"Even when it's a people problem, it's still usually something we can fix," she continued. "Ask any rescue group, there are countless dogs that have come from bad situations who have been rehabilitated. A little love goes a long way and has saved many lives.

"Today we're talking about a dog that was trained to be a therapy dog, to be a companion." She scanned the group of officials as she added, "This is a sweet, gentle dog who was lucky to come from a good place. All dogs should be as lucky as Lennox."

Riley set her note cards down, but kept the Bronze Star in her right hand, feeling more confident with each word. She looked at the mayor and city council members and saw that she had all of their attention. "I don't know whose decision it was to confiscate Lennox, but it was made with ignorance. I don't mean any disrespect, but the pit bull ban in our city is ludicrous and doesn't solve any problems, it just makes more of them." She noticed the animal control officer who she had seen picking up Lennox looked unimpressed with her words.

"The dog the city chose to die is not a threat to anyone, in fact, the bigger threat is euthanizing him, because you are putting a man's life in jeopardy."

Riley hoped she wasn't crossing a line here with Hawk, but she had to say it. "Lennox is a certified therapy dog who is assisting one of our veterans." She turned and pointed to Hawk. "This man sacrificed more for our country than most of us can even imagine, and you pay him back by killing his dog?"

She felt tears prick her eyes but willed them to stay away. The man across the aisle was watching her intently. "I'm sorry, but in my world, that's not how we treat those who sacrifice for us. I don't know about you, but I don't want to live in a city that treats its veterans this way."

There was complete silence in the room and Riley could feel her heart beating against her chest. She inhaled, then exhaled to calm her breathing and she heard a pair of hands clap, then more, there was applause from what sounded like the entire room, except from the animal control officer, the mayor, and city council members, though a few of them were smiling proudly. The man across the aisle showed no expression as he continued making notes.

When the clapping ended, Riley stood tall and said to the council members, "I really appreciate your time and the chance to speak for Lennox and Mister Hawkins. I think the city is about to make a really big mistake, and we don't want to see that happen. At the very least, I would like to see the city hire an independent canine behaviorist to evaluate Lennox before his life is taken. It's the least you can do for your citizens, especially one who has sacrificed more for this country than many of us ever will."

Riley turned around and smiled at Hawk. She walked up to him and put the Bronze Star back in his hand and said, "Thank you."

Half of Hawk's mouth turned up in a smile and he leaned down to give Riley a hug. She couldn't help the tears, they came streaming down her cheeks. "I hope I made them think," she said into his ear. "I hope I made a difference."

CHAPTER FORTY-FIVE

The Man Across the Aisle

Riley was sharing congratulatory hugs from her family and friends when she noticed the man across the aisle stand up. The Mayor and City Council had filed out and the audience in the room was dispersing. The man was huge, tall and broad, and he still had a stern face. Notebook in hand, he headed toward the exit.

Finn noticed Riley watching him. "Who's he?" Finn asked.

Riley shook her head. "No idea, but he was taking notes practically the whole time. I don't think he's a reporter, because they're all on the other side of the room."

"Maybe he's just a concerned citizen?" Finn suggested.

"Maybe, but he looked a little more intense than most of the concerned citizens that showed up." Riley shook it off. "Oh well, I'm starving. Maybe we can grab something to eat before we have to go to school."

Finn smiled. "Yep, my mom suggested we go to the Public House and your parents are cool with it."

"Good! Now that my stomach isn't so nervous, I can actually eat something and enjoy it!"

***

The Carsons, Murphys, Rycrofts, Harringtons, Mr. Felton, and Hawk were all seated in the smaller room to the right of the main dining hall at the Public House. The manager, Mr. Wood, came over to greet them. "Riley, I heard about your testimony this morning. Everyone's talking about what a great job you did!"

Riley could feel herself blush. "Thanks! I was pretty nervous, but I hope they will consider what I said and get an independent evaluator for Lennox. He's not a threat at all."

"I hope they do too," the smiling manager said. "It's a shame what they've done." He looked at Hawk who nodded with appreciation. "Well, it seems most of the town is on Lennox's side, and politicians don't like angry voters."

"Isn't that the truth," Finn's mom said.

"Any idea how long they'll take to make a decision?" Mr. Wood asked to no one in particular.

"They are supposed to start deliberating today," Riley's dad said. "I guess it depends on how many of them are in agreement as to how long it can take."

Riley was unconsciously fidgeting with her key again, hoping she had done enough, and Mr. Wood seemed to notice her anxious behavior. He smiled knowingly and said, "You have a lot of support around you, Riley. Based on what I've heard from folks who were in the room today, they are pretty confident that the mayor and council will make the right decision."

Riley let out a deep breath and felt goosebumps creep up her arms. "I sure hope so."

Mr. Wood had a look about him, a knowing confidence. "Let's have faith that they will make the right decision. When they do, we can all celebrate!"

Riley smiled. "That sounds like a plan."

As the waitress came to take their orders, Riley noticed the man from across the aisle at City Hall enter the restaurant. She had a clear view of the door and, as the hostess started to walk in their direction, the man seemed to notice Riley. He said something to the hostess and the young woman nodded, then turned direction and walked the man over to the other side of the restaurant, toward the back.

Finn was sitting across from Riley. "Earth to Riley," he said.

"Sorry, were you saying something?"

"Yeah, what's up?" Finn asked as he turned to see what Riley had been focused on.

Riley leaned in and in a low voice said, "That man from City Hall is here. The one who was taking notes the whole time I was presenting. The hostess was going to seat him over here, but I swear he saw me and asked to sit on the other side of the restaurant."

"That's weird," Finn said as he turned and looked back across the room. "I can't see him."

The wall between the two sections of the restaurant blocked their view of where the man had been seated. "She must have seated him near the back," Riley said. "They walked to the row of booths on the far side against the brick wall, and he pointed to the back of the restaurant. I wonder what his deal is?"

"I don't know," Finn said, "but let's not worry about it now. You did great today, let's celebrate that."

Riley smiled at Finn. He was so lucky he wasn't the worry-wart she was. "Okay, I'll try." Riley didn't want to celebrate yet, she hadn't accomplished her final goal of getting Lennox freed and safely back to Hawk. Even though she tried not to worry about that man, she couldn't completely shake him from her thoughts.

CHAPTER FORTY-SIX

Waiting For News

By the end of the day, they hadn't heard any news from the City Council. In a way, Riley was actually glad for all the homework she had because it kept her mind occupied. On Tuesday evening, still with no news, she again occupied herself with homework before the aromas called her downstairs for dinner.

"Hey, honey, can you set the table for me? Dinner's almost ready," her mom said as she checked on the lasagna in the oven. The television was on in the family room, tuned into the news and Riley peeked in hoping to see a headline banner with good news before heading into the kitchen.

"Sure," Riley said. She joined her mom in the kitchen and opened an upper cabinet to grab a stack of plates. "Is dad home yet?"

Her mom wiped her hands on a towel. "Yep, he's in the study working."

Riley set the last plate on the table and then went to retrieve silverware when the news anchor said, "We've got breaking news out of Roswell, tonight. A decision has been made in the case of Lennox the pit bull. We'll go live to Roswell City Hall after this break."

Riley's heart sped up and she set the pile of silverware on the table. "Dad! Come out here, they've reached a decision!"

While they could clearly see the television from the open kitchen, Riley and her mom walked into the family room. Her mom put her arm around Riley's waist and gave her a comforting squeeze. "It'll be good news, Roo."

Riley pulled her phone out of her back pocket and texted Finn. *Turn on the news, Lennox decision about to be announced.*

Riley's dad came into the room and stood on the other side of her. He gave her shoulders a hug and kissed her head. "It's going to be good news."

She wasn't sure if her parents were trying to convince themselves or her, but Riley was happy they were watching this together. Her phone chimed and she read the text from Finn. *We've got the news on and my dad called Hawk.*

Riley thought about Hawk, sitting all alone in the house across the street. She didn't want him to be alone when the news came, but depending on what it was, he might prefer the solitude. She could feel her heart beating fast, she said a silent prayer, one of hundreds already said, and waited.

Riley's mom ran into the kitchen to turn down the stove and rushed back in when the news intro started. "We have breaking news out of Roswell tonight, a decision has been made in the case of Lennox the pit bull," the female news anchor said. "Veteran reporter and dog lover, Trish Schneider has been following this case from the beginning and is at City Hall where a press conference is due to begin any moment. Trish?"

"Maria, we are here at Roswell City Hall where a press conference is set to begin any moment with news on the case of Lennox the pit bull. Earlier this month, Roswell passed a law banning certain breeds in their city, this law grandfathered in dogs already living in the city, but with certain stipulations. Residents from all over the metro area galvanized behind Lennox the pit bull and his owner when the dog was confiscated after a complaint was filed. Lennox was set to be euthanized, but residents petitioned the city and they heard the case for Lennox on Monday morning. I was in the chambers during the presentation, and young Roswell resident, Riley Carson, gave a very moving testimony on behalf of Lennox and his owner Calvin Hawkins. Viewers who have been following this case know that Mr. Hawkins is a retired Army Ranger who suffers from PTSD and Lennox is his certified service dog. That alone should be a consideration for the city, but we will see what their verdict is this evening."

Riley could see people walking out the front doors of City Hall and she noticed the mayor who led the proceedings on Monday as well as Hadrian Thornton leading the way. Her heart sank and she said, "I don't think Mr. Thornton will be on our side. I hope this isn't bad news." Riley tucked her hair behind her right ear and her mom gave her another squeeze around her waist.

"It'll be okay," her mom said. Again, Riley wasn't sure who she was trying to comfort more.

"This case has garnered attention from across the country and even internationally," the reporter said, "and we've had a group of protesters peacefully assembled here since Monday." Riley wished she could have been there with them, but with school and homework, it wasn't allowed.

The male news anchor was asking a question and the reporter said, "I'm sorry to interrupt, Paul, but it looks like we're about to hear the news. Let's listen in."

Hadrian Thornton took to the podium and Riley was surprised it wasn't the mayor. "Good evening, we understand that this case has been very important to many in our community, and we want to do right by our residents by making sure we are doing what's best for the city of Roswell and its residents."

Riley thought Mr. Thornton looked very pleased with himself to be standing at the top of those steep steps of Roswell's massive City Hall, speaking into cameras that were broadcasting across Georgia, and even the country and internationally. She thought he looked insincere as usual and was holding his hands in the weird way that politicians did. Never pointing, just gesturing unnaturally.

"After hearing the case of Lennox and his owner, the City Council has decided to have an independent canine behaviorist evaluate Lennox to determine if he is a danger to our residents. While we have a very qualified animal control team in Roswell, the fact that Lennox is a certified therapy dog is something that needs to be considered. Dr. Barrett Smith is a renowned animal behaviorist specializing in canine behavior. As a resident of nearby Dunwoody, Dr. Smith has agreed to evaluate Lennox and perform an independent analysis for us. We appreciate the passion of our residents and want them to know that their safety and security is of utmost importance to us. We will hold another conference after Dr. Smith has completed his evaluation. Thank you."

Riley noticed that Mr. Thornton wore his plastic smile, showing his perfectly white teeth as he declined to answer any questions from the reporters. She looked up at her dad. "This is a good thing, right?"

Riley noticed her dad eying Mr. Thornton on the screen before turning to her. "I think this is a good thing. They are giving Lennox a chance and it's good that they have a third-party behaviorist coming in. Lennox was already tested fully before becoming a service dog. There's no way he won't pass a fair and independent evaluation."

Riley smiled. "I think you're right, Dad." She pulled her phone out of her pocket. "I'm going to look this man up."

Riley's mom said, "The news channel beat you to it." She pointed to the screen and Riley saw the man who held Lennox's fate in his hands...it was the man from across the aisle at city hall.

Riley gasped. "That man was in the room when I gave my testimony!"

Her dad looked at her with concern. "Is that a bad thing?" he asked.

"No, it's just that he seemed so serious, and he was taking notes the whole time. I got a weird feeling from him. He came into the Public House when we were there and he asked to be seated away from us. I don't know, it was just odd."

"Oh honey, you and your imagination!" Riley's mom said as she headed back to tend to their simmering dinner. From what they just said, he sounds very qualified. He has a PhD in animal behavior and has been working with dogs for forty years. Try not to worry so much."

"I know, mom, I just don't want them to kill Lennox." Riley walked back to the kitchen and grabbed the silverware and continued to set the table.

Her dad joined them in the kitchen and put a hand on

Riley's back. "Have faith, Roo. There are still good people in the world."

Riley smiled. She realized she needed to have faith that good would triumph over evil, but she was finding that dealing with politics made that really hard to do sometimes.

CHAPTER FORTY-SEVEN

Lennox's Fate

Riley, Finn, and Eve were eating lunch in the cafeteria Friday afternoon. In between bites of her peanut butter and jelly sandwich, Riley said, "I hope we hear something about Lennox soon. I think Doctor Smith was supposed to finish his evaluation this week."

Eve was eating a banana. "Do you think the city council will make a decision quickly, or do you think it will take a while?"

"I don't know," Riley said. "We know Lennox isn't aggressive. I guess it depends on Doctor Smith's report and findings. Who knows with the city council, though."

"My mom said that the public outcry has been so huge that she thinks it has put a lot of pressure on the city. I don't think they thought the public would care this much," Finn said.

"Well, you take away a veteran's service dog and people are bound to make a fuss." Riley said as she grabbed her water and took a sip.

"Still worried about that stupid dog?" Riley didn't have to turn around to know that Corey Thornton decided to stop by. She figured his sidekicks Brad and Seth were alongside him as usual.

She took a deep breath and turned to face Corey. "Yeah, we still are, Corey, because we care about an innocent life."

Corey laughed. "It's just a dog."

Riley surprised herself by how calm she was. "No Corey, it's not *just a dog*. That's what people say who have never received unconditional love from a dog, or if they have, they don't recognize the power of that love. No life should be taken without very good reason and we know this dog—there's no reason to kill him. Besides, this dog also serves a retired veteran, so he's definitely not *just a dog*. I'm sure your dad realizes this too." She calmly turned back around, wondering if she should have left that last part out about his dad.

"Whatever," Corey said. "Come on, let's go."

Riley saw Corey, Brad, and Seth head over to another table to pick on some of the smarter kids in their grade.

"Wow, you sure shut him up!" Finn said.

"I'm just so sick of him," Riley said. "He's always picking on someone." She felt her phone buzz and pulled it from her pocket. "My mom said dinner is set for tonight. Can you guys still come over?"

"Yep!" Finn said.

Eve smiled. "Yeah, my dad said as long as something doesn't come up, we'll be there. Evan, too."

Riley smiled. "Good, she says to come over around six, dinner will be at seven." Riley tapped a short message back to her mom and put her phone away. "I'm so looking forward to the weekend. I need to sleep in."

***

Riley constantly checked her phone for alerts about Lennox

the rest of the day, but to her dismay, none came. As she helped her mom get ready for dinner, they had the local news on the whole time, but no news about Lennox came up. She was really starting to get nervous. They had invited Hawk for dinner, but he declined and she could understand why; he was probably too nervous about Lennox.

"I wish Hawk would join us," Riley said as she set the table in the dining room. Noticing his house across the street was dark as usual.

Her mom was placing candles in holders in the center of the table. "I know, honey. I'm sure Hawk is just busying himself with his work because of all that's going on. I told him to come over if he changes his mind, there will be plenty of food. I'm sure he's on pins and needles."

"Yeah, if I'm this worried, I can only imagine how he feels."

"Mrs. Powell really wanted to come too, but the doctors want her to rest," Riley's mom said.

"I'm so glad she's home and feeling better," Riley said. "When I called her after my appeal to the city, she sounded a lot better than she had before. She said she feels like she's about ninety-percent better."

Riley's dad came out of the study, finally detaching himself from his work. "It smells delicious out here! Your mom makes the best standing rib roast," he said as he gave his wife a hug and a sweet kiss on the cheek.

"I just love cooking it, and why not share it with our friends." Riley's mom looked very pleased, excited about entertaining in her home. She checked her watch. "Speaking of which, they should be here soon, let's get the appetizers ready."

While Riley and her mom were working, Hailey was still upstairs getting ready. Riley figured she was making sure her hair and make-up were perfect since Evan Rycroft would be joining them. Otherwise, she probably would have asked if she could make other plans. The news was on, but still not a word about Lennox.

After their guests arrived, Riley's mom was so busy entertaining that she had forgotten to turn off the television and put on music. Riley, Finn, Eve, and Evan were sitting in the family room snacking and talking and Riley made sure to face the TV in case of any late breaking news. Hailey was still getting ready, or trying to make an entrance, Riley wasn't sure which. Finn was in mid-sentence when the breaking news banner came across the TV with a photo of Lennox that had been taken in Hawk's backyard. Finn was sitting next to Riley and saw the image at the same time she did.

Riley unconsciously grabbed Finn's wrist. "Mom, Dad, come here! There's news about Lennox!" Riley stood up and grabbed the remote control to turn up the volume as the adults stopped talking and focused their attention on the television. Riley could feel her heart racing and she said a quick prayer.

"We're going live at city hall in Roswell tonight as we're told that the city council has made a decision on the fate of Lennox the pit bull," the male news anchor, said.

"That's right Paul, Trish Schneider here in Roswell, and we're expecting word any second now." As the reporter in the field was saying this, city hall's front doors opened and the mayor and city council members appeared through the doorway. Riley saw that Doctor Smith was with them and looked as serious as ever. She was trying to read his expression, but he had a good poker face and didn't show any emotion. Corey's dad took to the microphone again and Riley's stomach fluttered as she awaited the news.

"Good evening. As council members voted on by our citizens, the concerns of our residents are top priority for us. A lot of attention has come to this case and we wanted to make sure not to make any hasty decisions."

"Yeah, right," Riley said quietly to Finn. "This whole thing was a hasty decision."

Mr. Thornton continued. "The safety and security of our residents and visitors is also a top priority for us and after the horrific attack on one of our youngest, most innocent residents, we couldn't just stand by without doing anything." Mr. Thornton paused and looked directly into the camera, giving his best sympathetic look. "This has been a tough decision that has weighed on all of us and we want to do the right thing for everyone involved. As a whole, we feel that breed-specific legislation is still important to the safety of our residents."

Riley watched Doctor Smith's face to see if he reacted to this statement. All she could see was that he had inhaled sharply. "That's ridiculous!" She said to the television.

"We will still implement our ban on pit bulls and pit bull type dogs, nothing within that law changes. In the case of Lennox, after an independent evaluation, and all the evidence we've reviewed, the city council feels that this dog is not a threat to our community."

The whole house went wild, everyone cheering with glee. Riley hugged Finn then Eve, then Evan. Her parents came over and hugged her so hard she thought she might break. She was crying tears of joy as her sister finally came downstairs to see what was going on.

"Shhh, shhh, listen!" Finn said as he pointed to the television.

Mr. Thornton was still talking. "Doctor Smith has a few words about his evaluation." Mr. Thornton had that fake smile on his face as Doctor Smith walked up to the microphone. The two men shook hands, but Doctor Smith did not return the smile.

"Good evening. I know this is a controversial case so I wanted to give you a synopsis of my evaluation. I am an independent canine behaviorist with no connection to anyone in this case or on the city council. I have been working in canine behavior for forty years and have been exposed to all kinds of dogs. In my evaluation of Lennox, I found him to be a happy, loving, energetic dog who receives commands well. This is a smart dog who enjoys to work and I suspect that's what made him a good candidate for a PTSD service dog. He is very attentive to emotions and seeks to please. Even after being separated from his human and confined to an area where he has very little interaction with humans, Lennox showed absolutely no aggression. I am confident that this dog will not be a threat to anyone he comes into contact with."

The reporter from channel two hollered out a question. "Doctor Smith, how do you feel about the ban on this breed?"

Doctor Smith took a deep breath and Riley saw his jaw twitch. "With all due respect, I was not asked to comment on the law; I was asked to evaluate a dog. However, what I will say is that we shouldn't paint a breed with such a broad brush.

Each dog is a unique individual with different life experiences, just like humans." With that, Doctor Smith walked away from the microphone and let Mr. Thornton take center stage again.

The reporters hollered questions at Mr. Thornton, but he did a good job of telling them nicely that they were not going to get any answers. He smiled for the cameras with the rest of the city council members and then waved goodnight. Riley thought Doctor Smith looked like he just wanted to get the heck out of there.

"We have to call Hawk!" Riley said. "Do you think he knows?"

"I hope they called him before the news conference," Finn's mom said as Mr. Murphy started dialing Hawk's number.

Just then, the doorbell rang and Riley, Finn, and Eve ran to see who was there. It was Hawk and Riley thought he had the biggest smile on his face that she had ever seen. She gave him a big bear hug—she didn't care if he minded—though when she stepped back, she could tell he didn't.

Hawk squatted down so he was eye-level with Riley. "Thank you so much for all you did. You really made a difference for me and Lennox."

Riley was overwhelmed. "You're welcome! I'm so glad they listened."

Finn came up beside Riley. "When will Lennox come home?" he asked.

"They told me it won't be until Monday since they have paperwork to do and they came to the decision so late." Hawk looked sad about that but added, "I can wait a couple more days. At least he's coming home!"

Riley's parents and the Murphys came up and congratulated Hawk, welcoming him inside to celebrate.

"Come on," Finn said to Riley and Eve, "let's go enjoy the evening, we have a lot to celebrate!" He looked at Riley and said, "You did this, you know. You saved Lennox."

Riley felt herself blush. "I didn't save him, it was a group effort."

Eve said, "Your speech was really powerful. I think Finn's right. You really made a difference, you saved a life."

Riley felt uncomfortable taking the credit, but it made her proud to hear her friends say this. She was so happy she could make a difference, a difference that indeed had saved a life, maybe even two.

CHAPTER FORTY-EIGHT

Meeting Doctor Smith

On Saturday morning, Finn came over to Riley's house around ten o'clock so they could bake homemade treats for Lennox. Riley figured he needed some tasty snacks since he had been stuck in animal control so long. Who knows what they were feeding him.

While the dog bone shaped treats were baking, Riley and Finn discussed everything that had gone on recently. "I can't believe we actually did it," Riley said.

Finn was smiling at her. "You did a great job for Lennox... and Hawk. I guess that Civil War project really did help you prepare!"

Riley laughed at this. "Maybe, but I think it was also just that this was so important. Trust me, I was nervous and scared, but that didn't compare to how Lennox and Hawk must have been feeling. Mrs. Powell told me my heart would give me courage and now I know what she meant. When you care so much about something, it's easy to be brave."

Finn smiled at Riley. "Well, you definitely have a big heart for dogs. You did great!"

The oven timer beeped and Riley hopped off the bar stool at the island and went to retrieve the treats. "These smell really good!"

"Well, the ingredients are all stuff we eat, so I'm sure Lennox will love them."

"He'll probably scarf them down!" Riley said as she set the pan on the stove top to cool.

"You know it!" Finn said. "He probably hasn't had anything decent to eat since he was locked up."

"Let's get them ready to take to Hawk," Riley said.

"You never could wait to give a present," Finn said.

"I know! I just get so excited." Riley really couldn't wait. She was so excited that Lennox would be coming home soon and wanted to see Hawk. She heard her phone chime and pulled it out of her back pocket.

"What's up?" Finn asked.

"Eve's on her way over," Riley said with confusion furrowing in her brow. "She said she found something that she needs to show us right away."

Finn had started bagging the now cooled treats. "I wonder what's so important?

"I don't know. She should be here soon. She said that Evan was dropping her off." Riley said as they gathered the treats and headed to the front door.

When they got outside on the porch, Riley saw a large SUV in Hawk's driveway. "That's weird - I wonder who's at Hawk's."

Riley and Finn watched as a large man got out of his vehicle. He had on a baseball cap that Riley recognized as one that veterans wore. Hawk opened his front door and had a wide grin on his face. The man walked up and shook Hawk's hand. They talked for a minute, though Riley couldn't hear what they were saying. Then, they walked to the back of the man's vehicle.

When he opened the back, Riley could see the edge of a dog crate and heard whining.

"Oh my gosh, that must be Doctor Smith...and Lennox must be inside!" Riley could hardly contain her excitement.

Hawk opened the crate and Lennox wiggled all over, then jumped up, putting his paws on Hawk's shoulders. Lennox was trying desperately to lick Hawk but he couldn't - because he had on a muzzle.

"He still has to be muzzled because of that law," Finn said, noticing the same thing.

Hawk hugged Lennox and scratched his back and sides; it was as if Riley could see all the tension he had been holding inside melt away. When Hawk leashed Lennox, Lennox hopped out of the back of the car and pulled toward the front door.

Just then, Evan's Bronco rumbled up the street and pulled into Riley's driveway. Eve hopped out and saw the joyous reunion across the street.

Hawk saw Riley and her friends and said, "Hey guys, come on over!"

Riley and Finn ran down the porch steps and across Riley's lawn as they joined Eve and headed across the street to greet Lennox. Whatever Eve had to tell them would have to wait, Riley was dying to see Lennox.

"Let's go inside," Hawk suggested. "I want to get this muzzle off."

"I should be going," Doctor Smith said.

"No, please, come inside for a moment," Hawk said.

Riley noticed that Doctor Smith had a slight smile on his face now, and she read his cap which had "Vietnam Veteran" embroidered with yellow-gold thread.

After they got inside the house, Hawk freed Lennox from his muzzle and Lennox proceeded to lick Hawk all over his face. Then he rubbed his body along Hawk, like a cat would. Hawk stood up and shook Doctor Smith's hand again. "Doctor Smith, thank you so much. I don't think I could ever repay you for what you did."

"Please, call me Barrett," the man said in a deep voice. "There's nothing bad about this dog. When I read the story that he was a service dog, for a vet no less, I knew I had to step in." He looked at Riley. "This young lady did a wonderful job on your behalf. You are clearly a passionate dog lover."

"Yes, sir. Very much," Riley said.

Doctor Smith held out his large hand, which like Hawk's, enveloped Riley's small hand. "You did a great thing. You should be proud."

"Thank you." Riley thought for a moment. "Doctor Smith? I saw you at the Public House after I presented and you asked for a table on the other side of the room. May I ask why?

The tall man of few words said, "I knew if this dog was a certified service dog that you had a good case. I wanted to keep my distance so that no one could say I was influenced in any way. It was too important to get Lennox back."

Riley smiled. "That's funny because I saw you taking notes but you were so serious...I guess I was scared about you." Riley felt silly as soon as she said it and thought of how she had misjudged Hawk before getting to know him.

"Aww, that's okay," Doctor Smith said, a smile forming on his face. "My daughters always tell me I'm too serious, but I think I've lightened up in my older years." He now had a twinkle in his eye and smiled at Riley, Finn, and Eve.

"Oh, the treats!" Finn said. "We brought some for Lennox."

"Well, I'm going to let you enjoy having Lennox back," Doctor Smith said. "Any time you need anything, you've got my number...anything at all."

Riley could tell that Doctor Smith meant what he said and that it wasn't just about Lennox. As a Vietnam vet, he probably dealt with similar things as Hawk had, maybe even worse. She had learned about the Vietnam War from the programs that her dad liked to watch on TV and knew that the men who came back from it were treated pretty horribly. War was bad enough, but coming back to people spitting on you and hating you must have made those guys feel so much worse.

Doctor Smith left and Hawk, Riley, Finn, and Eve played with Lennox who seemed to have an immense amount of energy. When they took him to the back yard, he ran around like crazy, his bottom low to the ground as he dodged and darted around, stopping to roll around in the grass on his back.

"Welcome home!" A voice called out to them and they looked next door. Mr. Felton was on his deck, smiling and waving.

"Thanks, Jim!" Hawk called back. "We're glad he's home!"

"Me too!" The older man hollered back. He waved once more then went inside.

"Do you want to take him for a walk?" Riley asked. "We could go get Buster and Molly."

Hawk's expression hardened a bit. "Nah, then I have to muzzle him. If it's okay with you, I'd prefer to let him have his freedom for a bit."

"Of course," Riley said as she watched Lennox sniff around the back fence. "Sorry, I forgot all about that. We still need to get them to overturn that stupid law."

"I agree," Hawk said who was smiling again as Lennox had found one of his toys and pranced toward them with it.

"He's going to sleep well tonight!" Eve said.

"So am I," Hawk said.

Riley looked at Hawk and noticed that while happier than she had ever seen him, his face showed his stress and exhaustion. "Why don't we leave you two to hang out and start getting that rest?"

"Yeah," Finn said, "I bet you two could both use a nice nap!"

Hawk smiled at the kids, "I think you're right. Thanks so much for the treats." He looked at Riley, "Thanks for everything."

***

Riley's heart felt full as they crossed the street to her house and sat on the porch. She was so glad Lennox was finally home.

"So Eve," Finn said as he settled in a rocking chair, "What was it that you had to show us?"

Eve took off her backpack and pulled out a large book which Riley and Finn looked at quizzically. The book seemed to have notes sticking out along the side.

"*Gone With The Wind?*" Riley asked as she looked at Finn, then Eve who had a knowing smile on her face.

Eve nodded. "This is the copy that Mrs. Willnow lent me.

The one she got from the estate sale."

"So, it might be Mrs. Powell's?" Riley asked.

"I think so," Eve said. "And I think Mister Powell left some sort of clue in the back."

Finn and Riley were both on the edges of their seats. "A clue to what?" Finn asked.

Eve couldn't contain herself. "I think it's a clue to the tunnels...and maybe even treasure!"

A HEARTFELT THANK YOU TO MY READERS!

I hope you enjoyed book #2 in the Riley Carson Series! If you did, I would love a review on Amazon or Goodreads as it helps others find my books (ask your parent to help you if you're under 13). Tell your friends about the Riley Carson Series, so we can change the world for animals together!

Riley Carson will return in book #3, so stay tuned for more dogs and adventure! If you want to stay up to date with everything Riley Carson, sign up for my mailing list and get the free e-book prequel at **www.RileyCarsonSeries.com**

AUTHOR NOTES

Roswell, Georgia is a real town north of Atlanta. If there are any tunnels underneath the city, they are a mystery to me! The tunnels are my creation, but I think it would be cool if they really did exist. The Public House is real, but during the writing of this book, it changed ownership and is currently in transition. Mr. Wood was the manager of the Public House and was a wonderful steward of the building and its history. Fear not, after the Public House closed as it was, Mr. Wood purchased the Roswell Ghost Tour so he's still sharing the haunted history of Roswell! The Creepy House was real and was once a stop on the Roswell Ghost Tour, but it actually did catch fire and burned to the ground in December of 2014. To my knowledge, the cause of the fire remains unknown. There supposedly was a really nasty male ghost haunting The Creepy House, and some stories identify him as the town's hangman. I'm not sure if this spirit remains in the area where the house once stood. I never liked going near The Creepy House - it truly earned its name.

If you are familiar with Metro Atlanta, then you know the town of Dunwoody, which isn't far from Roswell. You may also think that I misspelled Dunwody in this book, but I assure you, I didn't. The family that the town is named after actually spelled their name with one 'o' but apparently the post office accidentally added the extra 'o' to the family name when the town's post office was established.

Roswell, Georgia has not passed or even proposed Breed Specific Legislation, in fact, you can see lots of great pit bull type dogs during events around town. Unfortunately, many municipalities around the world have passed laws banning pit bull type dogs and the law in the story was based on these bans. Sadly, there are many owners who have had to deal with the realities of laws banning dogs that look a certain way. When choosing a name for the pit bull character, I chose to honor a dog whose story did not end happily. Lennox was a pit bull type dog who was taken from his family by the Belfast City Council in 2010. Lennox was only five years old when he was taken from his family and was a beloved family member. He was a companion to a disabled girl who needed and loved him. Lennox's family was not able to see him when he was in quarantine; he spent 785 days alone and without them. In May of 2012, over two years after being confiscated, Lennox was killed. It broke my heart and the hearts of many around the world, so many people were advocating for Lennox and his family. Lennox had not done anything wrong, other than look a certain way. His story stuck with me for so long because it was so tragic, so senseless, so wrong. It is my hope that this book will shed light on Breed Specific Legislation so that we can educate others about this issue and stand up for the rights of dogs and their owners. Just as we should not judge people by the way they look, we should not judge dogs based on their breed or appearance. Just as each person is an individual, so is each dog. Please help us share this message so we can help those in power make better decisions.

For more information on Lennox's story and legacy, visit:
www.thelennoxcampaign.co.uk

Baby Girl was a dog that went missing in College Park, Georgia, near Atlanta on Christmas morning in 2013. Baby Girl and her dad were in a hotel room when a man and woman tried to rob them. Baby Girl got between her dad and the intruders and their gun went off. No one was harmed, but the gun shot frightened Baby Girl and she ran off. At the time of writing this, four and a half years later, Baby Girl has not been found. Like Lennox's story, Baby Girl's story stuck with me. Her family did so much to find their beloved girl and people shared lots of missing dog photos that looked a lot like Baby Girl, but unfortunately, were not her. If my memory serves me correctly, Baby Girl was microchipped, so if she had been found by a shelter, she could have been reunited with her family. It's possible that someone found her and just kept her. If you ever find a dog, please, please, please search high and low for the owners. Dogs can go missing for a long time and can be in rough shape when found...don't assume that there isn't a loving family out there looking for their beloved pup. While Baby Girl wasn't found, other dogs have been reunited with their families thanks to the work of those who love Baby Girl. In fact, the Facebook page dedicated to finding her still posts missing dogs in hopes of reuniting them with their owners.

Baby Girl is still missing, for more info visit:
www.Facebook.com/helpfindbabygirl

ACKNOWLEDGMENTS

As with everything, I thank God for the blessings He gives me, and writing these stories is indeed a blessing. My dear Michael, Finlay, and Riley...my everything, you inspire me and make life fun! My parents for your continued support and love. To my readers, thank you for reading my books and telling others about them, these books are nothing without you and I write them with love for you. Every writer needs a great group of beta readers, those who volunteer to read as I write so I can make my books the best they can be. Thank you to Joy Southerland–my constant and dedicated reader. You read each version with enthusiasm and without delay, you don't know what a huge help that is to me! Riley W, thank you for reading this around your school schedule and providing awesome and honest feedback. Catherine Campbell, my friend and run-on sentence wrangler - thank you! Lynn Harrington, Barbara Jones, Lauren Kramer, and Reena Nichols, thank you all for reading and giving me your feedback...it was appreciated and labored over! Jenny Bowman, my awesome editor, thank you for helping me see what needed to go and how to shape this novel while staying true to my message. Andy Suggs, my buddy and illustrator, thank you for helping my covers look amazing, I so appreciate you! Thanks to Don Freewalt for helping me with the back cover design.

To the families of Lennox and Baby Girl, your stories stuck with me and left an imprint on my heart. I hope you find some solace in your pups living on through this story and I hope their stories help educate others.

Sharon Swenson, for being my lifelong friend and allowing me to name a very important character after your dad. I love you so much. To Mike and Lynn Harrington, I hope I'm doing right by Tim and that you are enjoying his role in these stories. Mrs. Carroll and Mrs. Weingarten at Minor Elementary School, I can't thank you enough for sharing my books with your students and allowing me to come speak with them. It means the world to me. To the students at Minor Elementary School, you inspire me so much and I love your enthusiasm for my books! Keep reading and go after your dreams. You can be anything you want...you just have to work hard and dream big!

David Wood, thank you for sharing the stories of the Public House with me and agreeing to be in the novel! To my pals Sam and Marina at The Downtown Pooch on Canton Street in Roswell, Georgia, thank you for your support and always having a space for me on your front lawn for book signings!

A heartfelt thank you to all the people who work tirelessly for animals. You inspire me daily and I hope we can change the world for animals together, using the talents we have.

ABOUT THE AUTHOR

Michael Duisenberg

Megan Wargula is a self-proclaimed "dog nerd" - the kind of person who knows the dogs in her neighborhood better than their humans! A native of Atlanta, Georgia, Megan has always loved animals and has made it her mission to make the world a better place for dogs through her writing. When not at her day job as a graphic designer, Megan spends the rest of her time writing and enjoying life with her husband and dogs, Finlay and Riley. Megan is a fan of history and the paranormal which is part of the reason she loves the town of Roswell, Georgia so much. Many of the places in the book are real, so plan your visit!

Fun Facts: Megan, Finlay, and Riley were fortunate enough to get some training from Victoria Stilwell when she won a contest that included a piece in Oprah Magazine! Oh, and she invited a rock star to her prom back in the 90's and he said yes. She thinks it might have been the very first prom-posal, and is forever grateful to Evan Dando of Lemonheads for being such a nice guy.

91652848R00202

Made in the USA
San Bernardino, CA
23 October 2018